"YOU'RE ASKING ME TO TRUST YOU?"

"Is that such a difficult thing?" Faye parried. "Besides, weren't you asking the very same thing of me when you first approached me about this crazy business proposition?"

"Yeah. And as I recall you were damned reluctant."

"Okay, so we're both reluctant. We can start slow." She gave Seth a long level look. "You trust me a little and I promise I'll do the same."

He returned her gaze, his mesmerizing eyes having their usual effect on Faye. "I guess it's a deal," he finally said. "Shake on it?"

But as soon as her hand touched his, he twisted it lightly until their forearms were entwined. Then he lifted her imprisoned hand to brush it teasingly with his lips. "We'll see how far a little trust goes...."

ABOUT THE AUTHOR

Kentucky Woman is the sixth Superromance by
veteran Harlequin writer Casey Douglas. Fans will
be delighted to know that Casey's love of animals
shines through once again in this latest release set in
the world of horse breeding. California is now
the place Casey calls home, but she has traveled
extensively and whets her appetite for adventure
by writing.

Books by Casey Douglas

HARLEQUIN SUPERROMANCE

25—INFIDEL OF LOVE
56—PROUD SURRENDER
75—DANCE-AWAY LOVER
107—EDGE OF ILLUSION
131—TASTE OF A DREAM
194—KENTUCKY WOMAN

These books may be available at your local bookseller.

Don't miss any of our special offers. Write to us at the
following address for information on our newest releases.

Harlequin Reader Service
P.O. Box 52040, Phoenix, AZ 85072-2040
Canadian address: P.O. Box 2800, Postal Station A,
5170 Yonge St., Willowdale, Ont. M2N 6J3

Casey Douglas
KENTUCKY WOMAN

Harlequin Books

TORONTO • NEW YORK • LONDON
AMSTERDAM • PARIS • SYDNEY • HAMBURG
STOCKHOLM • ATHENS • TOKYO • MILAN

Published January 1986

First printing November 1985

ISBN 0-373-70194-2

Printed in Canada

To the real Kentucky women
who helped make this book a reality:
Pat Mathews, Brenda Light, Bettie Cloud,
and especially
Peg Rose Snyder

CHAPTER ONE

"OH, GREAT," Faye exclaimed softly as the heels of her suede boots sank down in the wet grass to the mud below. She had forgotten what country life was really like. The little she knew about dirt was confined to a clay pot of straggly ivy back in her San Francisco apartment.

The boots resisted her tugs, and she pulled harder until they popped out of the mud like corks from wine bottles. Gingerly she made her way to the top of the hill and the rickety fence that marked the boundary of the farm.

She leaned against the peeling rails and shoved her hands deeper into her jacket pockets. It had been raining off and on since she landed at Lexington Airport. Now the damp wind buffeted her cheeks and cast a gray gloom over everything.

Why did I come, anyway, she asked herself. *Gran's gone now. I should have let the bank's trust department take care of the estate. There's nothing left for me here in Kentucky.*

Faye's eyes roamed over the gray stone farmhouse built by her great-great-great grandfather who'd been mustered out of the Revolutionary Army. And she smiled suddenly, remembering a story Gran had told her once about one of their feistier female ancestors.

Timber dealers had swung through the county one summer, offering quick money for cut trees. All the cash-hungry farmers had jumped at the deal, only to realize

later they had sold way too cheaply. All except Cousin
Lydia, who'd invited a couple of dealers out to Indian
Creek Farm, plied them with elderberry wine and encouraged a wild bidding match for her walnut grove.
"She did real fine," Gran had told Faye, her eyes twinkling with pride. "Enough to buy a new buggy, a mahogany secretary desk and *still* put money by."

Faye laughed out loud at the memory. At least she
knew whom she'd inherited her grit from. Her good humor restored, Faye started to head back down the hill
when she saw a man come around the corner of the barn.
He moved with deliberate, even strides, his head bent intently as if he were pacing off the property to measure it.

She hadn't authorized any land assessor to come out.
What was going on? Faye turned away from the fence
and hurried down to the rented Ford she'd left parked by
the main road.

The farm gate was so badly warped that it dragged on
the ground, and Faye had to fight to open it far enough
to drive the car through. Her heart sank when she saw the
condition of the lane on the other side, as deeply rutted
and pockmarked as an old battlefield.

She drove at a snail's pace, grimacing every time the
wheels bounced into another hole. Although the house
and barn stood on a pretty rise of land, Faye was shocked
at how run-down everything looked. Weeds grew hip
deep in the yard, and last year's unharvested corn crop
dropped in long rows like defeated soldiers, all withered
and brown.

She flung open the car door and marched over toward
the man who was now scribbling in a pocket notebook.
If he was somebody official he certainly didn't look it,
Faye decided, as she took in his blue jeans and scuffed
boots.

"May I ask what you're doing?" she said curtly.

He looked up in surprise. "Who the hell are you?" he inquired, his eyes resting on the soft green scarf covering her hair. "If you're selling Girl Scout cookies, I ain't buying."

Faye bristled. If there was one thing she was sensitive about, it was her small stature. At five feet one and a half inches, she barely tipped the scales at a hundred pounds. Given that and the wispy light brown hair framing her wide hazel eyes, Faye knew she looked closer to eighteen than her actual age of twenty-eight.

"The name is Hunt," she replied, frostily meeting his disbelieving stare. "Fayette Lee Hunt. I happen to be the owner of this farm."

"Well, then, I happen to be buyin' it from you." He spit out the toothpick from the corner of his mouth and added in a matter-of-fact voice, "The name's Carradine. Seth Carradine."

This bozo's making fun of me, Faye thought indignantly, noticing the deep laugh lines that framed his green eyes even though he wasn't quite smiling.

"How can you buy something that isn't even for sale, Mr. Carradine?"

"Oh, yeah? Since when?"

"Since I—"

Her curt comeback was drowned out by a honking horn, and they both turned to watch a brown Cadillac come bouncing up the rutted driveway like an out-of-control bronco. Hollister Pettigrew was talking even before he'd squeezed his ample frame out from beneath the steering wheel.

"Mornin', folks." An ingratiating little laugh punctuated his greeting. "I see you're already getting acquainted."

"Listen, Pettigrew..."

"Mr. Pettigrew..."

"Now, now, just hold your horses." Despite the cool day, the banker was perspiring and red faced. "No need to get all riled up. We're all friends here."

"Friends, hell! I think we got a problem here, Pettigrew, and I'm holding you responsible."

Faye eyed Carradine with a bit more respect. He'd taken the very words out of her mouth. Maybe he wasn't such a bozo, after all.

Pettigrew spread his chubby hands placatingly. "All right, Seth, why don't you just let me talk in private with Miss Hunt for a minute."

Carradine shrugged and turned away to resume pacing off the old barn, which, even with its fresh coat of red paint, looked as if the next strong wind would send it toppling.

Faye herself was beginning to see red and getting more suspicious by the minute. From what she had seen so far, it seemed to her that the bank had only kept up the part of the farm visible from the road. The rest was gradually crumbling into decay.

She stared up at the big man pugnaciously. "Mr. Pettigrew, I demand an explanation."

"Now, Fayette Lee, why'd you have to rush out here like this?" His tone was aggrieved. "Your letter said you wouldn't even be arrivin' until day after tomorrow."

"And you'd hoped to have all the weeds cut down by then?"

"We've done our best to manage the trust, but this old farm's been unproductive for years."

Faye's eyes swept the property again, and she tried to ignore the disturbing image of Carradine measuring and scribbling as if the place were already his. "Mr. Pettigrew, by the look of things, you haven't even had a tenant out here."

"They're more trouble than they're worth, tenant farmers. I'm telling you this place is more of a drain on the trust than an asset." The banker mopped his face with an oversize handkerchief. "Why, it's only out of respect for your grandmother that we even bothered to keep the farm up at all."

"You call this keeping it up—planting second-rate crops that no one even bothers to harvest?"

"The price of corn was real bad last summer."

"Then you should have had a tenant out here growing tobacco," she pressed. "That's a solid cash crop."

"Now, Fayette Lee, what does a city gal like you know about crops?"

His condescension annoyed her, and her upturned nose tilted even higher. "Mr. Pettigrew, I work for a stockbroker," she said icily. "Part of my job is looking at crop cycles and telling commodities investors what to buy."

"My, oh my. Times aren't what they used to be, when girls were girls and not stockbrokers and highfalutin' lawyers and the Lord only knows what else." His nervous laughter cracked, revealing the shallowness of his bonhomie, but he recovered briskly. "All the same, Fayette Lee, the business you're in is all paper talk. This here is a real down-to-earth farm. Believe me, little lady, we know what's best."

Faye turned on her heel and walked over toward the barn, her mind whirring busily. Where had she heard that phrase before—*we know what's best*. Then she remembered. It had cropped up in a letter she'd received ages ago from Minah Willis, the black woman who had been Gran's housekeeper and, in those last years, her companion and friend. "Miss Courtney's worried, Miss

Fayette, even though the bank keeps saying they know what's best."

At the time Faye had brushed off her grandmother's fears as the sad ramblings of a senile woman. It had hurt Faye deeply to watch her grandmother's decline because they had been so close. Faye had spent every summer until she was eighteen on the Indian Creek farm. Then college and work had intervened and her visits had grown shorter, finally stopping completely five years ago when Courtney no longer recognized her granddaughter at all. Faye had been so saddened that she hadn't given a thought to what would happen to Gran's home. Now she felt overwhelmed by guilt and anger. Why hadn't she listened?

Pettigrew lumbered up behind her. "I can show you the books, Fayette," he panted. "Take my word, it's all down in black and white."

She pulled open the sagging barn doors, grateful for the complaining creaks that drowned out the banker's overeager explanations. Startled birds flew out from the rafters in a rush of wings and darted through the rear doors, which stood open to the clearing sky. The pungent, mildewy scent of rotting hay made her sneeze, but lingering there, too, was the more pleasant earthy odor of the horses and cows that had inhabited the barn.

Faye walked through the barn and stopped at the back door. She looked past the overgrown weeds and straggly corn to the neighboring spread. Alfalfa and bluegrass covered the lush, rolling hills. Dark creosoted fences crisscrossed the landscape, following the gentle dip and rise of the pastures in an unbroken line toward the horizon. Faye's spirits rose when a mare and two foals appeared at the crest of one of the hills, the gangly babies kicking up their heels while their mother grazed placidly nearby. This pastoral richness was the heart and soul of the Kentucky bluegrass. Tobacco, cattle, blooded horses—they were all a part of it. And it had all once been part of Faye, had enriched her life for many summers.

Maybe that's why Pettigrew's "We know what's best" had rung so falsely in her ears. The Farmers and Breeders Bank had held her grandmother's land in trust. *Trust—what an ironic word,* Faye mused. To her, it seemed more like a violation.

She turned around and saw Pettigrew, his rotund figure silhouetted at the front entrance of the barn. He hadn't followed her. He was probably afraid of soiling his expensive shoes with rotted hay and bird droppings, Faye thought contemptuously. She looked down at her own muddied boots and laughed ruefully. *Looks like I'm in this thing up to my ears,* she told herself. Squaring her shoulders, she marched back to confront the banker.

"Mr. Pettigrew, this farm's in no condition to go on the market."

Carradine overheard this stark announcement and came striding over. "Pettigrew, dammit, you told me—"

"Now just calm down, everyone!" Pettigrew shouted, running agitated fingers over the bald spot on the back of his head. He took a deep breath. "Fayette Lee, it's not as simple as that."

"Why not?"

Pettigrew slipped two fingers beneath his tight collar and stretched his pudgy neck. "Because there are other considerations."

"Such as?"

"We're going to have to talk at my office."

"How about now?" As she took a step toward him, Pettigrew backed away.

"No. I'll call you." He retreated another step and she followed.

"Mr. Pettigrew, how many people have bid on the farm?"

"Two, maybe three," he replied, still inching back to his car.

"I'm curious. Did you even bother to run an ad?" she persisted.

"This is the South, Fayette Lee," he said, pulling open the car door with obvious relief and wedging himself into the driver's seat. "We do things informally around here."

Faye watched in disgust as the Cadillac purred to life and disappeared down the hill. Carradine stood behind her, chuckling.

She turned and eyed him up and own. "What are you laughing about? Aren't you afraid of being next?"

"I don't scare so easily." His grin deepened, revealing a hint of a dimple in his right cheek. It occurred to Faye that some women might find this redneck rather attractive. "Besides," he went on, "I don't back down easily when there's something that I want at stake."

She gave him another exasperated look. "I've already told you, Mr. Carradine, this five hundred acres isn't for sale."

"Four hundred," he corrected quietly, no longer smiling. "The bank's already sold off a hundred back acres to pay taxes."

Faye tried to hide her shock. Pettigrew had never written anything to her about having to sell a parcel. She looked up at Carradine angrily. "Who bought it—you?"

He didn't say anything, and she sighed, murmuring half to herself, "Well, I guess I'd better find a lawyer."

Carradine walked her over to the car and opened the door, his expression unrevealing. "Don't go looking to make me your scapegoat, lady. Pettigrew didn't expect you to show up here at all. He was sure you'd tell him to sell off the property and that would be the end of it."

"Well, he was wrong." Her voice was surprisingly hard. "Dead wrong."

"Pettigrew said you hadn't been around for years. Why *did* you come back?"

Ignoring his question, she slid behind the wheel and rolled the window down halfway. "Goodbye, Mr. Carradine. You'll be hearing from me."

"Sounds promising." He leaned both elbows on the window, his green eyes teasing hers. "When?"

"I'm sure our attorneys..."

"Yeah, we'll let them work it out. In the meantime, would you care to have dinner with me?" His grin deepened until his eyes were half hidden in laugh crinkles. "I could show you a few sights."

"Thanks for the invitation." She put the key in the ignition and gunned the motor. "But I know my way around."

He gave a low, appraising whistle. "I'll bet you do, lady."

FAYE ATE HER SOLITARY DINNER in the Hyatt's trendy patio restaurant. The vaulted glass roof with steel buttressing below belonged more in New York or San Francisco than quaint old Lexington, she thought.

Quaint? Faye shook her head later as she walked down Braodway in the early-spring dusk. An elegant fountain, sparkling in floodlights, graced the new civic center complex where the sleepy corner of Broadway and Vine used to be. A taste of old Lexington remained in the row of Victorian shopfronts across Main. But their interiors had been gutted for remodeling, giving them an unreal look, rather like a Hollywood movie set.

Faye turned right on Main, strolling past the silent shops. At least some things hadn't changed. The old McAdams and Morford drugstore stood where it always had on the corner opposite the county courthouse. And the whole town still rolled up the sidewalk at six, she thought, smiling.

Faye suddenly realized that Lexington was the only real home she had ever known. All the rest had been a series of military-base houses shared with her widowed father. Long after he had died and Faye was on her own, she continued the "army brat" life-style, never living more than eighteen months in any one city as she job-hopped from one investment firm to another, climbing the junior-executive ladder.

She had been in San Francisco almost two years now, and Paine Webber was offering her a permanent position on their long-range-planning board. It would mean more money, more stability—permanence.

Faye shook her head, too tired to think about that now, with everything else on her mind. She turned and headed back to the hotel, remembering suddenly how much she'd looked forward every summer to coming "home." When and how had she lost that desire?

Gran had been a classy woman—lovely and funny and full of life. She had been the one to encourage Faye to get her degree in economics and tackle the man's world of high finance head-on. She was the one who always told Faye to think for herself. In her last years Gran had been struggling to do just that, even if everyone else insisted she was deluded, a senile paranoiac who had managed to convince herself that she was being defrauded.

Back inside the comfortable hotel room Faye kicked off her shoes and pulled the pillows out from beneath the bedspread to plump behind her. The file of letters and legal documents relating to the farm lay on the night-stand. She picked it up and leafed through the papers until she found Minah Willis's letter.

Miss Courtney's going fast, I'm afraid. Oh, she do know me right enough, but the way I was forty years ago, Miss Fayette, not the old lady I am now. It's just too hurtful. She's living in the past, except from time to time she rouses to complain about that old bank robbing her blind. Doctors say she got cute brain syndrome making her what they call para-noid. But I don't know. I always thought there was something peculiar, sneakylike, about that Mr. Pet-tigrew myself. Maybe that's just his way. I suppose we all do the best with what the good Lord gives us.

Faye dropped the letter in her lap and laced her fin-gers behind her head. *Right,* she thought. *What the good Lord's given me is a brain and two eyes in this head to see what's been going on. I'm with you, Minah. I don't trust Pettigrew, or Carradine, either, for that matter.*

She promised herself that she'd get to the bottom of the scandal for Gran's sake. The woman's heritage had meant too much to her to let it be undermined this way. Like it or not, that heritage was Faye's now. She couldn't ignore it.

CHAPTER TWO

FAYE TOOK ONE LOOK at the hotel's breakfast menu with its French quiches and California fruit plates and decided what she was really hungry for was old-fashioned fried eggs with grits and biscuits. Immediately she thought of Leroy's Café and wondered if the old place was still there.

She smiled when she saw it—the same tiny overcrowded parking lot and curtained windows with the daily specials tacked up to entice passersby. Before crossing the driveway entrance, Faye glanced back and nearly laughed out loud when she saw a sleek gray BMW waiting to pull in. The unpretentious little restaurant seemed to be attracting a fancier clientele than the local farmers and tobacco-leaf buyers she remembered. The driver motioned her courteously to go ahead, and she took a closer look.

Suddenly she realized she knew him. "Barry!" she cried, walking toward the car.

He rolled down the window and stared at her. It took him a second longer. "Fayette? What are you doin' here?" His blue eyes lit up. "I can't believe it."

He pulled into the lot, and Faye hurried over to join him.

Barrish Deshay Markham's family was one of the oldest in Kentucky. The Hunts and the Markhams had belonged to the same exclusive country club, where Barry and Faye had met the summer after high-school graduation. At the outset the Markhams had looked favorably on the budding romance between their son and Courtney Hunt's granddaughter.

"Barry, you haven't changed a bit," she teased him as he swung his long legs out of the car and stood beside her. "Still tall and blond and preppy as ever."

"Well, you sure have changed, Fayette." His eyes swept down her, taking in the stylish fox jacket and the beige jeans tucked into her pale suede boots, which she'd had to brush for twenty minutes to erase every last trace of dried-up mud. "Where'd you acquire your sophistication? You used to be a regular tomboy."

"Don't let appearances fool you." She winked and ten years fell away. "I'm still the same feisty hell-raiser I was back then."

He nodded slowly. "I can believe it."

She and Barry had been as different as champagne was from Bourbon. Where she was adventurous and indifferent to the opinions of others, he had been thoroughly conventional—half shocked and half enchanted by her antics. Faye had always wondered whether their romance would have cooled even if she hadn't gone elsewhere to college instead of applying to the University of Kentucky as Barry had wanted her to do. She was sure his mother would eventually have chosen a more sedate and decorous companion for her youngest son, not a roving army brat who'd apparently forgotten her roots and her rightful place in society.

"Well," Faye said, uncharacteristically at a loss for words. "Would you like to join me for breakfast?"

"I'd love to, Fayette, but all I've got time for is a quick cup of coffee." He glanced down at his watch. "I've got to be in court at nine."

"So you've stuck with law school after all," she teased him. "I thought you wanted to be a petroleum engineer and work on a rig out in some exotic part of the world."

"You know how things go."

She nodded, understanding. Barry had three older brothers who had already been immersed in the family's horsebreeding business when she had met him. While Barry was still in high school, Siperia Markham had decided the family needed a lawyer to handle the legal affairs of their small bluegrass empire.

"Are you married?" Faye asked after the waitress had shown them to a table.

"Divorced."

"Uh-oh," Faye said teasingly. "Bet that didn't go over too well with Mother Superior."

"I almost forgot you used to call her that." Barry grinned and shook his head. "Boy, Fayette, you really haven't changed a bit."

"And neither have you." She laughed. "I remember how you nearly had a heart attack the first time I made up that nickname for your mama."

"Yeah, well I got used to it right quick, as I recall," he teased her back. "Anyway. How about you, Fayette—did you ever settle down and get married?"

She shook her head, and suddenly neither one of them had much to say. The awkward silence was interrupted when the waitress slapped two mugs of coffee down in front of them.

Faye smiled again. "I'm surprised at how much Lexington has changed. I almost don't recognize it."

"There are a lot of new buildings, but underneath it's the same old town." He blew on his coffee before tasting it. "We're still doin' things the way they've always been done."

Faye saw him look at his watch again and quickly said, "Don't let me keep you, Barry." He nodded and started to signal the waitress but Faye stopped him. "No, Barry, please, this is my treat."

"Aha. One of those liberated women."

"Come on," she teased him back. "Wasn't I always?"

"Don't I know it!" He stood up, adding, "How long are you in town for?"

"I haven't decided yet."

"Well, if you're still here Friday night, how about dinner?"

"I'd love to," she answered immediately. "Call me at the Hyatt."

"I certainly will." He seemed reluctant to leave, oblivious to the fact that he was blocking the aisle. "You look just great, Fayette."

Barry took a step back and nearly collided with Seth Carradine, who had come in and was trying to squeeze around him. Ignoring Barry's distracted apology as he hurried away, Seth pulled out a chair opposite Faye.

She was definitely not in the mood for his company. "Look, Carradine..."

"I didn't think you'd mind if I joined you," he said with feigned innocence. "All the other tables are full."

Before she could protest further, the waitress returned with her breakfast. "You're sure a hit with the menfolk, aren't you, honey?" the nosy woman observed rakishly before turning her attention to Seth. "Mornin', good-lookin'. Your usual?"

"Right, Gerrie." As soon as the waitress had gone he said to Faye, "I see you didn't waste any time finding a lawyer."

"Not that it's any of your business, but Barry happens to be an old friend." She met Seth's questioning look head-on. "I have a feeling I'm going to need all the allies I can get in this town."

"Well, you could do better. Blue blood doesn't necessarily guarantee gray cells up here." He tapped his temple with a finger.

"What's your problem? Were you born under a cabbage leaf or something?" she retorted, stabbing her eggs. "Is that why you've got a thing against 'blue bloods'...because you don't have a pedigree of your own?"

"I'm no poodle dog, that's for sure, with a bunch of fancy names hung on me like laundry on a line."

Gerrie, her ears perked sharply for gossip, returned with Seth's coffee. She'd obviously been eavesdropping. Her gaze moved shrewdly between him and Faye. "You know, Seth, I was goin' to say this sweet little thing's not quite your usual—she looks a mite too young and innocent." The brassy-haired waitress dropped a couple of plastic creamer containers on the tabletop and grinned. "But on second thought, I get the feeling you just might have your hands full."

Faye's eyes sparkled her thanks at this unexpected vote of confidence. "She's right, you know," Faye said after Gerrie had gone. "I'm not going to let you and Hollister Pettigrew get away with anything."

"I'm not tryin' to get away with anything."

Faye sliced angrily through a hot biscuit, refusing to listen. She looked up as Gerrie swung by again. In high fettle now, the waitress was ready for more friendly banter, especially since she'd found an encouraging audience. "Know what your problem is, Seth?" Gerrie began. "You're used to gettin' your own way too darned much."

He grinned lazily. "Only where women are concerned."

Gerrie crowed in delight as she moved toward another table.

But Faye wasn't amused. "Not where this woman is concerned," she said softly, her eyes searching his. She found little warmth in their depths, and it hit her that his sexy good-old-boy act was just that: an act. Underneath that infectious grin she sensed the man was all business.

He seemed to have reached the same conclusion about her little-girl facade. "You think you're a hundred pounds of toughness, don't you?"

"I hope you don't forget it."

Their stony standoff was interrupted by a potbellied man in lowslung jeans who ambled over to their table. "Hiya, Seth. I got stuck out at the track," he said before turning to Faye with a polite "Mornin'."

"Tommy, this is Fayette Hunt," Seth explained.

"Pleased to meet you," he said amiably, pulling out a chair to join them. "I'm Lester Thomas, a trainer friend of Seth's. You can just call me Tommy, like everyone else."

"That's kind of you." Faye's prickliness only bounced off the mild-mannered trainer, and he turned unconcernedly to engage his friend in horse talk.

Faye was about to stand up when Tommy switched his attention back to her. "Know anything about horseflesh, Miz Hunt?"

"I know which end kicks and which bites."

"That's a start, anyway," he said, laughing. "You're from the West Coast, aren't you?"

"I've been there a couple of years."

"Goin' back?"

"I'm in no rush," she said and got a narrowed glance from Carradine.

Oblivious to that exchange, Tommy chatted on. "I'm a nomad myself. Used to run some horses out in California but mainly I'm in Florida. Hialeah in winter and back here in the spring. But I'm gettin' older now—wouldn't mind a stake of my own. Seth 'n' me have had our eyes on that place of yours for a long time." He added innocently, "If we can get the rest of it for what he paid for a hundred acres—"

Seth interrupted him. "Tommy..."

"You don't have to shut him up, Carradine," Faye interjected. "Something already told me you were the buyer and that you didn't pay full value."

"That acreage was run-down," he said shortly.

"Is that going to be the same excuse you'll use when it comes time to bid on the rest of the farm?" She pushed her plate away and crossed her arms on the table. "Is that the game plan you and the bank decided on—run the old Hunt place into the ground so it'll be sure to go cheap?"

Not bothering to reply, Seth pushed his chair back and stomped out of the café. Robbed of her target, Faye turned to the other man and asked sweetly, "Does he always leave you with the bill, Mr. Thomas?"

"You're wrong about Seth, I can tell you that right now," he said, eyeing her balefully.

"Then why did he walk out instead of defending himself?"

"Because he's got a temper, and he doesn't like bein' accused of conniving." His fist gently pounded the tabletop for emphasis. "No man does."

"Remember that old saying, mister? If the shoe fits..."

He stood up. "Excuse me, lady, but I believe you Northerners are a tad too hasty in formin' your opinions."

Faye watched him stomp out, too, and bit her lip. *Nice going,* she said to herself in exasperation. *If I keep making enemies at this rate, I'm going to have this whole town against me.*

Faye had always been proud of being outspoken. In fact, she often used her bluntness to prove to co-workers and clients that she was a "tough cookie," a far more sophisticated and assured woman than her little-girl appearance might lead them to suspect. But her brashness occasionally got her into trouble. She hated having to apologize, having to admit she might be wrong.

I'm not wrong in this case, she insisted. *And anyway, what do I care about making enemies as long as I can get this trust mess cleared up in a hurry? Lexington isn't home to me. I don't owe anyone here anything. Except Gran... and she's gone.*

Faye was so immersed in thought that it took her several seconds to realize Gerrie was hovering over her with a pot of hot coffee and a solicitous smile. "I just made it fresh, honey. Strong coffee'll perk up anyone's spirits, I always say."

Annoyed at having let her feelings show, Faye said stiffly, "There's nothing the matter with my spirits. I'd just like the bill, please."

"Well you're too late, Miss High and Mighty," Gerrie came back with a tart snicker. "Seth already got it. He left a ten-dollar bill at the register."

"I'll pay for my own, thanks." She dug around in her purse for her wallet. "I don't want to owe that man anything. I don't trust him."

Gerrie's laughter boomed out in earnest this time. "You ain't the first woman to say that, honey."

Faye looked up at her sharply, wondering what the waitress meant. But she was too proud to ask.

FAYE COASTED TO A STOP in front of the neat little cottage on North Limestone Street. In her grandmother's day, the whole area had been considered the "wrong side of the tracks." Now the thoroughfare was a pleasant tree-shaded neighborhood, its humble origins transformed by fresh coats of paint and masses of daffodils sunny with optimism.

She switched off the ignition and glanced down at the address she'd jotted on the back of her tourist map. Funny how it had never dawned on Faye that Minah Willis had had a family and home of her own apart from her duties at Indian Creek Farm.

The elderly black woman had expressed delight over Faye's unexpected phone call and insisted she come right over. Minah's house was the renovated "shotgun cabin" on the corner. Built by the score in the early part of the century, the simple cottages had one outstanding feature—a long central corridor so straight that a man could shoot a shotgun through the front door and see the pellet exit through the back. The Willis cabin, with its pale yellow siding and white trim framing the veranda like a lace collar, had a charming Victorian look.

Faye rapped firmly on the glass panel in the front door. She heard slow footsteps coming from a long way off and composed herself to wait patiently, though patience, like tact, wasn't one of her strong points.

Minah took one look at the young woman on the veranda, and her whole face lit up. "My, but you're the livin' picture of your grandmother, Miz Fayette. I'd a recognized you anywhere, chile. Yes indeedy, you sure have growed up a lot.''

"Thanks, Minah. Those are the nicest compliments I've had in a long time.'' They hugged each other, and Faye stepped back to regard her. Though the woman's hands were gnarled with arthritis and her back was slightly humped, her coffee-colored skin was smooth and clear, except for a sprinkling of age spots across her cheeks. "You look terrific, too.''

"Oh, such talk.'' Minah waved her hand deprecatingly. "This ole body's about worn down. All it feels like doin' is sittin' in the sun and rockin' away.'' But as if in denial of her words, the woman's eyes sparkled with life. "Now what are we doin' standin' here chattin' away on the porch! You come in right now and I'll make us a snack.''

The tiny front parlor was furnished simply with a gold brocade love seat and a low mahogany table set for tea.

Faye smiled. "You've gone to too much trouble.''

"Now I won't listen to no such talk, Miz Fayette.'' Her hands were gentle on Faye's arm as she guided her to the sofa. "You're like a fresh wind blowin' through here. Just lookin' at you makes me feel forty years younger.''

"Do I really look like her, Minah?''

"You've got the same eyes, chile, the same fine bones in your face.'' Minah shook her head and brushed away a tear. "Time passes too quickly for all of us. I still can't believe she's gone.''

"I shouldn't have stayed away,'' Faye confessed fiercely. "Gran must have needed me.''

"No, no, it woulda made no difference. She wouldn't have known you. What's done is done.'' Minah picked up the plate of cookies from the table. "Come on, now, take one. Don't you remember how you used to love my molasses snaps?"

"How could I forget? I always thought you were the world's best cook."

"Wish I still was." Minah rubbed her gnarled hands. "But I'm not complainin'. The good Lord gives and He takes away."

"Do you ever miss the farm, Minah?"

"No, I don't. It was a changed place after Miz Courtney took ill and the bank got involved in her affairs. The situation got real bad for me after that Mr. Pettigrew had someone else sent out to watch over your gran." Minah paused to pour out the richly aromatic tea, and Faye noticed it was the same English Breakfast blend her gran had loved. "The nurse warn't nice to neither one of us, though mercifully Miz Courtney didn't notice or care. Even then she was mostly living in the past."

"What right did Pettigrew have to order a nurse?"

"Miz Courtney trusted that bank. Lordie, she'd had dealings there for sixty-five years! Guess that's what made it easy for them to do like they did."

"Exactly what did they do? I'm confused."

"I guess I never wrote to tell you this. Didn't want you to worry overmuch, chile." Minah's hand shook a little as she handed Faye the china saucer and cup. "But one time that wretched ole she-cat nurse shooed me right out of Miz Courtney's room just before Mr. Pettigrew came by. He and Miz Courtney were holed up together a powerful long time."

Faye leaned toward Minah, her eyes intent. "What happened?"

"I didn't know at the time, Miz Fayette. I only knew he had a mighty pleased look on his face when he came out of your pore gran's sickroom. And it made me real mad." Minah's gentle features hardened. "I tole him right out, 'You oughten to tire a frail lady like that.' And you know what he answered me back, real self-satisfied like? 'She's got nothing to worry about now, Minah,' he tole me and waved a fistful of papers in my face. 'She's taken care of.'"

"Yes, I'll just bet she was."

Minah nodded unhappily. "It took me a while to figure out the situation. Before you know it that pretty farm started goin' to hell in a hand basket, that's how bad it was. And by that time Miz Courtney had to go into one of them nursin' homes, so I felt it was beholden on me to see the ole place didn't fall to ruin. I called the bank and you know what they tole me?" Minah ran her fingers agitatedly across the lap of her neat kettle-cloth apron. "They said the trust board had decided it was uneconomical to pour any more money into Indian Creek Farm. Uneconomical! A farm Miz Courtney slaved to make a go of after your grandpa died back in '39, and made a thrivin' concern of it, too. I'll tell you, Miz Fayette, it hurt me. It hurt me real bad to see what they were doin'."

Faye sighed in frustration. She was furious over the situation, even more furious with herself. She remembered vividly the day she had received her copy of the trust documents from the Farmers and Breeders Bank. She had been living in Los Angeles at the time, busy juggling a dozen new accounts for an aggressive stockbrokerage firm. Faye had only given the papers a cursory glance. She remembered how relieved she'd felt that everything had been so neatly and conveniently arranged by Gran's bank. They'd taken the burden off her shoulders, and besides, she had rationalized to herself at the time, Gran wouldn't have known the difference, anyway.

"Minah, I'm not sure what legalities are involved, but it sounds to me like Gran's signing those trust papers was a blatant case of coercion."

"What does that mean exactly, honey?"

"It means Gran was forced to agree to the trust when she was in no state of mind to make that kind of decision," Faye explained briskly, eager to put her own remorse on the back burner for a while. "And if we could get a witness to testify to that in court, I might be able to fight the bank's control."

"But I already tole you, honey, they just shooed me aside. I didn't hear nothin'."

"Think back, please, Minah. What did the nurse do after she'd sent you out?"

"Well, as best I recollect," she said slowly, "I believe she did stay in the room with Miz Courtney and Mr. Pettigrew."

Faye nodded in excitement. "Great. Now do you remember who she was, Minah—her name?"

"Ida Pinkowski." Minah's nose wrinkled with disdain. "How could I forget? That woman treated me like trash, Miz Fayette, and her with a husband who died an alcoholic and that pore crazy daughter of their'n." The elderly woman turned a bright piercing look on Faye. "Come to think of it, I heard she put the girl in one of them fancy private hospitals after she left Miz Courtney's. Now I ask you, where'd she get the money for that?"

Faye nodded. "I see you're beginning to think like I am, Minah, and the conclusions aren't pretty at all."

"I shoulda knowed—" Minah sniffed "—someone like her'd be all too happy to get paid off for doin' no good."

"Is this Ida Pinkowski still alive?"

"You know, I think I heard she died some years back."

"Oh, hell!" Faye swore in frustration, forgetting for a moment the nice Baptist woman next to her on the sofa. She caught herself too late and was about to murmur an apology when Minah cut her off with a soft chuckle.

"I've heard worse in my seventy-five years, chile." She reached out then, covering Faye's hand with her own gnarled fingers. "Now, never you mind no more. What's done is done. And like I always say, for everything that happens there's a reason."

"Oh, I agree," Faye said at once. "The reason was my own stupid selfishness."

"Hush, now!" Minah pulled herself up from the sofa and smiled down at her guest. "Listen, chile, would you like to see what your Gran gave me before her mind started to go? I was real touched." Without waiting for an answer Minah went over to a small desk beneath the window and took something out of the top drawer.

She came and sat down again, fondly brushing the padded fabric cover of what looked to be a photo album. The book was edged with lace. "My daughter Eunace made this for me in arts 'n' crafts class a few years back. Real pretty, don't you think?" Faye smiled, watching expectantly as Minah opened to the first page. "Miz Courtney and me spent practically one whole autumn winnowin' through dusty ole boxes of pictures. My, but we had a fine time, just two tired old gals, reminiscin' about the past." Minah's smile radiated up from her lips to her eyes. The lovely warmth there touched Faye.

"We saved all the best ones for you, Miz Fayette, but these extras she kindly gave to me."

"I'm glad she did, Minah. You shared so much more of her life than I did."

Minah was chuckling now, her finger hovering over a faded print that was brown with age. "Will you look at the beauty your sweet grandmama was! Put all the other girls to shame."

Faye smiled, too, at the old high-school group shot. Courtney must have been just eighteen in the photo, blond and perky looking in her baggy sailor-style uniform. Then Faye's eye was drawn to a smaller photo that she had never seen. She guessed it had been taken a few years later. Courtney, in a stylish cloche hat and drop-waist dress that just touched her knees, stood between a young man and a woman.

"Who are these people with Gran?"

"Why, that was Laura Bell Swann and her younger brother, Quentin. Them three were the best o' friends," Minah said, smiling at some private memory. "Young Mr. Quentin was head over heels in love with your gran. He was one of her very first beaux."

Faye was enchanted. "She never told me about him. But then I guess he never stood a chance once her cousin Catesby came home from the war, handsome and tall and 'dashing as all get-out.' She always used to tell me that my Granddad Catesby cut the most dashing figure in Jessamyn and Fayette Counties combined."

"Mr. Hunt did that, right enough! No, young Quentin Swann could never hold a candle to your grand-daddy. Miz Courtney always loved Mr. Quentin like a brother. She'd laugh and ruffle his hair and flirt like crazy, but she never woulda married the likes of him. To her he was a reckless little daredevil who never gave a serious thought to anything.''

"Except her, apparently,'' Faye corrected with a grin, enjoying the image of her lovely old gran as a sweet young heartbreaker.

"Excep'n her.'' Minah nodded absently, lost in her own memories once again, and turned the album page.

Together the two women sifted through the past. Faye stared down at the pictures of her two uncles, killed in the Second World War long before she was born, and her aunt who had died of polio in a terrible epidemic. Faye's dad, Carter, had survived the war and come out of it a career military man who had little interest in the family farm.

"It never dawned on me before how sad Gran's life must have been—losing so many people she loved. She never talked about it. I mean, she was always fun loving and enthusiastic about everything.''

"She'd a never put such a burden on you, Miz Fayette. Her character was strong and fine,'' Minah said, closing the book in her lap. "Still, she had her real low periods, too.''

"She confided in you a lot, Minah?''

"She did more and more as we both got older. 'Vulnerable.' That was a word I heard Miz Courtney use over and over again about herself—and you.'' Minah shook her head. "After your daddy died she used it even more. Well, you can understand how she must have felt, Miz Fayette, with all her kids dead and you just a young girl.''

"But she and Dad were the ones who taught me to be so independent. She saw me graduate from college, get established in a career. Why should she have thought of me as vulnerable?''

"Honey, feelings ain't got nothin' to do with logic." Minah's eyes sought Faye's, as if to make certain the young woman understood what she was saying. "What worried her most toward the end was that there'd be nothin' left for you, Miz Fayette. She feared that if the land was gone you'd have to be a wanderer like your daddy was. See, you got to remember your grandmama's whole life was tied up in the farm she inherited from your granddaddy. She come to love it fiercely and all the roots connected with it since they were hers, too."

Faye shook her head. "I didn't realize she'd worried about me like that."

"Her family and her land were the most important things in the world to Miz Courtney. She wanted somethin' fierce for it to go on." Minah began to wring her hands as if they were hurting. "How it all fretted her when she was in her right mind."

FAYE WAS EXHAUSTED by the time she got back to the hotel. Her conversation with Minah had drained her completely. She had found herself looking at parts of herself that she hadn't even known were there. Faye glanced down at her watch. Just two o'clock? She felt as if she'd relived a whole lifetime.

She did a quick calculation in her head. It was noon on the coast. Faye fought down the temptation to just lie down on the bed and sleep away the rest of the afternoon. If she called right now, chances were she'd catch Harvey still in the office unless there was an important client to be entertained over lunch.

Harvey Weinstock was Faye's boss and mentor at Paine Webber, an intense but genial workaholic who loved to tease his young assistant about her own tendencies in that direction.

Faye had made up her mind what she was going to say to him by the time she dialed the last digit. "Mr. Weinstock, please," she said crisply, twirling the cord around her finger while she waited for him to answer. "Harve? I'm glad I got you. It's Faye."

"Good to hear your voice, Shortstuff," he said breezily, and Faye could picture him at his cluttered desk, the phone cradled against his shoulder as he punched numbers into his calculator and tried to sip cold coffee at the same time. "How'd your trip go? Okay?"

"No, Harve, that's why I'm calling. I'm still here in Lexington. I've run into a few snags."

"Doesn't sound serious. Or are you pulling your famous act of underplaying the problem so you can prove what a cool little cucumber you really are?"

She laughed. "You know me too well."

"So what's up, Faye? Is something wrong?" After she'd sketched out the situation, he whistled. "Sounds fishy."

"Yeah, the whole situation stinks to high heaven."

"So, what are you going to say to the fat man when you go to his office?"

"I don't know." Faye sighed and sat down on the edge of the bed. "Maybe I can shake him up a bit, get some answers. Maybe I can even get some compensation for neglect."

"But is it worth going to court over? Your life's here in San Francisco, Faye. I don't have to remind you you've got a busy agenda coming up. You can't afford to waste energy on something like that."

"Right, but then you know me, Harve." She kicked off her shoes and leaned down to rub her sore instep. "I hate to walk away from a fight, especially if I think I'm right."

"Boy, do I ever!" There was a brief pause and then his expressive voice came over the wires, imitating the referee in a boxing ring. "Okay, fellas, let's make this a clean fight. No long holds, no hitting below the belt. Got me, kid? Go for the knockout in three rounds."

She was really laughing now. "I'll try, Harve."

"Seriously, take off the rest of the week. I can put your accounts on hold for that long. When you get back you can come over to Sausalito and we'll perk you up with a really fine vintage Pinot Noir. Lynette just made a run over to Napa to restock the cellar."

"Terrific!" Faye said with genuine enthusiasm. She adored Harvey's family. She thought Lynette was one very special woman to put up with her husband's long hours away from home. Even their four-year-old son, Jordan, was getting to be a trooper about it, although Faye sometimes saw the disappointment in his eyes when his daddy brought paperwork home on the weekend, too.

"And Harve? Thanks again. You're an angel to be so cooperative."

"Look, can I say one more thing?"

"Of course."

"Don't go bulldozing into this Pettigrew guy's office like a miniature army tank. Fight him with what he might not be expecting."

"And what's that?" Faye asked, curious.

"A little Southern charm."

She laughed. "What makes you think I've got any, Harve?"

"Come on, Faye," he teased her. "For months I've been hearing about that fine Southern lady you idolized. Now don't tell me the gracious Courtney Hunt didn't teach you a trick or two."

"Hmm. Maybe she did."

Faye hung up the phone in a much better mood. Hearing her boss's familiar voice was just the tonic she needed. She would be out of Kentucky in a week and she'd put this uncomfortable aspect of her life behind her.

Still, a little voice nagged inside. *Is that what you really want, Faye? To put aside something that used to mean so much to you...?*

CHAPTER THREE

HARVEY'S PARTING WORDS OF ADVICE were uppermost in
Faye's mind as she stepped inside the dim lobby of the
Farmers and Breeders Bank on Tuesday morning. She
intended to be as sweet as pie to Hollister Pettigrew if that
attitude would get her what she wanted: a fair and reasonable settlement of Gran's estate so that she could say
goodbye to Lexington with a clear conscience.

If she hustled she could be on a plane home by Thurs-
day night. That would give her another full day here to
go through things out at the farm and choose a few special keepsakes for herself before the rest was sold. Harvey had been generous in telling her to take the rest of the
week off, but she intended to be back at her desk bright
and early Friday morning.

Faye crossed the wide foyer toward the door marked
President. Before going inside she took a deep breath.

Ah, the smell of old money, she told herself wryly as
she breathed in the musty air that pervaded the building.
The bank had been in business at least seventy-five years,
its ups and downs mirroring those of the farming and
bloodstock interests it served.

Nowadays business should mostly be up, Faye re-
flected, thinking about some of the fabulous sums local
Thoroughbred breeders were getting for their stock. Why
should the bank's board of directors be so covetous of
Courtney Hunt's piddly little spread? It didn't make

much sense when you got right down to it. Shaking her head, Faye went into the office.

The banker's young secretary looked up from her typewriter and smiled inquiringly.

"Good morning. I'm Faye Hunt. I have an eleven-thirty appointment with Mr. Pettigrew."

The girl flipped open her desk calendar. "I see ya down here now," she drawled, quickly looking up again. "I'll buzz to see if you can go right on in." She continued to smile, her blue-shadowed eyes taking in every detail of Faye's outfit.

Faye smiled to herself, glad she'd worn the soft emerald-green wool dress that she had picked up for a song at the New York garment district last fall. The label was that of an Italian designer and the dress was beautifully made, with its slightly padded shoulders and a row of pleats across the bodice that narrowed to a fitted waist and long swingy skirt. The outfit oozed elegance and chic. Casually draped around her collar was a silky wool scarf in shades of green, gray and beige that her father had brought her from Japan years ago. Not quite acceptable according to the "dress for success" code, but then Faye had always been a maverick.

"You can go right in, Miz Hunt," the girl said admiringly as Faye moved around the desk toward the boss's door. "Mr. Pettigrew's expectin' you."

Faye knocked politely before entering.

"Good morning," she greeted the bank president in her best saccharine-sweet voice. "I think it's really kind of you to take time out of your busy schedule to explain things to..." She hesitated a fraction of a second, debating if she would be laying it on too thick to say "poor li'l ole me," decided it would be and finished with "...a newcomer like me."

Pettigrew stood up, slack-jawed at this radical change of manner, but recovered himself at once. "Set yourself right down, Fayette Lee. Like I always say, our first aim is to please."

"I realize that," she said demurely, perching on the edge of the chair he'd indicated. "And I must apologize for my behavior on Sunday. Sometimes I'm just too hot-headed for my own good."

Pettigrew spread his chubby arms wide, indicating his willingness to forgive, and Faye wished he'd hurry and sit back down. Towering above her like that gave him too much of a psychological advantage. But no such luck.

He continued to smile down at her benevolently, like a revivalist preacher gazing at his flock. "Now that's all right, Fayette. I could understand your feelings."

"Could you?" Her eyes flashed a sharp, inquiring look.

Realizing his error, he corrected himself quickly. "Now what I meant was you were just upset because you don't understand the whole confluence of events that led us to take your poor grandmother under our wing." He sat down and rested his hands on the thick folder before him.

"I'd be most grateful if you could clarify it for me, then." She gave a practice bat of her eyelashes and realized the whole business would have been more effective if she'd put on another coat of mascara.

Pettigrew preened a little and smoothed back the springy mass of reddish-brown hair that artfully hid his bald spot. "It's not a simple matter, little lady, but I'll do my best."

Had his voice actually deepened? Faye had to fight down a hysterical urge to laugh. "I'm sure you will, Mr. Pettigrew," she said, regarding him with naive, expectant eyes.

"This bank has been involved with the Hunt family for longer than you and me have been alive, Fayette Lee. You understand so far."

"What you're saying is," she said sweetly, "there was an attitude of mutual trust built up over those years."

He nodded, beaming, and then got all red faced with annoyance as the implication of her words sunk in. "Now, Fayette Lee, these are the facts," he said sternly. "After your grandfather died, it was real touch and go for your grandmama. She hung on, though, and built up Indian Creek Farm into a fine showcase. The older she got, the more it became an obsession for her to keep the place intact for her heirs—for you."

"So naturally, because Gran and the bank had this long relationship built on mutual trust, you immediately sold off a hundred acres." She couldn't help the sarcastic tone with which she spoke; it just came out.

"Who told you that?"

"It doesn't matter who."

"This is a financial institution, not a charity," he went on pompously, determined to regain control. "Once Mrs. Hunt started to decline, so did the farm. Now you can't go attachin' any blame there."

That much at least was true. Gran had given up the horses years ago. All she'd had was a small pension and the cash income from the tobacco fields she rented out to tenant farmers. But surely it had been enough to live on; she'd never complained.

Faye had to ask. "What happened? Did she have to come to you for a loan?"

"A small one. She had this crazy dream of gettin' that old barn renovated."

"And . . ."

"And shortly after that she started to go downhill. The workmen she'd hired turned out to be regular fly-by-nights. We did what we had to to protect our investors from a loss."

"That's understandable, but it still doesn't explain why you didn't keep the property up."

"Have you ever heard the saying 'Ain't no use in throwin' good money after bad'?"

"That was a fertile farm, dammit!" So much for laying on the Southern charm. "Land prices were going up five years ago. Indian Creek Farm would still have been a showcase for any buyer. Why'd you let it go downhill and why did you sell off a hundred acres without informing me?"

"Land tax came due," he said soberly, not quite looking Faye in the eye. "It had to be paid somehow."

"And what's going to happen this year?"

"I don't like havin' to be the one to tell you this." Pettigrew frowned and opened the file on the desk. "But I'm afraid there's a codicil to the trust that you might've overlooked."

"What codicil?" she asked in disbelief.

He slipped on his reading glasses and riffled through the pages until he found the one he was looking for. In a monotone he read the legal mumbo-jumbo out loud. When he'd finished he looked at Faye over the top of his glasses and cleared his throat nervously. "What this here means is that whether you as the heir want to or not, you might be forced to sell that property."

"Now I really don't understand," she said in exasperation.

"The stipulation is that the land is yours only as long as it supports itself, and the bank has the right to sell off pieces of the farm in order to pay expenses."

"That's the craziest catch-22 I've ever heard of! How can it be self-supporting when you've run it down into a dump?" Eyes flashing, she reached across the desk and pulled the file toward her. "I don't believe you."

Pettigrew's chubby forefinger stabbed at the paragraph and then moved down the page to show where Courtney had signed her agreement to the stipulation.

Faye took one look at the weak signature and demanded angrily, "Did my grandmother have legal counsel with her the day she signed this?"

"It wasn't necessary."

"Oh, really. Was that your fine judgment working, Mr. Pettigrew? I happen to have a witness who says Gran wasn't in sound mind and that you coerced her to agree."

"Who?" Small beads of perspiration had broken out on his forehead. "Not Id . . ." He didn't finish.

"What were you going to say?" Faye persisted, but he had recovered his aplomb.

"All I have to say is I've read about you litigation-crazy Californians," Pettigrew said self-righteously. "Always lookin' for trouble, lookin' for a way to make a fast dollar."

Faye shot up out of her seat. "I don't give a damn about the money. It's the principle, Pettigrew. All I can see is a banker who took advantage of a lonely old woman's weakness." She felt the sting of tears in her eyes and had to fight herself not to let them flow. "What I see is an institution that systematically and cruelly tore down the one thing that mattered most to her in the whole world. What I want to know is why." She leaned forward and pounded the desk almost under his nose. "Why? I smell some sort of ugly collusion here, Mr. Pettigrew."

"Those are slanderous words," he warned.

So she said them again. "I smell some sort of ugly collusion, and I swear I'm going to find out what it's about and who's involved. And when I do it's going to be your neck out there, Mr. Hollister Pettigrew. Scandal—in big capital letters across the front page of the *Herald*."

His small eyes seemed to retreat farther into their sockets. "You're talkin' wild now."

"I guarantee you'll find out I'm more than just a talker." With that she swept out of his office.

Once out on the sidewalk Faye took a deep breath to calm her jangled nerves. *Now the fat's really in the fire,* she thought. How could she have made threats she had no intention of carrying out? Or didn't she? The kernel of an idea implanted itself in her mind, but she tried to brush it away. *Come on now, Faye,* she chastised herself. *Be reasonable.*

As she began to calm down, Faye realized she was being jostled by passersby. Across the street in the courthouse park, brown baggers were taking advantage of the fitful spring sunshine. It was lunchtime, but Faye's stomach was too tied up in knots for her to be hungry. Still, she felt she had to sit down somewhere quiet and just think. Spotting a little café-bar on the corner, she headed that way.

Inside she perched on a bar stool and studied the wine and beer list posted on the wall. The bartender came up to her and desultorily flicked his towel over the shiny wooden bar. "What'll you have?"

She shrugged. "I guess just a draft beer, please."

"Are you kiddin' me?" The man grinned toothily. "You barely look old enough for sody pop, let alone beer."

With a sigh of exasperation Faye flipped her wallet open on the counter to show her driver's license. "From California, are ya?" He studied the license with interest. "Them hot tubs I've been readin' you got out there must be like them fountains of youth." When he saw she was in no mood for friendly joshing, he retreated tactfully to take care of other customers as they straggled in.

The beer was cold and slightly bitter, a perfect complement to Faye's feelings. She turned the mug around and around on the bar top, wondering what to do next. She had half a mind to take over Indian Creek and make it into a going concern, if for no other reason than to spite the sanctimonious Hollister Pettigrew. From the banker her thoughts moved in a natural progression to Seth Carradine. How did he fit in?

She sensed the attractive horseman was the wild card, the unexpected element. A man who played the easygoing charmer to get what he wanted. And it was obvious Indian Creek Farm played a key part in his plans. Faye sensed he was the type who was a little selfish, very ambitious and not afraid to go after what he wanted. *Someone very much like me,* she realized in surprise.

She left a dollar on the bar and went outside, feeling just as unsettled as she had before she'd gone in. She felt like a character she had seen in a cartoon strip once. The guy was standing on a piece of ice in the middle of a body of water. The ice started to separate beneath him. He looked down in a panic as his legs stretched crazily in two directions, but he couldn't move. *That's me,* Faye thought ruefully. *One foot in Lexington and one in California. Now what am I supposed to do?*

THE MANSION RESTAURANT stood just off the Newtown Pike. Its candlelit tables graced a series of small period rooms. The atmosphere was elegant and cozy, an unexpected combination not unlike Barry himself.

Faye lifted her wineglass and clinked it lightly against his. "It was sweet of you to move up our dinner date like this. I wasn't sure I'd still be around Friday."

"I should have thought of it myself, Fayette. Guess I've never gotten out of that old rut of working during the week and only socializin' on the weekend."

"Oh, don't apologize," she said with a smile. "It sounds like a perfectly reasonable way to live your life."

"And nothing like the way you live yours, I'll bet." Beneath his teasing, had there been a faint note of regret?

"Oh, yeah, it's great," she retorted airily, "if you happen to love three-ring circuses."

"You were always one to be the center of a whirlwind—one way or another." His tone grew nostalgic. "I sure missed you after you left."

"I'll bet your mother didn't, though. If I'd hung around any longer than I did, she probably would have killed us both," Faye said, determined to keep the mood light. "Anyway, you look content and settled now."

"I guess I am, more or less. Maybe fatherhood does that to you."

"Barry, you didn't even mention that before!"

"Corky's five. Five going on twenty-two," he added wryly. "Sometimes I can't believe how fast he's growin' up."

"Corky. That's cute." She grinned. "Whose family name is that?"

"My ex-wife's. Actually his name is Corcoran Willoughby Markham. But that seemed too much of a burden for such a little guy, so I started calling him Corky."

"Does your ex have custody?"

"I do, as a matter of fact." He looked a little embarrassed. "Belinda wasn't exactly cut out for the tame life. She's remarried now to some talent agent down in Nashville."

"I'm sorry," Faye said, not knowing how else to reply.

"Mama thought she was a real prize because Belinda's mother was a socialite and her daddy was a real bigwig at Louisville Downs. She was beautiful but a little spoiled."

"Well," Faye said forthrightly, "it sounds like you were better off to have dumped her."

"Actually it was the other way around."

"Then she was an idiot," Faye concluded in her typical straightforward style and turned her attention to the menu. "Now what do you recommend? I'm in the mood for something French and fattening. Definitely the veal in cream sauce, right?"

Since Barry still seemed to be hurting from his divorce, Faye did her best over dinner to cheer him up with stories about the eccentric clients she advised and about the old Victorian house in Pacific Heights she'd bought with two friends and converted into a three-unit condominium complex.

Barry perked up. "That must've been a good investment."

"It was, especially since we did most of the work ourselves."

"You?" he said, amused.

"Listen, I pound a mean nail." She cast a critical eye around the room they were dining in and added, "I could've taught these guys a thing or two about drywall." She was rewarded with Barry's laugh.

"Is that where you live now, Fayette?"

"No, I've got it rented out." She tapped her fingernail on the edge of the wineglass and listened to its bell-like tone. "No, I'm still in the same little furnished studio I found when I first got to San Francisco."

"Don't you ever think about settling down?"

She shook her head abruptly. "I'm happy with my life just the way it is."

She finished her wine in silence, grateful for the diversion of the beautifully laden pastry cart the waiter wheeled to a stop before their table. Proudly he pointed out each artful confection: rum trifle, caramel soufflé, chocolate almond torte, and the pièce de résistance—hothouse strawberries injected with liqueur and dipped in Swiss chocolate.

When he'd finished, Faye looked up at him innocently. "Don't you have just plain old chocolate chip cookies?"

"I'm afraid not, madame, though last night the pastry chef whipped up some chocolate chip mousse in a meringue shell. I could check to see if there's any left."

"Sorry, I'm a purist. That just wouldn't be the same," she sniffed, shooting Barry a sly, mischievous look. "Guess I'll pass."

Over coffee Faye allowed herself to get serious at last. "Barry," she began, "do you mind if I ask for some legal advice?"

"What is it?"

"I had a confrontation with Hollister Pettigrew today at the bank over Gran's estate. It's literally a mess, and I think the bank is culpable as hell." She paused. "Have you been out by Indian Creek Farm at all in the past few years?"

"I drive by it on the pike when I'm heading toward Versailles. Always makes me kind of sad to see the place so deserted. But otherwise I never noticed anything else."

"That's just the point, Barry," she said, agitated. "I think they deliberately planned it that way. When I was out there on Sunday I noticed how the grass was mowed only by the road."

"Now Fayette, that's not proof of negligence."

"Please let me finish," she returned. "As I walked over the grounds it dawned on me there was a pattern to it. They had reshingled the part of the barn facing the pike, but the far side was falling in. They painted the front of it, but inside it's a disaster area. Those trustees did just enough so the neighbors wouldn't complain." Her eyes flashed. "Only I bet Seth Carradine wasn't complaining. He was just waiting to swoop down and buy the farm cheap."

"Now don't go being hasty."

"Why does everybody keep saying that to me!" She ran her fingers through her hair, sending the neat blunt-cut ends into a flurry of wisps. "It's beginning to drive me nuts."

"Come on, relax," Barry said soothingly. "No use in getting riled up over Carradine, too."

"Oh, really? What do you know about him?"

Barry shrugged. "Just what I hear my brothers say. That he's one damned fine trainer but hard to work with. Stubborn as all get-out and hellbent on doing things his own way. Maybe he'll settle down now that's he's building up that spread of his own, but I doubt it."

"What do you mean?"

"I don't know." He shrugged unconcernedly again. "Just that some men have that fiery streak in them. The air kind of changes when they walk in. You know what I mean? It gets more electric, like you can feel the tension seeping out of them.''

"I think I do know what you mean," she said slowly, remembering how it was to be around Carradine. She'd felt on edge, prickly, all her senses on alert because she didn't know quite what to expect from him. Faye rubbed her arms and tried to brush the memory of him away. "Anyway, Barry, I want to know what you think about the whole situation. Don't you think the bank's been negligent?''

"Faye, what you're saying is just too outlandish. Hasn't it occurred to you that the farm has just slowly been declining for fifteen years? Once your Gran got older she wasn't quite so active and couldn't afford as much hired help. You can't go blaming a bank for that.''

"Barry, you're not listening to what I'm saying." Her voice rose. "Pettigrew deliberately took advantage of Gran's weakness to achieve some end of his own, or the bank's. I know it!''

"You can't go blurting things like that," he admonished her, glancing cautiously around the quiet dining room. "You never know who might overhear you.''

"I don't care who hears me," she retorted, though she did lower her voice to an impatient whisper. "For Pete's sake, Barry, I'm so burned up over the whole business I feel like marching up and down Main Street wearing a sandwich board that says 'The Farmers and Breeders Bank screws little old ladies.' Or running an ad in *The Lexington Herald* that says Hollister Pettigrew is a sanctimonious bag of wind and a cheat to boot.''

"That isn't funny, Fayette." He looked really upset now. "You aren't a kid anymore. People aren't about to put up with that kind of stuff. They expect a woman, especially one with a social standing like yours, to act with some decorum. No one wants to see dirty linen aired in public. It just isn't proper etiquette to go stirring up an ugly hornet's nest over who's cheating who.''

"You think I care about blue-blood etiquette when all these people are running around being unethical as hell?'' she said indignantly. "I can't believe you said that to me, Barry Markham!''

He reached across the table to touch her hand. "All I meant to say was you can't go running off all angry, making a fool of yourself. I still think you're imagining things,'' he went on quietly. "But even if it all was true, it still wouldn't matter.''

"What do you mean it wouldn't matter?''

"What I'm saying is, there isn't a darn thing you can do about it, anyway.''

"Listen to me, Barry—if you think I have a case, I could take them to court.'' She was on fire with enthusiasm.

"Look,'' he said patiently, "I'm going to tell you a few facts of life about the South that you may've forgotten or maybe you never knew. The lawyers here are like a fraternity. We sometimes have to close our eyes to each other's petty sins.''

"Petty sins?'' she repeated in disbelief. "In this case I'd say it's more like grand larceny.''

"Drop it, Fayette.''

"Are you telling me to just close my eyes to the whole business and walk away?''

"I'm telling you to pick up the pieces of what's left and be glad you got that much,'' he said firmly. "The time's past for bein' a rebel.''

"I think you'd better take me back to the hotel,'' she said, feeling defeated. "I'm awfully tired all of a sudden.''

They drove back to town in silence. Faye stared out the window, past the darkened high-tech factories that were gradually encroaching on the rural landscape. And she thought about what she had said to Barry when he'd asked her why she didn't think about settling down. *I'm happy with my life just the way it is.*

If that were entirely true then why did she wake up in the middle of the night sometimes and question where her life was going? Were a closetful of beautiful clothes, a red Alfa Romeo convertible in the garage and a few savvy investments what it was all about? Faye had been waking up like that more and more often now since Gran had died.

She remembered something Gran had said once about her youngest son, Faye's dad. It was the closest she had ever come to criticizing the life-style he had chosen. "I declare," Gran had said in a sad voice, "that man was simply running away from himself." Faye sighed. *Is that what I'm doing, too?*

Barry drew to a stop in the hotel's curving drive and started to climb out.

"Please don't bother, Barry. I can find my own way in. I'm a big girl."

"Fayette, stop chastising me, please. I don't want us to fight." He reached across to take her hand. "I didn't mean to sound so negative back at the restaurant; I was just trying to be a realist. I don't want to see you get hurt any more."

"That's sweet of you, Barry. Thanks." She started to disengage her hand, but he held it more firmly.

"I'd like to do this again before you leave."

"I'll let you know."

"Fayette..." He hesitated. "If you want me to look over those trust documents, I will."

She leaned across the seat and kissed him warmly on the cheek. "I should have married you back when I had the chance," she teased him. "You're an angel."

He laughed. "It's never too late."

Faye climbed out of the car and then poked her head back in again, her hazel eyes mischievous. "I'll keep that in mind."

She shoved her hands into the pockets of her jacket and watched him drive away. After he'd gone she hurried inside, eager to soak in a bubble bath and concentrate on nothing more demanding than the latest Stephen King novel she'd started on the plane.

FAYE HAD JUST CLIMBED out of the tub, all pink and blessedly sleepy, when the phone rang. She shoved her arms into her thin silk robe and rushed to answer, glancing at the travel alarm on the table beside it. Eleven-thirty! Who could be calling this late?

"Hello?"

"You sound all out of breath, Hundred Pounds."

Faye's hands tightened around the receiver. "Carradine, if I'd known it was you, believe me, I wouldn't have hurried to answer," she said in her best put-down voice. "You've got one hell of a nerve calling me at this time of night."

"Nerve, hell! I've been ringin' your room every half hour waiting for you to get in, and if that ain't persistence I don't know what is. I was afraid you were going to keep me up all night," he needled her, "and dammit, I'm a workin' man. I've gotta get up early."

"I can't believe you're for real, Carradine!" she fumed. "What do you think I am—an idiot who'd allow someone like you to put me on the defensive? You are very quickly using up my limited store of patience."

"Then I guess I'd better apologize."

"Yes, I guess you'd better apo—" She stopped in midword, suspicious all of a sudden. "Why did you give in so easily?"

"I just don't want to have you hanging up on me before I've spoken my piece."

He had her attention now; still, she wasn't going to make it easy for him.

"What makes you think you have anything to say that might interest me?" she bluffed. "What makes you think I'm not going to blow my rape whistle into your ear right this second?"

"Rape whistle? Ho-ly Hannah."

"Well, what makes you think I won't?" To prove to herself she wasn't completely bluffing, Faye picked up the phone and carried it around the bed. But the cord was too short. Her purse still lay out of reach on the dresser where she'd tossed it when she came in.

"I'll tell you why you won't. Because women are curiouser than cats."

"You mean more curious," she corrected his grammar smugly.

"Exactly," he replied with equal satisfaction. "I knew you and me would have to agree on something eventually."

"Carradine, I can't believe you're as dumb as you pretend to be."

"Do you always sweet-talk a man this way? I mean, it could become addictive."

She started to chuckle but caught herself. "Carradine, do you have something to say or don't you?"

"Yes, I do," he said soberly. "I've been thinkin' about it, and I've decided it was wrong of me to have stomped out on you the way I did the other morning. I apologize for that. I started considering things from your point of view, and I guess it looks kinda bad."

"Is this a confession?"

"Why—do you have a tape recorder running or something?"

"Don't worry. Taped confessions aren't admissible in court," she assured him. "They're only good for blackmail."

He whistled softly. "If you act half as tough as you talk you must be one mean critter, Fayette Lee Hunt. Makes me wary of trying to do business with you."

"What kind of business?" she demanded. "I've definitely decided not to sell."

"Yeah, I got the feeling you were one of those dig-in-your-heels types. That's why I'm callin' you now," he said slowly. "I've got a proposition to make."

"Do you usually proposition women in the middle of the night?" she countered. "You think their resistance is at a low point or something?"

His laughter drifted over the wires. "I just didn't want to take the chance of having you slip away."

Had he meant those words to sound so devastatingly seductive? She fought to quell the silly clamor of her pulse, but her blood was temporarily affected by the sound of that low, spontaneous, downright sexy laugh of his. Dammit!

"Look, bud," she said too loudly, "I'm not going anywhere for the time being."

"Glad to hear it." He chuckled, and a warm shiver went up her spine. "Can I come over?"

"Don't take me so literally! No, you cannot come over." The words tumbled out in a nervous squeak, and she found herself clutching her robe more tightly around her as if he could somehow see through it. "What is it about you that reminds me of a vulture, even when you're trying to be nice?''

"You've got a mean mouth, Hundred Pounds."

Thank heavens they were back to nice impersonal insults again. "Well, you know what they say, Carradine," she said, on surer ground now. "The best defense is a good offense."

"You've sure been that all right."

"I've been what?"

"Offensive."

She cocked her head like an affronted rooster. "Goodnight, Hardboots," she said tartly.

But before she could hang up, his soft, low laughter burst out again. "I don't have my boots on now."

With a click the line went dead, and Faye replaced the receiver with a shaky hand. Her blood was revving up again. She tried to tell herself that a good argument with a feisty sparring partner always did that to her. Carradine was a tonic, that was all, a necessary antidote to Pettigrew's oily smoothness.

But what accounted for that delicious sense of warmth deep in her belly, that unexpected aura of awareness of her whole body—like a prickly itch she couldn't quite scratch?

Faye drew a deep, shuddering breath. *Now let's just put things in perspective,* she counseled herself severely. *Seth Carradine is an uneducated, rough-around-the-edges hayseed and irritatingly macho to boot.* Not *my type at all.*

Yet she had to admit she was looking forward to seeing him again. She couldn't help wondering what on earth he had to propose.

CHAPTER FOUR

FAYE SETTLED BACK TO WAIT, her gaze moving idly around the office while Barry read over the trust documents she had brought. Before she talked to Carradine, she wanted to know if she had any legal leverage at all.

Walnut bookshelves rose to the ceiling behind Barry's desk. His law books had replaced the extensive bloodstock library that had occupied the space in his father's time. Otherwise, the traditionally furnished room bore the unmistakable stamp of the elder Markham, even though he'd been dead almost ten years. His favorite English hunting prints still graced the dark paneled walls and his rack of pipes stood on a sideboard, as if awaiting their owner's return.

Faye glanced back at Barry. Had he always had that slight nervous tic at the corner of his mouth? She noticed, too, how his long fingers drummed out a tense rhythm on the mahogany desktop as he read. Faye had thought of him as such a placid person, the easygoing type who would cheerfully settle into the life expected of him even if it didn't match his own private dreams. But maybe she was wrong.

She remembered that Barry had loved science and technical gadgetry, that he'd always had some funny little device or another lying around. Now his desk was almost too neat; except for a couple of framed photographs, it revealed nothing personal about its owner. He looked up then and Faye smiled overbrightly, feeling guilty about prying where she had no business to be doing so.

"Fayette, I'm sorry, but this looks airtight," he said, closing the thick file with an air of finality.

"So it's airtight from a legal point of view," she countered, refusing to be defeated. "But what about the ethics involved?"

"You know I can't answer that, Fayette," he said patiently. "I'm not a preacher, I'm a lawyer. And what you've got here is a trust document written by a whole phalanx of attorneys who know their business. This thing follows the letter of the law to a T."

"Oh, come on, Barry, there are always loopholes, aren't there?" she retorted. "People legally break contracts every day."

"I suppose they might," he conceded, "if they've hired a slick enough attorney of their own."

"Well, then," she said expectantly, looking at him.

"Boy, you're a stubborn woman. I thought we went over this ground last night, Fayette." Barry leaned back with a sigh. "I guess I was hopin' what I told you would sink in after you had a chance to sleep on it. I was hopin' you'd be a little more realistic about this." His blue eyes were apologetic. "I don't like to have to be the one to say this, but do you know what you are in the eyes of this town?"

"What—a vagabond? A hobo? A no-account Northerner?" she snapped. "Is that what you tradition-loving Kentuckians see?"

"Now, Fayette, I'm not necessarily saying that's how I see you."

"Barry, please stop trying to coddle me. Just spit out whatever it is you have to say, for heaven's sake! I can take it. You know I'm not one of those thin-skinned shrinking violets.''

His mouth tightened. ''Okay, I will. In plain and simple language, Fayette, you're an outsider. And this is a small, close-knit community. No one's about to cut his own professional throat to help you.''

For all her tough talk, the words hurt. ''What about friendship? Doesn't that count for anything?''

''I'm not a trust lawyer, Fayette.'' He scratched his head uncomfortably. ''What do you expect me to do?''

''You have friends.''

''They wouldn't help, Fayette. Like I said, everyone knows everyone else. They've got to do business with the Farmers and Breeders Bank every day. Why should they risk tanglin' with Pettigrew on your account?''

''Doesn't the Hunt name mean anything?''

''Fayette, as far as this town's concerned, your grandmama was the last Hunt. It's been ten years since you've spent any time here at all. You were a seventeen-year-old girl. Now you come back a woman no one knows.'' Barry's expression was sympathetic. ''I'm sorry, Fayette, but as far as this town is concerned you simply have not paid your dues.''

''I'm curious. Is that how you see me, too—as an outsider?''

He looked away. ''I don't want to be put in a position of having to choose between my loyalties to you and—''

She didn't let him finish. ''I didn't mean that as emotional blackmail, dammit. I'm just trying to get a clearcut picture of how I fit in. Did I ever really fit in at all?''

Their uncomfortable conversation was interrupted when the office door burst open and a small boy ran in.

"Hey, Daddy!" the child cried excitedly, his high-pitched voice a friendly drawl that was exactly like Barry's. "I'm home. Look what I made in kiddygarden."

Barry pushed back his swivel chair and Corky climbed up onto his lap. "My, that's real fine," Barry said with genuine enthusiasm as he examined the little house glued together out of Popsicle sticks. "Now, Corky, I want you to meet an old friend of mine. Say hey to Miss Hunt."

"Hey, Miz Hunt," he said shyly, sneaking her a quick glance from beneath long eyelashes. Before she could reply, Corky was talking to his dad again. "What do you think, Daddy? Miz Crabtree at school says I'm a fine artitect."

"Architect," Barry corrected him, smiling apologetically to Faye over his son's tousled blond head.

Faye smiled back, not minding at all. It intrigued her to watch their interaction. Barry had donned a whole new persona. The temporizing and lack of forcefulness that made Fayette impatient with him at times was no longer evident. Fatherhood had brought out a sureness in him that she'd never seen before.

She remembered the little bit he'd told her about his marriage breaking up and she wondered now about the untold part of the story. She wondered how his wife had felt about living at the Oak Hill enclave with the rest of the Markham clan. For a lively woman used to her own way, the Markhams' sumptuous but constrained life-style might have become a prison after a while.

After a quick kiss for his dad, Corky jabbered something about milk and cookies and took off as suddenly as he had appeared.

"Sorry about the interruption," Barry said.

"I'm glad I had the chance to meet him," she replied. "Corky seems like a terrific kid."

"He is."

Faye grinned. "Is he going to be a third generation Oak Hill breeder?"

"Not if I can help it."

The resentment in his voice shocked Faye, but she had no desire to pry. Barry's relationship with his family was no longer any of her business.

"Anyway, it looks like he has a promising future as an 'artitect,'" she said jokingly, as if she hadn't noticed anything. "Getting back to our discussion, Barry, I realize you can't represent me. But as my friend-who-happens-to-be-an-attorney, what would you advise me to do?"

"You know, you could just sell out and be done with it," he offered tentatively. "The price might not be as much as you hoped for, but it'd still be a tidy sum. You could invest in more promising real estate out in California."

"Oh, is that how I should see myself now—as a budding real-estate tycoon?"

He shrugged. "I guess I wonder how you do see yourself, Fayette. I've never quite figured it out."

"I've never thought about it much myself. I've been so busy working the past seven years.... And besides, I've never been one for all that introspective soul-searching jazz." Without warning her whole face lit up mischievously. "Actually, I share Popeye's philosophy."

"Popeye?" he repeated in disbelief.

"Yeah, you know what he always says—'I yam what I yam.'"

Barry shook his head. "Fayette Lee, you are a real card. Can't you ever be serious?"

"I'm trying to be," she retorted. "The truth is I just don't know what the heck to do."

"That's not what you told me last night. You said you were happy with your life just the way it is out there in California."

She shrugged offhandedly. "So I lied a little."

"Well, what would make you happy?"

"Oh, I don't know..." She stood up and put the file in her briefcase. "Fighting City Hall maybe...." She gave him a spunky grin. "And winning."

"You never were one for listening to sensible advice, were you?" he replied ruefully, walking her to the door.

"Look, before I give up I have a few cards to play."

"How long is that goin' to take?"

"Good question." She laughed ruefully. "I'm sure my boss is going to be asking the same thing."

"Well, are you goin' to share your strategy with me?"

"For one thing I think I'm going to talk to Seth Carradine."

Barry frowned. "Consortin' with the opposition? I don't think that's wise."

"I'm going to hear him out, anyway."

"Now you be careful, Fayette. He wasn't raised the way you and me were. I hear his daddy was a no-account alcoholic from the hills."

"Honestly, Barry, you can be such a stuffed shirt sometimes!" she exclaimed. "Do you think I'm in better hands dealing with a gentleman skunk like Pettigrew?"

Before Barry could reply, Corky came running out of the den and wrapped his arms around his dad's long legs. The boy stared up at Faye with his remarkably direct gaze.

"Say goodbye to Miss Hunt," Barry coached him.

"Bye, Miz Hunt," he said obligingly as he tried to pull Barry backward. "Come on, Daddy, I built a rocket out of Legos. I want you to see."

Faye winked at Barry. "I won't keep you any longer. I can see you're a busy man." She looked down at Corky then. "I'll see you around, Shortstuff."

"Shortstuff!" The boy was affronted.

"Look," she told him as if he were twenty years old, "there aren't many people I can say that to. And I'm sure by the next time I see you you'll be taller than me. You take care of your daddy now, okay?"

Satisfied, Corky smiled and nodded.

Barry put in, "I hope it's not that long until I see you again, Fayette."

She smiled. "I'll let you know how I've decided to handle things."

"Right. You take care now."

Outside Faye turned up the collar of her jacket and hurried across the wide veranda toward the stairs. But on the top step she turned to look back at the house. The sun had broken through the clouds long enough to cast shadows of the four massive white columns supporting the two-story portico. The decorative brass eagles flanking either side of the glass-paneled doors shone brightly.

Here was the essence of old-fashioned gentility, Faye realized. The graceful mansion had an air of wealth and pride in family lineage, an atmosphere of stolidity and permanence that she used to scoff at. Now she pictured Barry and his son sprawled comfortably before the fireplace in the den. The scene was a touchingly intimate one. Faye shook her head, reminding herself she wasn't the type to look back in regret. She ran down toward her waiting car.

Just as she was unlocking the door, another car drew to a halt behind hers in the curving gravel drive. A blond, heavyset woman climbed out from behind the driver's seat of the gray Mercedes Benz. Impeccably groomed in a conservative wool suit, she carried her weight with the grace of a laden ship under sail.

Faye recognized her at once and walked back to greet her with hand extended. "Hello, Mrs. Markham. It's been a long time."

"Fayette Hunt. Barrish mentioned you were in Lexington." Reluctantly the older woman accepted her outstretched hand. "A short stay, I'd imagine?"

"That all depends," Faye replied evenly. "There are still a lot of unresolved questions about my grandmother's estate."

"I was very sorry to hear that Mrs. Hunt had died. She was a true lady."

"Yes, she was."

"It's a shame you couldn't have spent more time with her, Fayette," the woman replied with a faint touch of asperity, "instead of being sent pillar to post all over the country with your father."

The implied criticism rankled Faye, and her nose tilted up in defiance. "I never felt deprived. In fact, quite the opposite," she asserted. "It taught me to make the best of things no matter what situation I happen to find myself in."

"There's only one danger, of course," Siperia Markham retorted coolly. "A person might find herself not caring if she'll ever truly fit in anywhere. I find that pitiable."

"I'm sure you do," Faye said between her teeth.

"Especially when I contrast it to my own family," Mrs. Markham went on sententiously. "*We* have always prided ourselves on our sense of belonging."

"Even when some family members might not want to belong?" Faye's determination to be on her best behavior had been shot sky high by the other woman's manner.

"I see you will never change, Fayette. You were a bad influence on Barrish ten years ago and—"

"I'd always hoped that Barry would be man enough to make his own decisions," Faye broke in crisply, "and not allow himself to be led by the nose by any woman—his mother included."

"Well!"

"Goodbye, Mrs. Markham." Faye turned and walked back toward her car, wishing now that she had kept her mouth shut. The last thing she needed was to antagonize that powerful woman.

Faye drove back toward town, deep in thought. She tried to be fair and to see herself from the Markhams' point of view—a drifter with no sense of commitment to anyone or anything. It wasn't a very pretty image.

An outsider. She repeated Barry's words to herself and felt sudden sympathy for the ugly little critter in *E.T.* Oh hell, I guess that's me, she thought in frustration. A "dang furriner" who doesn't quite belong anywhere.

CHAPTER FIVE

FAYE WANDERED up and down the aisles of the big toy store, trying to guess what would appeal to a five-year-old boy. Seeing Barry and his son together the day before had touched more than she cared to admit. It would be fun to send Corky a little something, and Barry would be so pleased by the gesture.

When they had dated she had always liked doing little things for Barry because he was appreciative. Whatever her personal feelings about Siperia Markham, Faye had to acknowledge the woman had done an exceptional job of raising unspoiled, hardworking, dutiful sons. Far *too* dutiful, in Faye's opinion. But then, who was she to criticize?

She paused in front of the construction-type toys and remembered that Corky had wanted his dad to help him build something out of Legos, whatever they were. Maybe there were some accessories she could buy. She picked up a package and was examining it when a pair of voices floated over the display.

"Yeah, Daddy, yeah, the Concorde. Will you hang it over my bed?"

"Now, I think that's a fine idea," came the reply in a deep quiet voice, at once steady and enthusiastic. "If we can find some nylon cord that's strong enough."

Smiling, Faye tucked her package under her arm and walked around the display. "Great minds think the same way, I see,'' she teased Barry, who was holding a detailed plastic model of the sleek supersonic jet.

"Fayette!" His eyes lit up with mingled amusement and pleasure. "This is the last place I'd have expected to see you. I thought you had a million loose ends to tie up."

"Well, this is one of them." She glanced toward Corky, engrossed now in examining a three-foot robot. "I wanted to get a little something for you-know-who."

The subject under discussion whirled excitedly. "What about a robot, Daddy? I need one."

"No." Barry's quiet voice was firm. "I want you to be thinkin' about our trip and what it's goin' to be like. That's why we decided on the jet model, remember?"

"Yes, sir." He glanced at Faye then, his blue eyes resting curiously on the package under her arm.

"Hi, Corky."

"Hey," he replied shyly, hesitating for a moment before adding with a note of pride, "Me 'n' Daddy are goin' on a jet plane over the ocean."

"Sounds exciting," Faye said. "Your first trip?"

"Yep. I never been on a super... superson..." He looked to his dad for help.

"Supersonic," Barry supplied, smiling at Faye again. "I'm taking Corky to Ireland for ten days. We're goin' to fly into London out of New York on the Concorde."

"Neat!"

Buoyed by her enthusiasm, Corky jumped back into the conversation. "Yeah, and we're gonna...we're gonna take a hot-air balloon over a river, an'...an'...." He couldn't get the words out fast enough. "An' we're gonna get a pokey old horse and a little gypsy wagon and ride through the country just like in old times. Daddy says we can sleep out under the stars."

Faye laughed in delight. "Gee, it's sounding like a better and better adventure all the time. Wish I could come."

"Come, then." This was Barry, and the look he gave Faye was no longer teasing but matter-of-fact.

"Is this the same old Barry I used to know?" she retorted, a little disconcerted. "I'm supposed to be the impetuous one, not you."

He laughed quietly. "I've changed a little in ten years, Faye. Not much but . . ." He hesitated for a second, the laughter going out of his eyes. "But enough."

As they made their way up to the cashier Faye gave him a sidelong look full of curiosity.

She paid for her purchase and then gave the bag to Corky outside the store. "Here you go, my man. Maybe you can build yourself an airport terminal out of Legos with this," she said, and added with a wink, "one big enough to hold your new Concorde when it isn't flying over your bed."

Corky warmed to her at that remark. "Thank you—" he paused and looked up at her with a smile exactly like his dad's "—Shortstuff."

She pretended to be shocked. "Hey, that's my line!" she said, reaching down to poke him lightly in the stomach until they were both giggling.

She straightened to find Barry's eyes on her again. "Faye, do you have time for lunch?"

"Sure," she said at once, picturing the three of them heading over to McDonald's.

But Barry had other ideas. "Come with me to leave Corky off at his friend Sam's house. Then we can have the afternoon to ourselves."

THEY DROVE THROUGH the quiet back country along U.S. 68, crossing a bridge over a wide, placid Kentucky River.

"Where are you taking me, Barry?"

"Doesn't this look familiar to you?"

"Silly question."

She smiled to herself, remembering all the times she had come down to the river with the local kids for picnics and paddleboat cruises just like their parents and grandparents before them had.

And she remembered Gran describing her family's trips from Jessamyn County to their Hunt cousins' Indian Creek Farm "way over a piece near Lexington." It had been a full day's journey along the narrow gravel highways twisting up through the palisades. Gran had talked about the picnic lunches they would pack to eat along the way and how their visits would last a week or more.

"It's nice to see you smiling, Faye," Barry said. "You've seemed awfully tense ever since you've been back in Lexington."

She sighed. "Guess I did need to get away from town a little while. Gives me a chance to put things in perspective a bit." She reached across to squeeze his hand on the wheel. "Thanks for suggesting this, Barry."

"I needed it, too," he said, his eyes fixed on the road. "I don't know, sometimes I think I'm suffocating."

"Is that why you planned the trip to Europe?"

"That's one of the reasons." Barry shot her a quick speculative glance, and Faye had the odd sensation he was wondering how much he could trust her.

The matter dropped as Barry turned in to a small gravel driveway on the Mercer County side of the river. An old stone-and-wood structure with a big central chimney loomed up, friendly and inviting.

"Murphy's!" Faye exclaimed in delight. "I had no idea it was still in business."

"Didn't I tell you things don't change around here?" Barry smiled a little as he opened the car door for her. "This place still makes the best catfish in three counties."

They were greeted by a plump, smiling middle-aged woman who showed them to a table overlooking the river and the steep palisades forming its far bank. Their waitress, who might have been a twin to the hostess, brought two tall glasses of sweetened iced tea and proudly rattled off their list of specials.

"I'll have the catfish," Faye said without even bothering to glance at the placemat menu. "And do you still make your cushaw squash and green beans cooked with country ham?"

"My, my, you know your way around our kitchen," the waitress said with a laugh. "And you don't even sound like you're from around these parts."

Faye smiled. "I used to be."

After the woman left, Barry reached across the table to touch Faye's hand. "I'm glad we ran into each other today. It bothered me to think you might just disappear out of my life again before we could..." He stopped and started again. "I just felt like I needed someone to talk to. Someone who...who really understands me."

Faye looked up from the tea she'd been stirring thoughtfully with a straw. "Talk about my looking tense," she said teasingly. "You should see yourself."

Barry let that comment pass. "I heard you ran into Mother yesterday after you left."

"Oh, it was a run-in, all right," Faye said lightly. "She made it obvious she wasn't too happy to see me back in town."

"I'm sorry, Fayette."

"Honestly, you don't have to apologize for her behavior. There's never been any love lost between us. And besides, you know me, Barry," Faye added with a rueful smile. "I don't help matters by shooting off my mouth."

"Faye," he said suddenly, "if I tell you something, will you promise to keep it under your hat?"

"Of course. What is it?"

"That trip to Great Britain I'm planning with Corky, well, it's not just a lark." Barry took a deep breath. "I've got an interview in London with Paul Bouvier Randall, the ambassador. He and my dad went to Duke University together. Mr. Randall is considering me for a job."

"Barry, that's wonderful!"

His face drained of tension. "I'm excited about it, Fayette. You know that's something I've always wanted—to live and work overseas for a while. Travel."

"But..."

"I know, Fayette, I know what you're going to ask. What about my family and Oak Hill? What about Corky? And I just don't know." His fingers drummed nervously on the tabletop. "I figure I'll worry about those things when and if Randall offers me the job."

"I still think it would be fair to Siperia to give her a little warning. After all, she must depend on you a lot."

His mouth tightened again. "Depends on me to be her yes-man. Fayette, I tell you I'm sick to death of it. I don't like Corky seeing her overrule my judgment time and time again. I'd like to get my son out of that household as soon as possible, before she starts layin' the guilt trip on him, about Oak Hill bein' in the family for six generations and how we have a responsibility to continue that tradition. Trying to tell him he's gotta be a lawyer or a horsebreeder when he might not want to be those things at all!''

"Oh, Barry, Barry, you've held it all in for so long," Faye replied, her voice soft and full of sympathy. "It's going to take a heck of a lot of courage now to try to break away."

"I know it, Fayette, but I'm ready," he said, a deep sureness in his tone. "It's so ironic, you breezing back into town just when I'm going through this crisis. More than anyone, you make me remember those old dreams I had. You're like a breath of fresh air in my life." He smiled. "Always have been."

"I'm glad you're taking this step, Barry."

"I have to," he said simply. "The only thing that worries me is keeping custody of Corky. I don't know how Belinda'd react to me taking him out of the country to live. Not that she pays all that much attention to him, anyway. But she is his mother."

"You're going to talk to her?"

"You think I should?"

Faye grinned. "You know my philosophy: take the bull firmly by the horns..."

By the time the waitress arrived with their lunch they were both laughing.

As Barry talked about Rome and London and Paris, Faye found herself being swept up by his excitement, seduced a little by this new side of him. In a way Barry reminded her of her father now, afire with plans for the future. A basically conservative man, Barry was now eager for new adventures and experiences.

"Fayette," he said seriously, after the waitress had cleared their plates away and brought them fresh hot coffee, "I meant it before when I said you're someone who really understands me. If...if we hadn't run into each other today I'd have called you. After we talked in my office it dawned on me you weren't really thrilled with your life in San Francisco. And I thought to myself why couldn't you and I..."

"Barry..."

"No, Fayette, don't interrupt me now. I fell in love with you once when I was a kid. And I'm one of those firm believers in lightning striking twice. It worried me that you'd probably never been around children much," he rushed on, "but then I saw the way you interacted with Corky. I...I think the three of us could build a real nice life together. Get out of Lexington, put this behind us. You could forget your bitterness over Pettigrew and that damned bank. We could start over again."

"Barry, I'm overwhelmed," she said, touched by his heartfelt outpouring. "But really, I hope you don't expect any kind of a coherent answer from me. My life's in a turmoil right now. I don't need this!" She bit down hard on her lip, not knowing whether she wanted to laugh or cry.

"I'm sorry, Fayette. But I had to get the words out. The thought of you flying out of my life again—"

"Don't flatter me," she interrupted teasingly, trying to inject a light note into the conversation. "I just may be staying around longer than I'd planned to. Once the novelty wears off you might be wishing you'd never talked."

Barry looked confused. "What do you mean you might be staying?"

"I'm not a quitter, Barry. Every little barrier I run into—Pettigrew, Carradine, your dear mother—makes me all the more determined to stick around and fight.

They all think I'm an outsider who doesn't belong. Well, maybe I don't. But that doesn't mean I can't roll up my sleeves and stand up to them for a while. Go out with my guns blazing and all that," she said, laughing.

"Lord Almighty, Fayette, I should have guessed you might pull a stunt like that." He shook his head in admiration. "But what about your job?"

"I don't know," she admitted sheepishly. "I haven't worked out minor details like that yet."

"Well..."

"Well," she echoed him.

"Fayette, I won't bring up what we discussed again," he promised. "Last thing I want is for you to feel uncomfortable. If you ever...want to reconsider, just let me know."

"You bet." She grinned. "But I certainly won't hold you to it."

As they drove back into town Faye played their conversation over in her mind, touched and amused all over again. How ironic that yesterday after she'd left Barry and Corky at Oak Hill she had briefly fantasized about what it would be like to marry and settle down. At the same time Barry was fantasizing about sweeping her away to distant corners of the world.

That puppy love she'd felt for the tall handsome blond high-school senior had long faded, though she still cared for Barry deeply. What would happen to them if she did stay? The last thing in the world she wanted to do was hurt him.

Faye sighed, thinking back over all the men she had dated in the past ten years. She'd always felt she could take them or leave them. It worried her sometimes that she might be incapable of feeling a deep abiding passion. Maybe the right man just hadn't come along yet.

Suddenly she laughed a little to herself, remembering her late-night phone conversation with Seth Carradine in her hotel room. Now there was a man capable of arousing feelings in her—intense dislike, boiling anger—all good, healthy, passionate responses.

"What are you smiling at, Fayette?" Barry asked.

"Nothing."

She looked out the window, wondering what she was going to say to her boss when she called him. Wondering what on earth she was going to do with the rest of her life.

CHAPTER SIX

FAYE STOOD in the middle of the farmhouse living room. Cramming the phone between her ear and shoulder, she reached out to pull a dust cover from her grandmother's heirloom secretary desk.

"Oh!" She coughed and spluttered, trying to fan away the motes settling in her hair and eyelashes.

"Faye, what's going on?" The voice on the other end of the phone sounded sleepy and a little confused.

"Harve, I told Lynette not to wake you up if you were still in bed. I know how you like to sleep in on Saturday morning."

"Are you kidding? All she had to say was you were calling from Kentucky. That was enough to make me sit up straight," he said, his voice cracking. "I thought you'd be on a flight home by now."

Faye glanced around at the familiar soft yellow walls, their corners full of cobwebs. Outside, an overgrown dogwood tree leaned against the front window and creaked in the wind. Its branches were in bloom, the blossoms a soft pink against the Wedgwood blue of the sky.

"It's a long story, Harve," she said finally. "The reason I'm calling is to ask you for a leave of absence. I've already mailed in a formal written request, but I didn't think it would have been fair to have smacked you with that Monday morning without some warning first."

"You're kidding," he said in disbelief. "This is a really critical period in your career. Opportunities don't come along like this every day, you know. How much time are you asking for?"

"Six weeks."

"You're nuts," he said flatly. "Only a miracle could hold that planning-board position open for that long. Are you sure you know what you're doing?"

"No, I'm not sure." Faye paced between the desk and a beige velvet overstuffed chair, waving her hands in agitation. "It just feels like something I have to do. I can't explain it."

"Where are you now?"

"I've moved into the house. I had all the utilities turned on yesterday. Now I'm just trying to—" she stopped and sighed, not knowing where to begin "—get things organized. To make it feel like a home again."

"You mean the fat man just handed over the keys without a whimper?"

"Are you kidding?" she snorted. "I had to raise a ruckus. I told him I was going to march right down to the newspaper office and give them their juiciest feature story of the year. 'Young heiress denied access to ancestral home.'" Faye's tongue rolled lovingly over the words. "It would have made a great headline, wouldn't it, Harve? Pettigrew must have thought so, too, because he practically fell over himself running to the file to get me the keys."

Harve started to chuckle despite himself. "You mean it was as simple as that?"

"Not really. All I've actually gotten is a temporary grace period," she admitted. "The bank's agreed to give me a couple of months to show the place can be turned around and made profitable. Otherwise it has to go back on the market."

"A couple of months to turn things around!" It was Harve's turn to snort impatiently. "Who do you think you are—Mickey Rooney and Judy Garland rolled into one? What are you going to do—put on a show to save the old homestead?"

"I could do without the sarcasm, Harve."

"Look, I'm just trying to play devil's advocate here. I'd just like to know what the hell you really hope to accomplish."

"At least I can spruce the place up a bit and have some sort of input about the asking price and who the property sells to," she said quietly. "At least I'll have the satisfaction of wresting some of the control out of Hollister Pettigrew's grasping fingers."

"That's all very noble. But what are you going to live on in the meantime?"

"I have a bit in savings."

"You're talking to Uncle Harve, remember, Faye? The guy you complain to about never having enough left over at the end of the month? The guy who's always teasing you about being a great money manager for other people but a lousy one for yourself?"

"Do you have to rub it in?" she said coldly. "If worse comes to worst, I can sell my condo. I've got a lot of bucks wrapped up in equity."

"Faye, don't be crazy. That's the only nest egg you've got. You don't want to burn bridges that way." He sighed in frustration. "I don't know what to say—it's like you're running away from everything you've started to build here. What are you going to do if this venture of yours falls to pieces—just drift someplace else and start all over again? I'm beginning to think you thrive on that kind of scenario."

Faye closed her eyes. It hurt her to hear him saying the same awful things Siperia Markham had put her down for. "Harve, please," she begged, "I'm not in the mood for a lecture right now."

"Okay, I'm sorry. But you know what I'm saying is motivated out of my wanting what's best for you."

A tear squeezed out from beneath her lashes. "Thanks, Harve," she whispered huskily, trying desperately not to cry. It had been a long time since anyone had said anything like that to her, and a wave of loneliness suddenly washed over her. "I . . . I'd better go now."

"One last thing, Faye," he said more gently, perhaps sensing her fragile mood. "If you need a loan to tide you over, just let me know. I don't want to think of you getting roly-poly on fatback and grits because you can't afford anything else."

The ridiculous image made her laugh. "Don't worry. When I was scouting around yesterday I found an old patch of collards gone to seed in the back garden. At least it'll be fatback and greens."

"Yech." He laughed, too. "Keep in touch, okay? I'll try to hold that job open as long as I can. I think you're going to be back here, Faye. Sooner than you think."

"Maybe you're right." She sighed. "Bye, Harve. And thanks again for everything."

She hung up, feeling as if she'd just cut herself off from her last friend in the world. But she refused to cave in to self-pity. Halfheartedly whistling "My Old Kentucky Home," Faye gathered up all the old dustcovers and carried them out to the laundry room. On her way back through the kitchen she stopped to check the work list she'd stayed up writing until two in the morning. Grabbing some supplies from the shopping bag on the table, she headed for the dining room.

Faye squeezed caulking compound onto the loose windowframe and then spread it evenly with a putty knife she pulled from the hip pocket of her jeans. After a while she was whistling in earnest, thoroughly engrossed in her repairs. When the telephone rang a few minutes later she looked up in surprise.

Without bothering to wipe off the putty knife, she shoved it back into her pocket and hurried to pick up the phone. Who was it, she wondered. Carradine, maybe? He had left a couple of messages for her at the hotel but she hadn't been ready to talk yet. She was leery of the deal she was sure he was going to offer her. On the other hand, what if he offered her too much money? Then she'd have no real reason to hang on here except sheer cussed stubbornness. She wasn't yet ready to admit to herself that the place might be working its way back into her heart.

Faye picked up the phone. "Hello. Faye Hunt here." There was a pause and she could hear the caller breathing on the other end of the line. "Hello?" she said more loudly.

"Miz Hunt?" The voice was muffled. "I got a message for you."

"Yes, go on."

"If I was you I'd get myself off that farm right away."

"Who is this?" she demanded indignantly.

"Because if you don't," the voice went on like a slow-talking robot, "you might just get your head shot clean off. I could make a real quick job of it. All I'd have to do is stand on the hill above your place and you'd be a sittin' duck. Easy as pie."

Faye gasped as the line went dead. Her hands were shaking so badly she could barely replace the receiver. A chill went right through her, as if a cold wind had suddenly blown through the bright room.

Had it been a prank, a stupid practical joke played just to annoy her? Faye rubbed her hands up and down her arms, with the hope that the action could force her numbed mind to work. No, the call was too vicious to have been a joke. She knew how visible the house and barn were from the road; she'd stood there herself last Sunday and looked down at the place. The thought of someone on that hill watching her, and waiting, made her skin crawl. Desperately she tried to place the caller, but she was pretty sure it was the voice of a stranger. Young and male, but who?

Faye went back into the kitchen and dug around in the pantry until she found a dusty bottle of Bourbon that looked as if it had been there for years. "Aged to perfection," she tried to joke to herself as she pulled off the cap and poured a shot of the amber liquid into a juice glass. She tossed it back in one gulp, feeling her courage return little by little as the liquor's fiery warmth spread through her. Even so, she realized she was still holding on to the edge of the sink for dear life as she stared outside.

The lonely isolation of the farm had never occurred to her before this. The gray stone farmhouse sat snugly within its gently rolling acreage, her nearest neighbor a half mile away. Picturesque and peaceful. At least it had been until a stranger had shattered her peace of mind with an ugly phone call.

Gradually, as Faye's terror subsided, anger began to take its place. What coward had pulled such a rotten, sneaky trick? She wasn't about to be frightened off that easily. Remembering the old rifle that Gran had kept downstairs, Faye moved quickly toward the basement door.

The .22 stood where it always had in the glass-walled cabinet, looking serviceable and efficient even if it hadn't been shot in years. Faye went to the ledge above the window where Gran had always kept the gun-cabinet key. It was still there.

She lifted the rifle gingerly and ran her hand lightly down the barrel. Faye poked her head back inside the cabinet and came out with a box of shells. She hesitated only a second before loading the rifle.

Upstairs in the dining room once again, she laid the weapon within easy reach and picked up her tube of caulking compound. She tried to whistle, but it was a hollow sound now. Every minute or so she found herself glancing around furtively, as if the windows of the home and the overgrown fields beyond had become enemies to be feared.

When the phone rang again a few minutes later, she almost jumped out of her skin. She turned and stared at it tensely. It rang five times before she could gather up the courage to answer.

On the sixth ring she picked the phone up. "Hello!" she barked. "Who is this?"

"What the hell you bitin' my head off for?" a familiar voice drawled. "I'd sure hate to be your old man."

"Carradine," she breathed in relief and sank down into the velvet armchair, oblivious of the sticky caulking mud on the back of her jeans. "I thought you were somebody else."

"Whoa," he said, his tone at once amused and questioning. "Who you mad at?"

"I'm not sure."

"That's a new one," he teased her. "Or are you just mad at the whole world?"

"Actually." She paused to take a deep breath and to make sure she could carry off a lighthearted response. "Actually, I just got a weird call from some bozo. Other women get your average garden variety obscene calls. But not me," she said. "I...um, thought it might be him calling back."

"What exactly'd he say?" All the lazy amusement had fled from Seth's voice. And after she told him he asked immediately, "Did you recognize him?"

"Who do you think you are—a detective or something?" she snapped, loath to have him guess how scared she had been.

But he'd obviously guessed, anyway. "Do you feel like some company?" he asked her gently.

A wave of relief washed over her, but she answered in a cool, Clint Eastwood deadpan tone that had required a dozen viewings of *Dirty Harry* for her to master. "Why not? I guess we have to talk sooner or later," she said indifferently. "Especially now that we're neighbors."

Faye finished her caulking in the dining room and then began to work on the small window above the sink. She sat scrunched up on the kitchen counter. When the front doorbell chimed she started, bumping her head on the cabinet behind her.

"Ouch," she murmured and jumped down to the floor. She was halfway across the room before she remembered the rifle lying on the table. Without hesitating, she picked it up.

With her thumb wrapped around the stock and her finger resting lightly on the trigger, Faye flung open the front door.

Seth Carradine stood on the porch, his left hand shoved into the pocket of a sheepskin-lined jacket and his right holding on to the collar of the biggest German shepherd dog Faye had ever seen.

"Hi," she said, meeting his surprised stare head-on.

"Hi, yourself." His gaze shifted to the gun in her right hand. "You know how to use that thing?"

She gave him a contemptuous look. "I don't bluff, Carradine. For your information my gran taught me how to skeet-shoot when I was twelve. I can hit a moving target at a hundred feet," she informed him, "and I guarantee I will if I have to."

Seth bit his lip as if he didn't want to smile, but that dimple in his right cheek seemed to have a mind of its own. "You might just try a warning shot if someone's prowlin' around."

"Not on your life," she flung back with cool outrage. "Anyone who threatens me won't have the courtesy of a warning."

"Sounds like you mean business, lady."

"You better believe it, buster."

He really did smile then. His eyes lit up first, sparkly green as a country pond glimmering under the afternoon sun. The effect was dazzling, Faye decided. *Too* dazzling. And for some crazy reason she noticed his teeth. White against his tanned skin they were and a bit crooked—a nice kind of crooked that seemed to say "Nothing phony here."

She must have been staring at him because he was staring back at her with a warm calculating gleam in his eyes. Nervously she rubbed her nose and was shocked to feel a blob of caulking mud on the end. Then to her horror she felt herself blushing, something she hadn't done since she was in junior high school. To cover her confusion she frowned down at the dog, which had taken a step into the foyer and was licking her trigger hand.

"Who's your friend?" she asked disapprovingly.

"I call her Jenny." He ruffled the dog's head affectionately. "I thought you might need some protection in case your telephone admirer decides to come callin' in person."

Faye edged her hand away from the friendly slobbering tongue. She'd never had a dog and didn't like the looks of this one. "What'll she do—kill him with kisses?"

"I've been overpowered that way a few times myself." He laughed, that damned low intimate laugh that insinuated all sorts of things and made her pulse go haywire.

"Hmph!" she sniffed and turned on her heel to lead the way back to the kitchen. "Why do men always have to brag about their sexual prowess?" she tossed back over her shoulder.

"Who's braggin'?" he retorted innocently, though she could still hear the laughter in his voice. "And for that matter, who's talkin' about sex?"

Aren't you, she thought as she turned to face him in the kitchen, her eyes taking in the taut fit of his jeans over his thighs and measuring the breadth of his shoulders. And she realized with some chagrin that she was accusing him of her own sin. He was so damned masculine she had reacted the way any red-blooded female would. It was one of those instinctive physical responses that bypassed reason. To cover herself, Faye made a pretense of being busy. She filled an old pottery bowl with water and set it down for the dog. Then without looking at Carradine, she resumed her perch on the kitchen counter and started caulking again. She felt those green eyes watching her, though, which made her all the more self-conscious.

Finally he asked, "So who do you think it is that's tryin' to scare you off?"

"Why shouldn't I suspect you, for one?" She looked over at him, her jaw thrust out slightly and her eyes alight with mischief. "You seem to want this farm so badly. I'd say that was motive enough, wouldn't you?"

"Bull," he swore and strode over to her. "That's not my style and you know it."

"I don't know a damn thing about you, Carradine," she said huskily, wishing he didn't have to stand there like that with his hips pressed against the counter. Wishing she didn't have to notice how that full, attractive mouth of his curved down on one side when he was angry.

She glanced away and he leaned both hands on the counter, boxing her in. When she looked up again, she was unnerved to find they were practically nose to nose. Faye understood now what she had been accusing him of and she wondered if he realized it, too. She was much too attracted to him, and she knew he was a far more subtle and devastating threat to her feminine vulnerability than any crank caller.

"Back off, Carradine," she whispered, but he ignored her.

"You say you don't know a damn thing about me," he said slowly, the muscle in his jaw jumping tensely. "Well, maybe it's time you found out."

She licked her lips nervously and was appalled to see his eyes following the movement of her tongue.

"Well, what do you say, Hundred Pounds?"

"I..." She hesitated, afraid of being trapped no matter how she answered. "I think the dog wants out."

Jenny stood by the back door, looking back at them with expectant eyes. Stifling an oath, Seth went over to let it out and as he did so Faye slid down off the counter.

"Why'd you bring that silly dog over here, anyway?" she asked peevishly, feeling embarrassed now that the moment had passed.

"Her name's Jenny."

"Whatever." Faye turned to watch the dog through the window as it sniffed excitedly beneath every bush. "How do I know she won't be your inside man, keeping tabs on everything I'd—" She broke off her sarcastic rebuke. "Hey, your dog's got something in its mouth."

Jenny bounded back up to the house and pushed open the screen door with her nose. She came right up to Faye and dropped a dead gopher on her Adidas. "I don't believe this," Faye said, wrinkling her nose in disgust.

"You see, she likes you already," Carradine replied, trying to keep a straight face as he picked up the dead gopher and went to dump it in the trash can outside the door.

Faye glared at the dog who stared up at her with bright attentive eyes, its tongue lolling goofily. "With friends like her, who needs enemies?"

"She's a good watchdog," Seth defended Jenny, squatting down beside the dog to pat it affectionately. "Barks like hell."

Faye squatted, too, regarding Carradine suspiciously over Jenny's back. "Why should you care if I'm protected or not?"

"Maybe I just like you." He teased her with that grating sultry laugh of his, his grin deepening as Faye stood up abruptly. "Or maybe I'm just protectin' my investment."

"What investment?" she retorted, going back to the sink to pick up her putty knife. She shot him a quick sideways look and caught him looking at her, the expression in his eyes measuring and thoughtful. She worked in silence awhile, until curiosity finally got the better of her. "Okay, Carradine, so what is this proposition you've been dying to discuss?"

"Simple, really. I was thinking I'd like to put some money into that old barn of yours down the way. Once the renovation work's done, I'll lease the space from you to keep my new brood mares."

"Why don't you build your own barn—on your own property?"

"Cheaper this way," he explained succinctly. "And besides, I think we'd both come out ahead."

"Why should you be so philanthropic?"

"Let's just call it smart politics. If you see the sense in what I'm suggestin', we can make a deal. When it comes time to sell, all I ask is that you give me first shot at this property."

"Pettigrew's allowed you that perk already, from what I can see," Faye retorted, her voice rising over the sound of the water she'd turned on full blast.

"But I'm not dealing with Pettigrew now," he said slowly. "I'm dealing with you."

She shut off the water and turned to face him, her expression blatantly suspicious. "How do I know he hasn't set you up to do this? Your offer just sounds too pat, Carradine. It comes too close on the heels of my talk with Pettigrew down at the bank." Faye casually wiped the putty knife dry on the side of her jeans and dropped it on the table. "I still think you two are in cahoots."

"There's a difference between me and him," Carradine said, picking up the knife she'd dropped and testing its sharp edge with a callused thumb. "If Pettigrew is bound and determined to run this place into the ground, that ain't any of my business."

"But it does happen to be my business."

His green eyes flickered. "That's between you and Pettigrew. What he's doin' is foolish. I don't know why he's doin' it and, what's more, I don't care. But I'll damn well take advantage of the situation if I can."

"So I've noticed," she snapped.

"Maybe what you haven't noticed is this: you and me got the same stakes involved . . . we both want to see this place built up into a goin' concern."

"I don't trust you."

For an instant his eyes revealed his amusement. "You don't have to, honey. Trust's got nothing to do with it. I've seen many a partnership built on mutual need."

"Didn't you mean to say greed, Carradine?"

"Call it what you want. The way I look at it is, if I build a barn for you now it's just a matter of investin' in my own future."

"What you're banking on is my failure," she answered caustically.

"Maybe I am," he admitted. "But maybe, just maybe, I'm givin' you the only opportunity you'll get to pull your act together. You can take it or leave it."

"What an ego you've got!" Faye glared at him as she perched on the edge of the table. "I've got plenty of other options. For one thing," she blustered, waving her hand airily, "I've got my fertile tobacco land."

Seth caught her hand in midair, and with a grin he turned it palm up. "Yeah, I heard your know-it-all spiel about crop cycles when you were talkin' to Pettigrew. But this doesn't look like a farmer's hand to me." His forefinger lightly traced her curving life line and brushed the sensitive skin on her wrist. "I think you're all talk, Fayette Lee Hunt."

She jerked her hand away, annoyed by the little shiver that had run up her spine in response to his touch.

"Well . . . ?" he asked.

"Well, what?"

"Are we gonna shake on our little gentlemen's agreement or aren't we?"

"Only one problem," Faye retorted wryly, "neither one of us is much of a gentleman."

"Speak for yourself," he teased her back.

Faye gave him another long, considering look. For all his lighthearted banter, she sensed his tenseness and wondered if he could see through her bluffing, as well. The truth of it was that they did need each other. Right now, Carradine was just another small-time hardboots, training and breeding on a limited scale. The Hunt farm could give him the stature she sensed he wanted so badly. And maybe, just maybe, with rent coming in from the barn she could scrape by long enough to keep Pettigrew at bay until she could think of another plan to counter the bank's legal ploys.

Still, she hesitated. "How much do you think a renovation job'd cost? I'd imagine labor's cheaper around here."

"Five thousand or thereabouts. Depends on how much has to be done."

"You'd make me sign a personal note for the amount?"

"What do you think?" he said lazily. "I ain't Santa Claus."

"That's what I like about you, Carradine," she needled him. "You've got such a nice healthy self-interest."

"You're no fool and neither am I," he growled. "I've been jerked around enough in this world to know I'd better look out for number one, because if I don't nobody else will."

His outlook didn't surprise her, given what Barry had intimated about Carradine's background. In fact she was suddenly curious to know more about him. "How long have you owned that piece of property next door?" she asked.

"I bought that fifty acres out of my first big stakes winner. I made a promise to myself I'd reinvest every penny I'd ever make off a horse and that's what I've been doin' the past three years. This Bluegrass stake was something I'd been promisin' myself for a long time." He said it fiercely, as if he was challenging Faye or anyone else to try and take it from him.

"Were you raised around here?" she asked.

"I was raised on the road." He picked up the putty knife and started toying with it again. "My old man trained cheap claiming horses—he used to like to gripe he was two steps ahead of the bill collectors and one step ahead of the glue factory."

"Why didn't he just quit?"

"That was all he knew—horses." Carradine looked up at Faye, wondering how she was taking the whole sordid little tale. "The sad thing was he was a dreamer, always sure the next broken-down hack would be a fast-gallopin' Cinderella that nobody else saw the potential of, except him."

"So you're not a dreamer, I take it."

"All my dreams've got a firm footing in reality."

"Meaning what?" Faye asked, curious. "Property and prime bloodstock?"

"What else is there?"

She grinned. "Spoken like a true Kentuckian. You are that, at least, aren't you?"

"I was born over Louisville way," he conceded.

"Is that where you learned to ride—working at the Downs?"

He laughed shortly. "There and at every other track between Frisco and New York. Like I said, we didn't stay put too much."

"I guess we've got something in common then. My dad was a major in the army, so we were always on the move, too."

"You liked that?"

Faye shrugged. "A kid gets used to anything. Actually, my dad made sure I'd never be an outsider for long. He coached me in softball until I was the hottest little second baseman wherever we went. And believe me, he was a demanding coach. He used all the same disciplinary tactics he kept his men in line with."

Seth whistled. "Sounds like a tough old bird. I guess you're just a chip off the old block."

"I guess I am like him." Faye grinned. "People around here keep telling me I'm still infected with his wanderlust. I can't shake it."

Carradine gave her an appraising look. "If that's the case, then what are you doin' settling down here at Indian Creek?"

"Settling down? Are you kidding!" she shot back at once. "I hardly consider it that. This is more like an adventure I've decided I can't turn my back on."

"Strange sense of adventure you got, Hunt," he said with a slow shake of his head. His eyes had that telltale trace of amusement Faye was beginning to like. "Patchin' up holes and talkin' to weird kooks on the phone."

Faye's nose went up in the air. "That guy didn't scare me."

"Either you're a liar or a fool."

She tried to stare him down, but he was more stubborn. "Never mind, Carradine," she said finally in exasperation. "Are we going to shake on this deal or not?"

"I didn't know we had one."

"I'll tell you why I'm going to go along with your business proposition," she said suddenly. "I found out from Pettigrew that one of the last things my gran wanted was to renovate that old barn of hers. It might have been a crazy dream, but that's what she wanted. I decided it'd be nice if I could do that much for her. That's why I'm going to go along with your deal."

"Now that's real touching," Seth replied, as if he didn't believe a word of it. "Sounds like you've got a heart, after all, underneath that stainless steel exterior."

Slowly he put out his hand and even more slowly she took it. They shook, both of them wary. It was as if their sharing confidences had had the opposite effect it should have had. Their little talk only underlined in Seth's mind what he'd already suspected about her. Faye was downright cocky and competitive, a woman who liked to play only if she had a good chance of winning. Someone a shade too much like himself. He had an uncomfortable feeling their little deal could backfire right in his face.

"Well, I guess I'd better be goin'." He stood up. "It's already startin' to get dark."

Faye glanced nervously outside. "You can stay for dinner if you want." She hoped she sounded casual enough. The last thing she wanted was for him to guess that she was still a little shaken up by the phone threat, so she added, "I'd like to hear what your plans are for the barn."

"That's neighborly of you." His eyes warmed up enough to tease her. "I'm not averse to samplin' California cuisine."

"Fine," she said briskly, though inside she quailed at the term *cuisine*. She was a lousy cook, but she consoled herself by rationalizing that a guy like Seth, who probably grew up on grits and ham hocks, wouldn't know the difference, anyway.

"You sure you want to cook?" he asked with a grin.

"I offered, didn't I?" she said huffily, causing him to grin wider.

"I'll leave you to it, then," he said, moving toward the back door. "In the meantime, I think I'll go take a more serious look at the barn, now that I know we got a deal."

"A tentative deal," she couldn't resist calling after him.

CHAPTER SEVEN

FAYE TRIED to cut through the thin pork chop, but it was as resistant to the knife as shoe leather. She sneaked a glance at Seth and realized he was having the same problem. Finally she managed to hack a slice off and popped it into her mouth; it was horrible. So much for that "foolproof" recipe for tomato-soup-slathered chops. She took a forkful of the potatoes O'Brien she'd cooked from a frozen-food package; they were still half-frozen. Faye looked up again just as Seth looked across at her.

"You cook this way all the time?" he asked dryly. "Or is this something special just for company?"

His words broke Faye up. "Actually it's what I call diet food," she said through her laughter. "You see it and die at the thought of having to eat it."

Seth was laughing now, too. "I can see you're a woman who'd play havoc with an unsuspectin' man's constitution."

"Oh God, I am sorry," she said, wiping away a tear of merriment. "Do you think we should call out for pizza or something?"

"Now let's not go rushin' to admit defeat," he teased her. "Have you got any more of these potatoes left?"

"Half a package."

"You got eggs?"

"A brand-new dozen."

"Let's go, then, Fayette." He reached across to pile her dish on top of his and headed for the kitchen.

"Listen," she said, following him out, "since we seem to have graduated to a first-name basis, would you mind just calling me Faye? Every time someone in this town calls me Fayette I feel like I'm twelve years old again."

"You got it, Faye." His eyes crinkled. "Now let me at those eggs."

She pulled over the step stool and sat down, content to watch him bang around.

"Onion?" he asked, swirling oil into a big iron skillet.

She glanced into the pantry. "There's a jar of onion powder, here. Probably pretty stale."

"We'll chance it."

Quite soon the appetizing aroma of frying potatoes filled the air, almost obliterating the smell of burned tomato soup left over from her culinary disaster.

She watched him break a half dozen eggs into a bowl and beat them. "What are you making—an omelette?"

"It's called a tortilla."

"Now wait a minute," she protested, "a tortilla is something Mexicans make enchiladas out of."

"That's the Mexican version," he said, deftly running a knife around the edge of the pan to loosen the eggs. "This is Spanish."

"Guess I'll have to take your word for it," she said skeptically, though her mouth began to water as he divided the food onto two clean plates and slapped butter on the English muffins he pulled from the toaster.

"Whatever you call it, it's delicious," Faye said a few minutes later, savoring every bite. "Where did you learn to make it, anyway? Were you in the service over in Europe?"

"No." He laughed slyly. "But I did date a Spanish señorita for a while."

Faye lifted an eyebrow. "Oh, yeah? What else do you cook?"

"Let me see," he replied, his eyes glinting. "Where should I start? I make a mean spaghetti carbonara, a wild Indian curry, and naturally, I can put together a real irresistible Southern dumpling."

"Naturally," Faye said dryly. "I'm sure the recipes took a lot of...experimentation."

"Women and food just seem to go together, you know what I mean?" He laughed softly. "Tasty morsels all around. In fact, I just can't help lickin' my lips."

His words were so hypnotically sensual that she almost found herself licking her own lips in expectation. But she caught herself in time and with a little shake of her head stood up to clear the table.

He followed her into the kitchen. "Tell you what," he offered casually, "I'll make us some coffee and get a fire going in the livin' room while you wash up."

"Did you bring your slippers, too?" Faye retorted. "It sounds like you're ready to move in, Carradine."

"It's Seth now, remember?" he corrected her, his dimple working again.

"Seth," she repeated in exasperation. "Now, in case you've forgotten, this is my house and *I* call the shots."

"Yeah, Toughstuff, I'm waiting."

She opened her mouth to say I think we should call it an evening, but the words didn't come. Because the truth of it was coffee and conversation by the fire sounded delightful. She hated to admit even to herself how lonely and vulnerable she was feeling.

"Well?" he prompted.

"Just one question." The corners of her mouth lifted in a reluctant smile. "D'you think you can make your coffee strong enough to scare away the bogeyman?"

"Between your rifle totin' and havin' Jenny around, I think that bogeyman's got a hell of a lot more to worry about than you do."

"Thanks for the vote of confidence, but I still like my coffee strong."

"Don't need to tell me that," he teased her. "I sorta figured you weren't the Milquetoast type."

"I'm glad I made an impression." Faye gave him a wry look before turning back to crank the water faucet on full blast.

"Oh, you did that all right," he murmured behind her.

Her hand froze on the bottle of dishwashing liquid on the windowsill as Seth reached around her waist to stick the teakettle under the running water.

"You could have asked me to move."

He winked. "More challenging this way."

I'll just bet it is, she thought, all too aware of the unsettling warmth stirring deep in her belly. She watched the water splash into the kettle and finally run over the sides.

"All right, it's full," she informed him tartly.

"Mm, I see." His soft breath tickled her ear. "Too bad."

He moved away with a show of reluctance, and she made a great pretense of scrubbing vigorously at the dirty dishes, glancing sideways every second or two to make sure he didn't sneak up on her again. She didn't relax until she heard the sound of his boots receding down the hall.

In her usual slapdash fashion she finished the washing up. As she wrung out the sponge, Faye happened to catch her reflection in the window. Automatically she reached up to fluff her wispy bangs, and she saw her own eyes staring back at her—big eyes brimming with life and yet somehow wary. She wondered if she always looked on the world with those vaguely suspicious eyes.

For some reason she thought again of the dozens of men she'd dated over the past several years. She'd man-hopped more often than she had job-hopped, a nervous bird determined not to have her wings clipped by anything or anybody. Barry's proposal had touched her, though she wasn't about to take it too seriously. *That's me,* she thought, *a cool little heartbreaker.* Faye nodded vigorously at her reflection, taking courage from the thought as she went to join Seth in the living room.

The man did nothing by half measures, that was for sure. A blazing fire crackled cheerfully in the grate, spilling its warmth into the room. Seth had pulled one of the crushed velvet throw pillows from the sofa and tucked it under his head. He lay stretched out beside the hearth where he'd set a pair of steaming mugs and the bottle of Maker's Mark Bourbon Faye had opened earlier in the day. Jenny lay half drowsing beside him, her big head resting on her paws. As Faye approached, the dog looked up alertly. Seth opened one eye and gave Faye a lazy smile. "Come join the party," he invited. "We saved you room."

"Three's a crowd, don't they say?" she replied, curling up into a chair and setting her notebook on the arm. "Besides, the last thing I'd want to do is come between a man and his dog."

He pulled himself up onto one elbow, poured a healthy shot of Bourbon into the mugs and handed one to Faye. She lifted hers in mocking salute. "To the perfect host."

He laughed. "Next time you can wine and dine me over in my trailer."

"Trailer?"

"That's right," he shot back. "What'd you think I had—a fancy mansion like your friend Markham lives in?"

She heard the slight edge in his voice; she sensed again his hunger for that kind of roots, for the prestige they bestowed. She realized how badly he must have wanted—and still wanted—the rest of Indian Creek Farm, *her* farm.

With a flick of her wrist she tossed her notebook and a pen down to him. "Show me what you had in mind for my barn."

His brow burrowing slightly in concentration, Seth drew a sketch with swift, sure strokes. Faye cocked her head, trying to follow the plan from where she sat.

"Okay, let me see," she said impatiently, as if her whole future were riding on the simple drawing.

"No, you come down here," he replied. "It'll be easier to explain."

"Just give it to me," Faye demanded crisply. "I call the shots. It's my property."

"Yeah, and it's my money."

Seth gave her a long look and she stared back defiantly, not about to concede an inch. Faye suddenly realized it was crazy for two people with the same "take-charge" mentality to consider working together, but it was too late now.

"How often are you going to rub that in my face?" she snapped.

He shot her a crooked grin. "As often as I need to, to keep you in line. You're a pain in the ass."

Faye shot up out of the chair indignantly and made a grab for the notebook. Seth caught her arm and pulled her down nearly on top of Jenny. "Now, here, have a look."

She frowned as he shoved the page under her nose. "Why do you only have ten stalls drawn?"

"Because your gramma's stalls are too confinin' for Thoroughbreds."

"If they were good enough for Standardbreds..."

"That don't mean they're good enough for me."

She let that drop for the moment. "How much income will I get from them?"

"Five hundred a month."

"That's chicken feed," she said with a disdainful lift of her nose. "How much if I take care of the horses for you?"

"You?" He snorted. "What the hell would you do with a high-strung Thoroughbred when you're even afraid of old Jenny here?"

"I am not," she answered stiffly. "Besides, I can learn. You can teach me."

"Maybe I can," he said, his eyes crinkling, "seein' as you're such a willing pupil."

"They're only horses."

"Only horses," he repeated in disbelief, laughing a little. "I'd like to hear you say that to Sheikh Mohammed just after he's paid a cool eight million for a year-old colt."

"Why shouldn't I say it to him or anyone else?"

"You know something, Faye," Seth said, laughing a little. "I like your spunk."

"Oh, yeah?" She gave him a tart look. "A lot of men are intimidated by it. What makes you different, Hardboots?"

"Maybe they're scared off because they think you're stronger'n they are."

"Maybe I really am."

"And then again, maybe you aren't," he said, stretching out again comfortably as if the house were his.

She looked at him sharply, a little disconcerted by the teasing challenge she found in his eyes. Instead of arguing, she shifted her attention to the dog, which made a nice safe barrier between her and Seth. Tentatively Faye reached out to stroke her thick fur and was pleasantly surprised at how warm and soft the dog felt. Jenny responded by looping her paw companionably over her newfound friend's arm, and Faye had to smile at the silly, if rather endearing, gesture.

Seth's eyes followed Faye's very gesture and expression. "You know," he said after a while, "for such a hard-assed little woman, you've got a real gentle touch, Faye."

"It's just a ploy to lull men into a false sense of security." She shot him a mischievous look, rolling her small hand up into a menacing-looking fist. "See? This is the real Faye Hunt."

"I'll take my chances," he remarked softly as he caught her fist and pulled her toward him over the dog's supine form. Jenny yelped and snaked out from beneath Faye.

Her heart beat faster as she fell against his chest, their chins nearly bumping. "Hey," she protested, her eyes smoky as they met his. "I usually make a man beg for these kinds of favors."

"Not this man," he whispered huskily. "I prefer to take what I want."

"Just try."

The softly murmured challenge sparked a hot current of expectation between them. His strength excited her as much as her softness honed his desire.

To her surprise, Seth loosened his grip on her wrist. Almost disappointed, she started to draw back. Then he surprised her again, catching her off balance to flip her down gently onto her back beside him. "I've got you pinned, doll face." He laughed down into her eyes, deftly punctuating his victory by throwing his leg across hers. "Now what do you have to say?"

"What can I say?" she murmured, fluttering her lashes provocatively. "To the victor belongs the spoils."

He lowered his face toward hers, and Faye waited until his eyes closed. Then she made a fist again and brought it up to jab him lightly but squarely in the solar plexus. His breath escaped in a startled "Oomph" that made her laugh.

His eyes shot open. "Sly little bitch," he swore softly as soon as he got his breath back. "I see I'm going to have to teach you a lesson you won't forget."

He caught her fist and brought it up to his bared lips. He grazed the clenched knuckles, and using his lower teeth as a lever, he forced her little finger open, nibbling down the length of it. A deep well of pleasure spurted inside her when she felt his wet tongue circling the sensitive pad of her palm. He unfastened the shirt button at her wrist and began to kiss the pale, soft underside of her forearm.

She had expected his lovemaking to be of the rough-and-tumble variety, a grab-and-squeeze assault leaving no room for subtlety. She hadn't expected this slow, sensual advance that left her swaying tipsily. Losing that fine edge of control made her nervous, confused.

"Seth, please..." she murmured, hazily aware that they had somehow shifted position again. She was sprawled atop him, her hips and breasts and thighs sweet touch points of fire.

"No need to beg, Hundred Pounds," he teased her softly. "You got me right where I want me."

"Quiet, Hardboots," she shushed him, grasping for some shred of control in their private little game. "You talk too damn much sometimes."

Saying that, she lowered her mouth to his until their lips just touched. The moment spun out into a long quivering thread of expectation, and then the touch became a kiss. Her lips parted slightly, pillows of softness that beckoned and invited his returned pressure. She felt his hand lightly cupping her neck, his thumb caressing the sensitive lines of her jaw and throat. The hand held her captive, made her mouth prey to the slow brushstrokes of his lips, the teasing foray of his tongue against hers— a wildly delicious give and take that aroused soft little contractions of pleasure deep inside and made her reckless.

Her hands curled around the edges of his shirt, and she unfastened the row of snaps with one crisp tug that exposed his bare chest. She lowered her lips to the hard band of his pectorals, brushing the mat of hairs there until they lay moistly against his skin. He smelled good to her, clean and fresh, no cologne to mask the completely natural, sexy maleness he exuded.

His breath escaped in a sigh of pleasure. "Faye, honey," he murmured, "I just knew that wicked tongue of yours had to be good for something."

"Watch it," she growled softly in return, "I can bite, too."

"So can I, sweet stuff." And with that he pulled her up to nuzzle her neck and tickle the rim of her ear with his tongue until her tough little growl became a gentle purr.

She pulled herself to a sitting position astride him, smiling as she ran her hands down his chest and stomach. His build was square, hard and compact, with that sinewy unselfconscious strength of a working man's body.

"My turn now, Faye," he said, reaching up to unfasten the top button of her pink oxford-cloth shirt. Slowly he unbuttoned them all, one after another until he could push the blouse back off her shoulders, trapping her arms in the soft folds of cotton. Deftly he undid the front clasp of her lacy bra. Her breasts stood out small and firm, their full pink tips upturned.

Seth's big square hands could easily have engulfed them. Instead he reached up with a sensitive forefinger to trace their curves in ever-smaller concentric circles until he brushed the nipples, sending quivers of pleasure radiating outward to the rest of her body. His eyes were more rapacious than his hands, hungry and caressing.

"You remind me of a drawing I saw once," he said, now teasing the underside of one breast with a long easy brushstroke. "You're soft and small and fragile as a dancer. Beautiful," he breathed. "All woman. Now come down here, Faye, and let me kiss you."

He pulled her to him, his lips closing gently around a nipple, his teeth lightly grating. Faye moaned, shocked and delighted by the subtle magic of his playful teeth and wet tongue. She felt her breasts burgeoning beneath his caresses. Until now, she'd always been sensitive about their smallness, aware they would never match up to centerfold standards. But Seth drove away that concern; his words as much as his touch made her feel more physically a woman than she had ever felt before.

Seth drew her down to lie beside him, his hands moving in long lazy twirling motions over her torso until her flesh seemed to cry out its own separate engulfing pleasure. Their legs were entangled, and she felt the gently compelling pressure of his knee against her mons, an intimate gesture that sent little warning flares of sensation pulsing along her inner thighs. She felt as though she were already his, as though the sensual persuasion of his body and his tongue had bypassed her will.

"You're sweet as honey, Hundred Pounds," he whispered against her breast. "I could lick you up all night long."

She moaned again as he unzipped her jeans and slipped his hand inside. He found the soft fullness of her womanhood, his fingers moving beneath the lace banding her thigh.

Without warning she felt him jerk against her, and she was about to console herself philosophically that a woman couldn't have everything. When he jerked again, punctuating it with a bellowed "Ouch!" it dawned on Faye that maybe he wasn't climaxing prematurely.

"What is it, Seth? What's going on?"

He had sat up and was wincing as he tried to reach behind him to touch his back. "Damned sparks out of the fireplace. They got me."

"Oh, no, let me see." She sat up, too, and turned his shoulders around to examine the two white welts raised on his skin. The fireplace chose that moment to send another cascade of sparks onto the rug, and she clambered over to them on all fours to beat them out with her shirt cuff.

Seth by now had forgotten his pain and reached across to pick up where they had left off, his hands cupping her breasts and curving intimately around her hips to pull her back to him. But she wriggled out of his embrace, at the same time putting her loosened bra and blouse back into some semblance of order.

"What the hell you doin'?" he demanded.

"Don't you believe in signs?" she joked though her eyes were still smudged with desire. "I wouldn't put it past my sainted gran to toss a few hot coals around. That'd be just her style."

"You're talking crazy, Hundred Pounds."

She sighed and looked down at her shirt, belatedly realizing she'd buttoned it wrong, but she didn't redo it for fear of igniting another delirious lovemaking session with Seth.

"I think you'd better go," she said quietly. "It's late."

"Oh, hell," he groused, "I thought sparks were supposed to start fires, not put them out."

She looked up again, a reluctant smile creeping back into her eyes. "Now you know differently."

"Come on now, Faye."

But she'd already stood up. "For crying out loud, Seth, we don't even know each other. You think I do this every time I meet an attractive man? You just caught me at a vulnerable time. It's not going to happen again, I assure you."

"What's the big deal? We were just bein' neighborly."

She glared at him. "Oh, is that all it was. Well, I think you'd better leave. Like I've told you before, I don't trust you, Seth Carradine."

He strode over to her and poked her shoulder with an angry finger. "Baloney," he said. "You don't trust yourself, tough stuff."

"Good night," she said, marching into the hall and holding the front door open to the cold night air. "And you can take your dog with you."

"Jenny stays," he said flatly, tucking in his shirttail and grabbing his jacket off the hook. "I guess I'll be talkin' to you in the morning," he added in an aggravated tone, as if that was the last thing in the world he'd want to do.

She slammed the door soundly after him.

AS HE HEADED DOWN THE WALKWAY, he thought in irritation, *Oh, hell, what am I getting so worked up about? She's not even my type.* Invariably his dalliances were with wealthy, sophisticated women. The kind of women who liked to play games; women who were temporarily bored with the Lexington-Palm Beach-New York carousel. Of course, they'd get bored with him, too, eventually and drift off, leaving nothing behind but a faint whiff of some hundred-dollar-an-ounce perfume or another. They were all the same to him, all part of the game.

That explained his fascination with Faye, of course: she wasn't his type. His romancing her tonight had been one of those reflex reactions—cold night, warm woman. Hell, he'd never have guessed in a hundred years that the little straight-talking half-pint with her stubborn lower lip and the rubber cement in her hair would have made him explode like a firecracker.

He relived that little scene by the fireplace and a shiver ran up his spine. "Aaoww!" he barked up at the moon, as he climbed into his Blazer and roared off down the bumpy driveway.

What was it about her, anyway, he asked himelf. What intrigued him? Methodically he ticked off her characteristics in his head, as if he were rating a new mare he was thinking of buying. Faye was sweet but tough, feisty and independent as hell and pretty as a damned painting. His left brow lifted lecherously at the thought of her perky breasts. He'd get her to come around, Seth consoled himself, trying to ignore the hunger still gnawing in his loins.

They could have something real nice together—for a while, anyway. That's what he liked most about Faye; for all her cocky down-to-earth sweetness, she was more allergic to permanence than he was. No danger there of him accidentally getting caught up in something serious. Nope, he decided, no danger at all. They'd have their bit of fun and then he'd see her packing for California, leaving her fine piece of property right where it belonged—in his hands, for his horses. In Seth's life women came and went like the seasons. He had only one abiding passion—horses.

Driving the short way down the road to his place, Seth tried to concentrate on the chores he'd set out for the morning, to think about the ailing colt he wanted the vet to come out and see.

But inevitably his thoughts drifted back to Faye. He could still feel her mouth against his, tasting of roses and wine. *A damned sight too intoxicating,* he swore as another shiver went down his backbone. *Gotta get that woman off my mind.*

CHAPTER EIGHT

THE CHIMING DOORBELL startled Faye out of a deep sleep. Groggily she lifted her head off the pillow and peered at the luminescent hands on the bedside clock. Who'd have the nerve to come calling at seven in the morning? One guess, she thought.

Her eyes half closed, Faye got up and dragged a robe over her nightgown. She nearly stumbled over Jenny, who was pacing restlessly in front of the closed bedroom door, her bushy tail waving uncertainly.

"You think it's him, too, huh?" Faye laughed softly down at the dog. "I swear, your master's got no manners at all."

As soon as Faye opened the door, Jenny bounded out ahead of her and down the stairs to the hall. She was sniffing furiously at the front door by the time Faye caught up with her, and had begun to growl.

"Okay, calm down now, girl," she admonished Jenny. "I don't think you should show how much you missed him. It'll just give him a big head."

Tightening the belt around her waist, Faye flung open the door. But the smart remark she had all ready for Seth died on her lips. Nobody was there at all.

Confused, she pushed open the screen door and caught a glimpse of a figure hurrying away through the early-morning mist. Faye ran to the edge of the porch, oblivious to the cold concrete under her bare toes. "Hey!" she shouted.

The man threw a furtive glance over his shoulder and quickened his pace. His reaction immediately made her suspicious, and she concentrated on imprinting his appearance in her mind.

As she turned back toward the house, Faye saw a long white box propped up next to the door, and she felt a little sheepish. It looked like a simple florist's box. The guy must have been a deliveryman, after all. Curious now, she picked up the package and went inside. She didn't even notice Jenny shoot past her into the yard.

A puzzled smile tugged at the corner of her lips. Long-stemmed roses, she guessed. Now who could have sent them—Seth? Hardly. She shook her head, remembering their phone conversation the day before.

"Think you can see things from my point of view this morning?" he'd asked her impatiently.

"Why should I want to look at things from the point of view of a lecherous male?"

"Aw, hell, I'm not talking about *that*."

"Good. Neither am I." She had paused then. "What *are* we talking about, anyway?"

"The barn, remember?" he prompted. "The sketch I made ya?"

"Oh, that," she said airily. "I don't know, Carradine. I mean, there are twenty stalls now. If I did things your way, I'd be cutting way down on my potential income. I think you're being impractical."

"Yeah, and you're being downright inhumane if you think my high-strung Thoroughbreds could live in that barn the way it is. Those stalls are like straitjackets, for cryin' out loud."

She knew he was right because she'd gone out herself to have another look at the run-down structure. Still, she couldn't bear to give in too easily. She had to show him their romantic interlude was a crazy fluke that hadn't softened her attitude toward him one bit.

"Yeah, well," she bargained coolly, "I think we should have twelve stalls at the least."

"Twelve at the absolute maximum," he retorted in irritation.

Faye smiled at her own cleverness. "Agreed. So when do we start work?"

"I can get a crew out there tomorrow, if you're willin' to cooperate."

"Aren't I always cooperative?" she asked sweetly.

"Right," he had snorted. "About as cooperative as a cornered weasel."

Could she seriously expect to get roses from a man who'd say something like that?

So maybe it was Barry Markham who'd sent the flowers. They had spoken a few times since lunch at the river, their conversations always warm and friendly. It seemed they'd made an unspoken agreement not to mention his proposal. Barry seemed genuinely pleased that she was staying, but a little concerned, too. Faye hadn't mentioned the phone threat, mainly because she wouldn't have put it past Siperia Markham to try scaring her off. The woman was no fool. She must have sensed her son's vulnerability after his divorce and guessed he might be drawn to an old flame who suddenly showed up in town.

Yes, Faye decided, the flowers had to be from Barry. It was just the kind of Southern-gentleman gesture he would make.

Eagerly now, she opened the long white box. But the smile in her eyes died as she stared down at the dozen long-stemmed buds. They were all black and wilted. Dead.

Her hands shaking slightly, she opened the card inside. A poem was scrawled across it in smudgy felt pen.

Roses are black
My sentiments are true
I know that these lack
A pretty coffin for you

"Dear God," she whispered in horror. "This is really sick."

If her enemies had meant to frighten her badly, they had succeeded. Faye put a hand to her mouth and took a deep breath, willing herself not to panic.

Instinctively she groped for the security and warmth of Jenny's presence. Hurrying over toward the door, Faye tried to whistle but fear had dried out her lips too much. She felt the hairs rising on her arms as she stared out into the cold gray morning. The mist lay closely on the hills, shrouding her from the rest of the world.

She started when a dark figure emerged suddenly out of the fog and then breathed a sigh of relief. It was only Jenny, come back.

Faye held the screen door wide open and Jenny bounded in, her eyes bright with the look of conquest. The dog dropped a scrap of gray cloth at her feet. Faye bent to pick it up and gave Jenny a hug. "Good job, girl," she said with a shaky laugh, examining the ripped trouser cuff. "I hope you gave him a damn good scare."

If someone had told Faye two weeks ago that she would not only be hugging dogs but holding one-sided conversations with them, she would have flatly told him he was crazy. Now she wasn't at all sure she wasn't the one who was nuts.

With a shake of her head, Faye stood up again and carefully locked and chained the door. Then she leaned back against it, staring down at the scrap of cuff in her hand.

Upstairs in the bathroom, Faye splashed some cold water on her face. She was afraid to take a shower, afraid her morning caller might come back. And she realized that must have been the intent of the episode—to make Faye a victim of her own fear. It was a game of ugly psychological warfare.

Angrily she ran a brush through her hair. She wanted to fight back, but how could she when she still wasn't certain who her enemy was? Much as she wanted to peg the blame on Hollister Pettigrew, the whole threat business seemed a shade too subtle to have been thought up by him. Then who?

She wasn't used to feeling so damned helpless. She remembered what the people here thought of her—an outsider, a loner who'd long ago given up her right to the vital network of friends and allies in the Kentucky community.

Making a determined effort to shake off the helpless feeling, Faye pulled on jeans and a sweater and went down to the kitchen to make coffee. She was just about to pour herself a cup when her hand froze on the pot. Had she heard the rumble of a motor outside? Faye grabbed her ever-present rifle.

A white pickup slowly lumbered up the bumpy drive. Her heart beating quickly, Faye marched out into the yard to confront the three men in the cab.

"Who're you and what do you want?"

"Would you mind pointin' that weapon the other way, Annie Oakley?" the driver said good-naturedly, pushing his painter's cap back on his head. "Makes me kinda nervous like."

"Who are you?" she insisted.

"Cal Darby." He jerked a broad thumb toward the words Darby Construction painted on the side of the truck. "Seth Carradine sent me and my crew out to do some work on that barn of yours down there."

"Do you have a work order?"

He climbed out of the truck and rummaged in the oversize pocket of his overalls, pulling out a briarwood pipe, which he stuck in his mouth, and finally a rumpled sheet of green paper, which he handed to Faye.

She scanned it quickly. "I guess it looks okay. Go on ahead."

"That's right neighborly of you." Darby's voice was dry as sandpaper. "What were you expecting, anyway— an Injun attack?"

"I've been having problems with…trespassers. I want to show them I mean business."

"I guess a pointed rifle'll do that, all right." He nodded, more sympathetic. "You live out here alone?"

"No, I've got the dog."

Darby glanced approvingly at Jenny, who stood watchfully by Faye's side. "He looks mean enough for two."

"She," Faye corrected, a hint of a smile lightening her stern expression. "And she *is* mean enough for two—just like her mistress."

"I believe you, ma'am." With a grin, Darby turned back to his men. "Come on, boys, let's get to work now we got our adrenaline pumping."

Her hand resting on Jenny's head, Faye watched them drive on down to the barn. She smiled again, remembering how Darby had called her Annie Oakley. She did feel a little like an Old West heroine, making a stand to protect what was hers. The strange part was that if someone had offered her even a pet rock a few months ago she'd have turned it down because she wouldn't have wanted the responsibility of lugging it around. What on earth was happening to her?

Maybe for the first time in her life she'd found something worth hanging on to, worth defending. She only wished things weren't moving so quickly; having to deal with Pettigrew and Barry, with the threats, and Seth, was proving to be almost too much for her. And even though she didn't trust Seth much, she was coming to depend on him, and she didn't like the idea. Faye was sorely tempted to sell her Pacific Heights condominium and plow all the cash into the farm, until she remembered Harvey's warning.

No, it was smarter to let Seth's money work for her. Logically, that decision made sense; emotionally, she was torn. Gran had lost her husband, her sons and daughter, and yet instead of giving up she'd gambled everything on running the place herself. Faye admired that kind of gutsiness.

Looking around the yard, she remembered how Gran had taken pride in every blossom and leaf, in every blade of grass. What a sorry spectacle it had become. Faye's eyes gleamed suddenly. *Shoot, if Gran could do it,* she told herself, *so can I.*

Distantly she heard the phone ringing and hurried inside to answer.

"Hello," she said breathlessly. There was no immediate reply, then Faye heard breathing on the other end of the line and her hand tightened on the receiver. She half expected to hear the voice again, whispering more threats of violence, tauntingly asking how she liked the flowers. "Hello!" Fear made her voice sharp, angry.

"Fayette?"

She slumped against the wall. "Yes. Who is this?"

"Siperia Markham."

Faye blinked. The rush of terror had subsided as soon as she'd heard the female voice, but upon realizing who it was, Faye became alert once more. She sensed the woman's manner was as sharp and watchful as her own.

"Fayette, are you there?"

"Yes," she replied carefully. "I'd been wondering if you'd call."

"Had you?"

"I'm sure you've heard that I'm settling onto the property here. And it occurred to me you might be worried about my seeing Barry again."

"You were never one to mince words, were you?"

"No." There was another brief silence.

"Actually, the reason I called is to invite you to our monthly luncheon meeting of the Summerton Club on Wednesday."

Faye nearly laughed out loud at the unexpected invitation. "How very kind of you," she said in an ironic tone, "but I don't think I can make it."

"I want to talk to you. I thought a neutral location like that would be best."

"What do we have to talk about?" Faye asked innocently, as if she were unaware of the woman's growing frustration.

"All right, if you want it more directly, then I'll say it. My son's future matters deeply to me, Fayette. He's just extricated himself from one bad marriage..."

"And you don't want him rushing headlong into another."

"Will you come on Wednesday or won't you?" Mrs. Markham demanded.

"Is this an ultimatum?"

"Let's just say it would be in your own best interests to come, Fayette," she said in a more conciliatory manner. "Really, this isn't something I care to discuss over the phone."

"I'll let you know," Faye said, her eyes on the dead flowers on the coffee table. "Goodbye, Mrs. Markham."

In your own best interests. What was that supposed to mean? She was becoming paranoid.

STRAINS OF FRANK SINATRA'S "New York, New York" belted out of the cassette player on the front porch, while Faye worked her way down the walk, pruning the overgrown rosebushes. She had already tackled the pretty dogwood tree outside the living-room window, her trial-and-error tactics resulting in an only slightly lopsided shape.

She stopped and flexed her cramped right hand. Even wearing the gardening gloves she'd found in the basement, she could feel the blisters rising on her soft palms. The release hard physical work offered was just what she needed. Her conversation with Siperia Markham had been so odd and unsettling. Faye wouldn't have put it past the woman to engineer the wearing psychological assault on her nerves. Now here came this direct attack and a ridiculous invitation to a women's club meeting. Faye knew she had to go, if only to satisfy her own growing curiosity.

She looked up at the sound of a car approaching. Seth's dusty blue mini-Blazer came jolting up over the last bump in the driveway, and he roared to a halt at the end of the walkway. Dolly Parton's melodious twang poured out of his car like sweet syrup. Faye breathed a sigh of relief when Seth switched off the engine and Dolly faded away, leaving Frank's sophisticated crooning unchallenged.

Seth sauntered down the path toward her with his nonchalantly sexy stride, grinning as his eyes swept over Faye's sweaty, dirt-streaked face. "You look like you been wrestling with a hog, and the hog won."

"What's the matter?" Faye retorted, snapping off a particularly thorny branch with her shears. "Haven't you ever seen a real country woman before?"

"A real country woman wouldn't be pollutin' the airwaves with that crap." He jerked his head critically toward the cassette player up on the porch.

"Your redneck's showing over your collar, Carradine," she needled him. "There's more in this world than Grand Old Opry stars with big boobs."

"Ah, now you're talkin' my style," Seth replied with a husky, appreciative laugh that made Faye want to poke him with her shears. "That lady's got what it takes."

"Yeah, a built-in ledge to hold all her Grammies," she snapped.

"Don't tell me you're jealous!"

"Don't be ridiculous." Her shears snipped cruelly at an innocent branch. "I just don't happen to be a fan of country corn."

"Blue-blood snob."

"Bluegrass hick," Faye shot back with relish, realizing what a dumb argument this was but not caring. It was a relief to be arguing about something so silly for a change. She needed a break from the far more serious, tension-filled confrontations that seemed to be piling up against her lately.

She shot Seth a wry grin. "I should have put some music on the other night when you came over to dinner. We might have stayed out of trouble that way—we'd have been too busy arguing."

He shook his head slowly. "Uh-uh, Hundred Pounds," he teased her. "At least we know there's one area where we can get along just fine."

Faye bit her lip. *Yes,* she thought wryly, *that's just what I'm afraid of.* She turned back to her pruning, and Seth couldn't help playing sidewalk superintendent.

"Here, give me those things, Faye," he said, taking her shears. "You got this bush too lopsided." He clipped away in silence, pausing every now and then to cock his head and squint as if he were surveying a sixty-story building site instead of a little rosebush. "There," he said at last with satisfaction. "You're gonna have this place all shipshape by the time I take it over."

The offhand remark cut her like a knife. Just like that he had killed the easy mood between them.

"Don't be too sure," she replied coldly.

"I told you I was a realist, Faye." His shrug was easy, unconcerned. "I'm not a man to back long shots; I only go for the sure thing."

"Is this your way of trying to psych me out—pretending to help me with one hand while the other stabs me in the back?" Her clear eyes darkened with hurt.

"If you're so damned oversensitive, you'd better get out, Faye, because I'm tellin' you right now," he warned her, "things are only going to heat up around here. I'm a man who goes after what I want, and I usually manage to get it. I'm makin' no bones about it. I want this farm. Do I gotta put it any more naked than that for you?''

She smiled grimly. "Was that other message from you, too?"

"What other message?"

"The flowers."

Seth looked genuinely bewildered, but then Faye thought maybe he was just a clever actor. "What flowers?"

"Come on into the house a minute. I want to show you something."

The macabre bouquet lay untouched in its box on the living-room coffee table. Faye picked up the accompanying poem and handed it to him to read. "I'm curious, Seth," she said. "Is this your way of saying thanks for the other night?"

His eyes snapped up angrily. "If I got something to say, I say it to your face, dammit. I don't play these kinds of weasely games."

"Why should I believe you?"

"Because you don't have any other choice, Faye," he said slowly. "Because I'm the closest thing to a friend you got."

"Then heaven help me."

"Heaven ain't gonna help," he murmured, eyes glinting. "This is going to be a one-on-one between me and you."

The softly spoken words, half threat and half promise, sent a shiver of anticipation up her spine, and she knew she had to break the spell.

"Oh, boy, I can't wait," she responded sardonically.

"You don't have to," he said in the same soft hypnotic way, coming around the coffee table toward her. "I'm here right now."

Faye blinked in surprise. The last thing she'd expected was to be out-brazened by him. She backed away and knocked the florist box off the table. Grateful for the distraction, she bent to pick it up but Seth was right beside her, grinning. He knew he'd won that little skirmish.

Annoyed, Faye gave him a withering look as she stuffed the blackened rose petals back inside the box. "I should have known this wasn't your style," she needled him. "I bet you never sent flowers to a woman in your life."

"Wrong." He laughed slyly. "I send 'em all the time. But not when you'd think."

"What are you talking about?"

"Actually, if you want to know the truth, I use flowers to cool a romance down, not to heat it up."

Faye was intrigued now. "I don't understand."

"You ever hear of bachelor's buttons?"

She stared at him for a second, wondering if he was putting her on. "I have to say that sounds like you. No one could ever accuse you of being a diplomat, that's for sure," she said, her eyes reluctantly mirroring the amusement in his. "I'm curious. Do your poor lady friends usually get the message?"

"Loud and clear. One of them called it my bachelor's shove."

"God, you're cruel," she said biting her lip so she wouldn't smile. "That waitress down at Leroy's didn't exaggerate one bit about you."

With a mock-innocent shrug, Seth turned his attention back to the flowers in question. "Any idea who sent this nasty bouquet? My guess is it's the same creep who's your telephone admirer."

"Yeah, and I barely caught a glimpse of him." Faye shoved the lid back onto the box with a purposeful air. "I'll tell you one thing, I'm going to get to the bottom of all this. I'm going to find out who's doing this to me. And when I do..."

"And when you do?"

"I don't know." She sighed. "Maybe by then if I have something conrete, Barry will be more willing to help me."

"Markham couldn't find his way out of a paper bag," Seth grumbled. "The guy's a pussycat."

Faye grinned. "You're jealous of Barry—just because he happens to be handsome, influential and rich."

"Jealous, hell," Seth retorted irritably. "No use talkin' to you. I'm going to see how Darby's getting along."

Faye followed him out onto the porch and watched him swagger down to the barn. *I'm jealous of what Dolly Parton's got, and Seth is jealous of what Barry's got,* she thought with a shake of her head. But didn't Seth realize he had what most men only dreamed about? He was so damned sure of himself. It wasn't just his terrific eyes or his dimple that were so seductive to women; it was his strength, his knowing exactly what he wanted out of life and going after it. Faye found that terribly attractive— and threatening. They were headed on a collision course. Faye just hoped she could keep her head. She shivered deliciously. *No more cozy nights by the fireplace,* she swore to herself. *My system couldn't take it.*

CHAPTER NINE

MIDMORNING ON WEDNESDAY, Faye found herself driving along twisting country lanes, heading for the Summerton Clubhouse. She remembered it vaguely, a rustic hunting lodge tucked into a forested nook off Grimes Mill Road. Gran had taken her out there on a few big social occasions—the blessing of the hounds in the fall before hunt season began, a festive barbecue in the spring. Now Faye was headed out there on her own, about to face thirty Chanel-suited matrons casting grim, disapproving eyes over her.

She smiled mischievously to herself in the rearview mirror. Eyes shadowed with a repellent Day-Glo lime green glinted back. Nothing like a touch of the outrageous to perk up one's spirits. There was nothing wild about her long-sleeved yellow jersey T-shirt dress. But her plastic earrings, along with the patent leather belt and shoes she'd picked up at the five-and-dime to match her eye shadow were another matter.

Faye rolled down the window and started whistling happily. The day was gorgeous. She should have been grateful to Siperia for getting her out of the house to enjoy it.

Wild mustard, bright as newly minted gold, grew densely along the high banks beside the road. By summer they would be gone, lost in a riot of orange Virginia creeper and frilly white Queen Anne's lace. A few tobacco fields still wore long thin sheets of white canvas, protection against frost for the tiny seedlings.

The landscape had a peaceful, fulfilled look. She breathed in the country air, nostalgia pricking her as she drove past the little limestone church of St. Hubert's with its stained-glass windows depicting animals of the hunt.

By the time Faye pulled into the grassy parking area in front of the lodge, she was wishing she hadn't gone *quite* so overboard in her attire. As a sop to convention she unfastened the wide shiny belt at her waist to let the dress hang straight. Climbing out of the car she glanced down at the green sandals that looked pretty tacky all of a sudden. *Nothing I can do about those, or my hair,* she told herself philosophically as she squared her shoulders to go face the dragon.

Siperia Markham was just rapping the meeting into session as Faye walked in. She acknowledged the newcomer with a dignified nod of the head, and dozens of eyes turned to regard Faye. A stir went up in the crowd as their collective gaze took in her attire. For a second she felt like a renegade daffodil about to be blown over by an ill wind, and then Siperia spoke coolly. "Welcome, Fayette. I hope you'll bear with us through our business meeting."

For more than an hour Faye sat, her back ramrod stright, forbidding herself the luxury of shifting position. She refused to show any signs of restlessness, though her stomach was beyond the range of her discipline. It growled embarrassingly from time to time in impatient answer to the mouth-watering odors emanating from the lodge kitchen.

For the first fifteen minutes Faye had been furious. How dared that woman invite her here to endure this excruciatingly boring session. And then, bit by bit, as she sat stewing, it dawned on Faye just what Siperia's game plan was. You think you want to return to Lexington, she could imagine Siperia challenging her. Well, this is the reality, Fayette. No excitement, no glamour here, just a small town getting on with its existence. No place for a restless, devil-may-care career woman used to the bright lights and the cosmopolitan sophistication of San Francisco. You'd be bored silly within a month. Bored with my son. Bored with the quiet, contained life we lead at Oak Hill Farm.

And so Faye sat, with a look of feigned interest plastered on her face, determined not to show that she knew she'd played right into Siperia's hands with her outlandish punk look.

At long last the meeting ended. The president had barely returned the gavel to its box when the club members turned eagerly in their seats to speak to Faye. Most of them had known Courtney Hunt and remembered her fondly as a lovely, hardworking, independent woman—"an inspiration to us all." "How wonderful to have a Hunt with us again." "It's refreshing to have some young blood around for a change."

Faye listened in surprise to their kindly chatter and grew keenly aware that Siperia Markham, Hollister Pettigrew, Seth Carradine and whoever else begrudged her return to Lexington were a small minority. These women hadn't been judging her when she walked through the door; their eyes had been full only of lively curiosity and interest. They had literally opened their arms to her, and for the first time since she arrived, Faye smiled genuinely.

Siperia must have realized that her carefully plotted game plan was unraveling because she threaded her way through the milling women to take Faye's arm and lead her to a place at her own table.

Though the meal of grilled pheasant with herbed sauce was delicious, Faye barely tasted it. Each attempt at conversation with the other women around the table was skillfully deflected by Siperia.

"Do you plan to settle in Lexington?" one of them asked Faye.

Before she could reply she heard Siperia's gracious drawl responding for her. "Fayette is her father's child. You remember Carter? Could never stay in one place too long."

"But that farm's been in the Hunt family for generations," another woman broke in. "It'd be a shame to see it go to strangers."

Faye opened her mouth to reply and again Siperia cut her off, smiling as she twisted the dagger. "But you're forgettin' that Fayette herself is a stranger, too. Now how many of you honestly would have recognized her in the street if I hadn't told you Miz Hunt's granddaughter would be with us today?"

They looked at Faye obliquely, as if noticing for the first time her ridiculous green eye shadow and grape lipstick, the wildly blown-dry hair sprayed heavily to maintain the Tina Turner look.

There was silence and then a small voice chirped up. "I would have," an elderly woman said, pale eyes twinkling behind her glasses. "I remember a dinner dance Catesby and Courtney came to back in the thirties, when those Dolores del Rio movies were all the rage. Courtney came decked out in a hat piled up with real fruit. Darnedest thing you ever saw. She caused quite a stir." The woman smiled and patted her own neatly permed white hair. "Guess you might say Fayette is a chip right off the old block."

Faye shot her unexpected ally a spunky grin. "I never heard that story. But then maybe Gran didn't want to encourage me too much in that direction."

The faded blue eyes twinkled more brightly, as if reflecting off Faye's yellow banana-shaped earrings. "A fat lot of good it did her."

"Well," Siperia broke in, seeing that the conversation had gotten away from her, "I think we can all adjourn. I planned to show Fayette over the grounds while the sun's still high."

Seeing that Siperia was so anxious to get her alone, Faye purposely dawdled, shaking every hand and exchanging small talk with each woman as she departed. Finally the last club member had gone, and Faye turned to her hostess. "You wanted to talk to me?"

Siperia gestured to the rear door, and together they went out into the garden. They walked in silence along the high creek bank, Faye savoring the faint gurgle of the water flowing swiftly in its rocky bed.

"Nothing daunts you, does it?" Siperia said after a while, her annoyance giving way to bemused curiosity.

"Why should it?" Faye retorted. "One thing I've learned in life is resilience. I adapt quickly."

"A chameleon."

"Lizards have more fun."

"Honestly, Fayette, I don't understand what Barrish sees in you."

Faye stopped and turned to confront the older woman. "I'll tell you what he sees in me, Mrs. Markham. I'm alive and open to new things. I like adventure. I like to laugh and be crazy sometimes. I represent everything he's never had."

"He's in love with you." It was less a question than a statement.

Faye flushed. "I suppose he is."

"Are you in love with him?"

"You have no business asking me that."

"Fayette, listen to me," she nearly pleaded. "Just hearin' you talk right now, I know it would never work between you. I'm sure you've figured out why I invited you to this meeting. I wanted you to get a taste of what it's like living here in this town day in and day out. You'd be like a scrappy little blue jay caught in a cage."

"Maybe I'm ready to be caged," Faye said argumentatively, though inside she couldn't help wondering if she didn't really mean it. "Am I really the one you should be worrying about, Mrs. Markham? You think you can read people so well. What about your own son—what do you think he wants?"

Siperia shot her a questioning, deeply suspicious look. "I don't know what you mean."

"I didn't mean anything," Faye said, realizing she had no right to even hint at Barry's dissatisfactions. She had given him her word. "I really think this discussion should end. It's pointless for us to be talking like this."

She started to turn away but Siperia's firm hand on her arm detained her. "Pointless?" she repeated in disbelief. "Fayette, I have to know what you want. I have to protect my son. If you're not in love with him, what are you after? Do you think by marrying Barrish you can ease the financial burdens on that farm of yours? Do you think you can talk him into runnin' Indian Creek? He'd be a fool to take on such a marginal property when he's got a lifetime of excellence behind him at Oak Hill."

Faye stared at her, aghast, not knowing what to be insulted over more—the insinuation that she would marry for money or the criticism of Indian Creek Farm. "Mrs. Markham, I'll thank you to mind your own damned business."

"My family's welfare is my business."

"You don't give a damn about Barry's welfare," Faye said dangerously. "All you care about is Oak Hill—controlling it and your sons."

Siperia's mouth tightened. "How much do you want, Fayette? Name your price," she said slowly and deliberately. "I will see that you get comfortably out of debt if you promise to stay away from my son."

"I'm not interested in your bribes, Mrs. Markham," Faye said, almost shaking with anger. "No matter what you might think of me, for God's sake, give me credit for having an ounce of integrity."

"How much, Fayette?" she insisted.

"Dammit, didn't you hear me!" Faye shouted, tears burning her eyes. "I am not for sale."

"Fayette, I'm warning you...."

"Don't bother," Faye flung over her shoulder as she turned away. "I've already been warned off twice. You'll have to stand in line."

She moved swiftly back along the creek bank, her head pounding. Damn her, Faye swore over and over again as she hurried around the old lodge and found her car. By the time she slid behind the wheel her hands were shaking so badly she could barely get the key into the ignition. Mercifully it started up first try and she sped half blindly out of the parking lot.

CHAPTER TEN

AFTER A RESTLESS NIGHT'S SLEEP imagining intruders on the stairs and monsters under her bed, Faye dragged herself from under the covers. It was no use. She might escape the nightmares but the fears would stay with her throughout the day.

And she could turn to no one. She was a pariah, an outcast nobody wanted around. Even dear Barry with his offer of marriage had presented less an offer of commitment than a promise of escape for them both.

Dammit, I'm not going to be driven off by Siperia Markham or anyone else, she resolved. First things first: she would find out who hated her enough to go to the length of threats. Faye's vow to Seth that she would "get to the bottom of all this" hadn't been pure bravado. She relished the idea of playing detective. If nothing else, it would give her a sense of being in control of her life again.

Jenny padded loyally down the stairs behind her, curling up on the kitchen rug while her mistress brewed coffee and dropped a couple of slices of bread into the toaster.

Ten minutes later they were both munching whole-wheat toast liberally slathered with butter and raspberry jam.

"What should I do first?" Faye asked her friend rhetorically.

Jenny licked her chops, eyeing Faye's last bite of toast.

"Try to get Pettigrew off my back," Faye answered herself, as she lifted the coffee mug to her lips thoughtfully.

She had to try to build up a case against the bank's manipulative and borderline criminal interference in her grandmother's affairs. The only strong lead Faye had was Ida Pinkowski. Even if the woman had died, as Minah Willis seemed to remember, someone in her family might remember something that would be helpful.

She jumped up and ran to find the brand-new telephone book she'd picked up at the phone center. Anxiously she ran her fingers down through the *P*'s. Dozens of Pettigrews and Pittmans, but not even one Pinkowski. What next?

Faye thought for a minute before answering her own question again. Nurses' registries. Surely as a licensed vocational nurse, Ida Pinkowski had worked through one of them. Faye turned to the yellow pages, and moistening a forefinger, she began to flip through. Within a few minutes she had jotted down the addresses of the four registries in town.

Pleased by the start she'd made, Faye went back upstairs. With Jenny planted outside the locked bathroom door and her loaded rifle inside, she treated herself to the luxury of a long soak in the tub.

BY 10:30 A.M., Faye sat slumped behind the wheel of her rented car, demoralized. Her hot little strategy had fizzled to nothing. Armed with the addresses and her city map, Faye had methodically visited each registry. None of them had a record of Ida Pinkowski, L.V.N., as none of them kept records beyond four years. They couldn't even give Faye a shred of proof that Hollister Pettigrew had ever hired the woman to care for her grandmother.

"Now what?" she asked herself in aggravation, not quite ready to give up. She decided she might as well pay a visit to the county courthouse, to find out if the elusive Ida had truly existed at all.

After several false starts, Faye was directed to the right department and a helpful clerk in the vital records section tracked down a copy of Mrs. Pinkowski's death certificate. Faye jotted down the date, thanked the clerk and went out into the warm spring morning.

"Talk about a cold lead," Faye muttered to herself with gallows humor. "I might as well be chasing ghosts."

She was about to climb back into her car when she realized she had forty-five minutes still left on the meter. "Oh, what the heck," she decided on impulse, "might as well walk up to the library and check their newspaper files." Wasn't that what detectives always did in books when they were looking for a lead? Maybe the woman's obituary would mention survivors or something.

The reference librarian obligingly pulled out the microfilm cassettes of the *Herald*'s back issues and showed Faye how to use the machine.

She set to work with more enthusiasm than she felt, turning the handle briskly until the social columns and Meyers department-store ads, the stories on horse sales and editorials on tobacco subsidies dissolved in a gray blue through the viewfinder. Faye slowed down occasionally to check the date in an upper corner. Eventually she found what she was looking for, a miserly three-sentence obituary notice on Ida Pinkowski that mentioned nothing about survivors, and nothing that might have linked the deceased nurse to the Farmers and Breeders Bank.

"Hell." Faye swallowed her disappointment and idly began to flip through the other issues. She stopped here and there to read a wedding announcement or study a photograph, but the names and faces meant nothing to her.

Faye was about to turn off the microfilm machine when her eye was drawn to the photograph of an elderly woman that illustrated a brief feature article. Something about the woman's features tantalized Faye's memory and she read the caption: "L. B. Wainbridge, the former Laura Bell Swann, has run Boar's Head Farm singlehandedly for thirty-five years, compiling an enviable record in the world of Thoroughbred breeding and racing that even few men can match."

Laura Bell Swann. Faye recognized the woman's maiden name at once. Courtney Hunt and the young Laura Bell had stood with their arms around each other's waists in the old photograph Minah Willis had shown her. Faye remembered what Minah had said about Courtney, Laura Bell and her brother, Quentin. *"Them three were the best o' friends."* Thoughtfully Faye made a photocopy of the article before turning off the machine.

"Is there a pay phone?" she asked the librarian after she'd returned the microfilm cassettes.

"You'll have to go down to the courthouse."

Faye smiled her thanks and hurried down the broad old-fashioned staircase, suddenly feeling optimistic.

She found Boar's Head Farm in the telephone directory and dialed the number. She wondered to what extent the powerful Laura Bell Wainbridge would remember the friendship that had gone back sixty-five years, and if the woman might be moved enough by sentiment to help the granddaughter of her old friend.

"Good morning. Boar's Head Farm," a voice said briskly. "May I help you?"

"Yes. My name's Fayette Lee Hunt. My grandmother was Courtney Hunt. She and Mrs. Wainbridge were—" Faye hesitated only a fraction of a second "—the best of friends. My grandmother's dead now, but I've moved back to Lexington and I was wondering if I could pay a social call."

"One moment please. I'll have to check."

While she waited, Faye pulled out the photocopied news story and studied the woman's photograph. Her strong-boned face had withstood the ravages of time very well; no doubt that's why Faye had been able to recognize her at all. She looked at the eyes staring out at her. Even the fuzzy newsprint couldn't blur the hard, uncompromising light in her eyes, and Faye wondered what her gran's old friend was like.

The telephone line clicked back to life. "Miss Hunt?"

"Yes?" Faye said eagerly.

"I'm very sorry, Miss Hunt, but this is breeding season now," the secretary explained. "Mrs. Wainbridge regrets she's too busy to receive any visitors."

"I...I see," Faye replied, deflated by the rather transparent rebuff. "Thanks, anyway."

Had she been naive enough to think the woman might still think about or even care about the past?

Faye stepped out of the telephone booth and ran nearly head-on into Barry Markham.

"Fayette!" he greeted her. "I was just thinking about you."

"Oh, hi, Barry. What a nice coincidence."

He smiled. "Hey, you're not in the big city now, remember? In this town you're supposed to be surprised if you *don't* run into someone you know."

"You're right." She nodded ruefully. "Small towns have eyes..."

"And ears," he finished for her. "Can I buy you lunch, Fayette?"

"I'd love it. Just let me throw another quarter in the meter."

"Is this your car?"

"It's a rental. My Alfa's on the way from California," she explained. "I'm having it delivered through one of those drive-away agencies. My friend Harve packed it up with a couple of boxes of my clothes and stuff."

"Sounds like a permanent move."

Faye made an effort to sound lighthearted. "Permanent for now."

They managed to find a quiet booth in a bustling little deli nearby that featured lacy curtains in the window and ferns in hanging baskets.

"Boy, I might as well have stayed in California," Faye said, her eyes taking in the trendy but nevertheless cozy surroundings. "Lexington's taking on some real airs."

Barry ignored her remark. His gaze was fixed intently on her. "Fayette, are you okay?"

"Why shouldn't I be?" she retorted a little sharply.

"This town has ears, remember?" he said. "I've been hearing rumors of trouble out at your place."

"Nothing I can't handle." She brushed off his concern. "Barry, did your mother tell you she invited me to her club meeting last Wednesday? She made sure I got a big dose of small-town life. Her own brand of scare tactics."

"I hope they worked," he said, surprising her. "Fayette, have you given any thought at all to my...my offer?"

"Hey, you promised me you'd let it drop. Barry, my life is in such a jumble I've got enough trouble concentrating my wits just so I can make it day to day. Don't you see?" she said, looking at him with an intensity that was not like her. "I have something I have to do here."

"Fayette, I don't understand you. It's like you're changing and I'm changing, but we're both going in different directions." He fiddled with his water glass. "You're thinking of staying put here, aren't you?"

"I don't know."

"What happened to your famous sense of adventure?"

She looked at him, surprised at his sarcastic tone. "Barry, I've been footloose since I was born. It's the only life I've ever known. For me this is as big a step into the unknown as you going off to join the diplomatic corps."

He smiled a little. "I like hearing you say that, Fayette. Makes my dream feel concrete, real."

"Have you discussed it with your family?"

"Not yet."

"You have to, Barry, It's only fair to your brothers and your mother."

"If you were behind me, I'd feel easier doin' it."

"I *am* behind you. But I don't want to get involved in family conflicts. Believe me, Barry, the way your mother feels, if you had me come over to give you moral support, I think the whole thing would backfire right in your face."

"You're probably right." He smiled ruefully. "She tried to give me an ultimatum—not to see you again."

Faye's eyes flashed. "And?"

"I told her very politely to get stuffed."

"You didn't!"

"Well, I implied it," he amended. "I could see Corky taking in the whole thing, and I'm damned if my son is going to see his daddy getting pushed around."

"Bravo," she teased him. "A rebel with a cause."

"Better late than never, right?" he said. "You're a terrific catalyst, Fayette."

"Why, no man's ever said such a thing to me before," Faye replied in a teasing flirtatious manner. "I do believe you're sweet-talkin' me, Barrish Markham."

Barry laughed. "You're the only woman I know who'd rather hear that than be told she's pretty."

"Pretty. How dull."

"See what I mean!" he exclaimed. "But I don't care, Fayette. I'm going to say it, anyway. You are pretty—a lot prettier as a woman than you were as a girl."

"I'm tougher, too, Barry," she said. "It goes with the territory."

"If you're trying to scare me off, Fayette, it won't work," he said good-naturedly, "because I'm going to ask you to dinner, anyway."

Her answering smile was mischievous. "I accept . . . as long as you take me to the Cheviot Country Club and I can flaunt myself in front of the local aristocracy. One other thing I inherited from Gran was her membership in the club. They might as well see for themselves there's another Hunt back in Lexington. And she's not about to be cowed."

"Spoken like a true blue blood," Barry teased her. "Even Mother would approve. There's hope for you yet, Fayette."

She winked as the young waitress bustled up to their table. "Champagne for two," Faye ordered imperiously.

"Now, Fayette, I got to work this afternoon," Barry started to protest and then reluctantly nodded his assent. "I can see you're going to force my hand—make a renegade of me whether I'm ready or not."

"I don't have anything to do with it," she countered, her eyes serious. "You're finding the courage all on your own, Barry. And I deeply respect you for that."

"Respect. That's a mighty long way from love," he said quietly. "But I'm a patient man, Fayette. I think you'll get tired of playing the country gentlewoman. Sooner or later the grass is goin' to start itchin' under your feet." His eyes sparkled, "And when it does, I'll be ready to whisk you away."

"I'll remember that," she promised, laughing.

After lunch Barry excused himself to return to the courthouse and Faye stared after him as he walked hurriedly on his way, smiling at his slightly flushed cheeks and the usually perfectly groomed hair that had gotten a little mussed from his running a hand through it. He was such a fine person, she thought to herself, conscientious and good and gradually coming into his own as a man. He so much wanted her to be a part of his future, but Faye couldn't make that kind of commitment.

She flushed, thinking of Seth. She was usually so adept at keeping men at a distance, at controlling the situation. What on earth was it that happened to her whenever he was around?

She tried to shrug him off, to think of other less disturbing things. She thought about knocking 'em dead at the country club—about setting Siperia Markham back on her heels again. Small-town life indeed, she scoffed. It didn't have to be dull!

Faye decided to postpone the drive home long enough to do a little window shopping at an exclusive boutique she'd noticed in the Hyatt Center.

Multipaned windows of beveled glass gave Panache the air of a small French couturier's shop. The sexy and elegant woman behind the counter with her auburn hair and sultry green eyes looked like a young Joan Collins.

"Afternoon," the woman greeted Faye with a lazy drawl, giving her customer a quick up-and-down from beneath plum-shadowed eyes.

"Hi," Faye said crisply, fingering the exquisite fabrics while wincing inwardly at the prices.

"Is there something I can help you with?"

"Yes. I'm looking for something gorgeous, sexy..." Her eyes sparkling, Faye paused a half second before adding, "And on sale."

The woman laughed. "I just have something that might suit you to a T. Follow me."

Faye did, noticing enviously the way her curves filled out to perfection the elegantly simple skirt and sweater she was wearing.

The shop owner pulled out a dress from a rack. "What do you think?" she asked, her green eyes amused. "Most of my clients are older and conservative, so this mini kind of got overlooked. But you just might be the type who could carry it off. Looks like it should fit you; it's a size three."

Faye took the pale pink cashmere sweater dress and held it up to herself in front of a mirror. The effect was scrumptious.

"I'll try it."

The dress was even better on. While the front had a fairly modest boat neckline, the back plunged in an extravagant and totally unexpected V. Faye turned her head over one shoulder and then the other, checking out the effect.

There was a polite knock on the dressing-room door. "How you doing in there?"

Faye flung open the door. "All set."

The woman whistled softly. "I knew that pretty little thing was just waitin' for the right taker." She smiled. "And it's on sale, too."

Faye glanced at the tag. The price was still a little steep, but by this point she didn't care. She needed something very beautiful and slightly outrageous for her country-club debut. "I'll take it."

A few minutes later they were facing each other over the counter. "Are you just passing through town?" the woman asked conversationally as she took Faye's Mastercard and rang up the sale.

"No. As a matter of fact, I've taken over a place out off the Versailles Pike."

"All by yourself?"

"I happen to like challenges."

The woman's well-brushed eyebrows rose a fraction of an inch. "D'you know Seth Carradine by any chance?"

Faye's head snapped up from the charge slip she was signing. "Why do you ask?"

"Seth owns a little spread off the Versailles road. I thought you might be neighbors."

"Is he a friend of yours?"

The shop owner's well-defined lips lifted in an intimate little smile that made Faye's hackles rise. "I suppose he is."

Faye realized by the way she said it that this woman hadn't received any bouquet of bachelor's buttons. "You don't look his type," Faye said snippily.

"So you do know him! You were holdin' out on me."
The woman laughed throatily. "Sounds like he's been
holdin' out on me, too. I'll have to ask Seth about you."

"I'll have to do the same," Faye shot back. "What's
your name?"

"Parris Harper."

"How charming," Faye responded with a smile so
sugary sweet that she was sure she'd give herself a cavity.
With that she picked up her bag and sashayed out of the
shop, even though she knew she couldn't hope to compete with the elegant Ms Harper's mesmerizing hip
swivel. Faye realized she was behaving childishly but she
couldn't stop.

Jealous, she scolded herself roundly as she tossed the
elegant shopping bag into the rear seat of the car. *You're
just plain jealous, Faye Hunt, and it's not like you one
bit.*

CHAPTER ELEVEN

FAYE BRAKED behind Cal Darby's truck and went into the barn to see how their job was progressing. She nearly fainted when she saw the dizzying maze of scaffolding holding up the barn and Cal's two assistants perched high up in the sturdy metal webbing, their electric saws cutting through the huge horizontal beams that had once supported the roof.

She rushed over to Darby who was absorbed in cutting two-by-fours for new frame supports in the expanded stalls. "Mr. Darby," she said breathlessly. "What's going on—what are those guys doing?"

He straightened and shook his head. "We found dry rot in those beams. They gotta be replaced, Miz Hunt."

"I would have appreciated being consulted first."

"You weren't around and Carradine was." The man shrugged philosophically. "So I got him to give me the okay."

"I see. Is he around now?"

"Said he'd drop by sometime this afternoon to check on how things are going."

"Thanks," she said shortly, doing her best to contain her dismay. The situation wasn't Darby's fault.

Faye started up to the house, only to remember the package she had left in the back seat of the car. As soon as she saw it, the elegant paper bag smote her conscience. What had she been thinking of to have blown seventy-five dollars on a little wisp of a dress, when her property was practically falling down around her on all sides? Her impulsive purchase was downright irresponsible. Faye sighed, angry with herself, angry with the situation she had gotten herself into.

Her attention was distracted by the sound of a vehicle approaching. She smiled grimly when she recognized Seth's Blazer, relieved to find a new outlet for her frustration. She marched over toward his truck, her arms crossed stiffly over her stomach.

"Hey there, Hundred Pounds," he greeted her. "I been tryin' to get ahold of you all day."

"I'm right here."

His eyes narrowed at her tone. "Yeah, well, you weren't this morning when Cal found that dry rot."

"So you went ahead and gave him the okay to spend what—another four or five thousand of my money?" she said furiously.

"Your money, hell!" He slammed the door shut with a vengeance. "I'm the one layin' out the cash. As far as you're concerned, the costs are just on paper, anyway."

"Just on paper!" she repeated in disbelief. "Have you forgotten I've got to get this place in the black—on paper—or I'm going to lose it? Another five thousand in the red 'on paper' is going to sink me a whole hell of a lot deeper." She gave him an accusing look. "Or maybe that's what you intended from the start."

"I warned you once before, Faye," he said in a low, controlled voice that was far more threatening than an angry shout would have been. "I warned you not to go makin' me your scapegoat. You understand me?" He jabbed his finger an inch from her upturned nose. "Now, this construction crew's costing us two hundred bucks a day, and I wasn't about to have them sit idle while I tried to track you down to get your damned permission for work that's gotta be done, no matter what."

"That's a matter of opinion," she said icily.

"Well, then you go on in there and tell them the job's off, because I'm not about to put my bloodstock in a barn where the roof might fall down on their heads."

"I'm not saying I want it called off," Faye retreated. "I'm saying I'm tired of being manipulated into situations where I'm always the potential loser."

"Now that's pure bull and you know it, Faye," he said angrily. "I'm sure a savvy little woman like you has investments squirreled away for the future. But you aren't gonna touch them. You know why?"

She stared back at him, eyes blazing. "Why?"

"Because at heart you don't give a damn about this place. It's just a game for you, Faye, a paper chase that doesn't mean a thing. And when the game's over you'll count your cash and thumb your nose at me and Pettigrew and the rest of this town on your way out."

"That's not true."

"The hell it isn't," he swore, leaning back against the truck and resting his elbows on the hood. "Let's you and me be honest with each other for a change. You're using me as much as I'm using you. We both think we got a good chance at winning, so we're willing to gamble. But when you get right down to it, you haven't laid a damn thing on the line."

The accusation cut bone deep. "What about my life, dammit! I've been threatened twice just for being here," she whispered in a choked voice.

"And how do I know you didn't manufacture those threats yourself, just to get my sympathy?"

"Damn you!" she burst out, and turned to run up the hill toward the house.

But Seth was too quick. He caught her arm and spun her back around to face him. "No," he commanded. "We've got to settle this here and now." She shook his hand off and stared up at him pugnaciously. "Maybe I went a little too far with what I just said. But I think the rest of it was fair. Now, I want to know—are you gonna kick in the extra money for those beams, or aren't you?"

Faye sighed and rubbed her hands over her face, sending her bangs into wispy disarray. Finally she looked up at him again, some of the fight gone out of her wide hazel eyes. "I can't," she murmured in a barely audible voice. "Every spare cent I've got has to go for living expenses over the next few months. All my investments you think I've got squirreled away like acorns are consolidated in one little remodeled condominium I own in San Francisco."

"You gonna put it on the market?"

Faye managed to give him a steady look. "I don't know yet."

"In other words, you still want me to refinance the whole remodeling job?"

"I'd like you to make the additional expense in the form of a personal loan, Seth," she said, her self-confidence buoying up again. "I don't want that jerk Pettigrew to find out how big a hole I'm digging for myself."

"You think I give a damn about your feud with the bank?" He ran his fingers through his curly brown hair in agitation.

"What difference does it make, anyway, how or why I want you to finance our deal?" she retorted. "You'll have the condo as collateral."

"Yeah, and I think I'd be a fool to count on collecting a debt on some property I never even saw."

"What are you being so cautious about?" she snapped. "One way or another you'll get every penny back, especially if I have to sell out here."

"Yeah, but you're forgetting one thing," he said coolly. "Once the barn's been upgraded, the land assessment's going to be higher. I could wind up paying for this damn barn twice over. It's just too risky."

"Oh! So now you're suddenly afraid of taking risks," she flung back with a deliberately provoking laugh. "As if you don't gamble every day of your life in the business you're in. With every weanling one of your mares drops and every yearling you keep to race, you're taking a big chance, aren't you? I'll tell you one thing, Seth Carradine," she said, striding over to plant herself directly in front of him, "I think I'm a heck of a lot better risk than any of your horses."

Seth straightened, abandoning his casual stance. "You know something, Faye? Sometimes you remind me of a bitty balloon that's got itself way overinflated." He reached out and poked her lightly in the chest with his finger, his eyes glinting with sardonic amusement. "I'm gonna get my kicks waiting for you to burst."

Faye willed herself not to explode, since that seemed to be what he was expecting. She took a deep breath and when she did finally speak again it was in a surprisingly gentle voice that Seth had never heard before.

"Seth, all I'm asking is that you trust me. I need to make a go of this farm." She was almost pleading. "I want to get back at that bank and show them they can't push us Hunt women around."

Seth noticed the irrepressible bravado creeping into her voice again and he smiled a little. "So you're asking me to trust you?"

"Is that such a difficult thing?" she parried. "Besides, weren't you asking the very same thing of me when you first approached me about this crazy business proposition?"

"Yeah. And as I recall you were damned reluctant."

"Okay, so we're both reluctant. We can start slow." She gave him a long level look. "You trust me a little and I promise I'll do the same."

"I guess it's a deal. Shake on it?" But as soon as her hand touched his, he twisted it lightly until their forearms were entwined. Then he lifted her imprisoned hand to teasingly brush it with his lips. "We'll see how far a little trust goes."

"Mm," she murmured, taken aback, realizing too late how much like a sigh of pleasure her reply must have sounded.

"Mmm-mm." His low husky voice mocked her playfully.

Faye drew a ragged breath as warmth surged through her. The delicious little moment had caught her unawares. It had made her realize once again how incredibly vulnerable she was where Seth was concerned.

He released her hand at last and Faye looked away hurriedly toward the barn. "How long do you think it'll be before the work's finished?"

"A month maybe," he said lazily.

"A month. I guess a lot can happen in that amount of time." She sighed and gave him a rueful sidelong glance. "You have any faith in miracles, Seth?"

To her surprise he threw back his head and laughed. "Funny you should ask, Hundred Pounds. It seems like us horse folk get by on little else but that sometimes. As a matter of fact, I want you to come on out back," he said suddenly, and somehow Faye's hand was in his again. "I want to show you something."

"What is it?" She tried to hang back, but he was pulling her forward.

"Just do somethin' without arguing for a change, will ya?"

They brushed through the high weeds on the south side of the barn and came around to the sturdy new post-and-rail fencing that marked the boundary between their adjoining farms. Seth hoisted himself up onto the fence and Faye joined him there.

"Okay, now I'm here," she said, a trace of suspicion still in her voice. "What's to see?"

"Just a second." Seth put two fingers to his lips and gave a long piercing whistle.

In response to his call, a beautiful Thoroughbred appeared over the rolling crest of a nearby hill. Bright sunshine had broken through the billowy clouds in the spring sky, and the mare's chestnut coat gleamed brilliantly. The animal pricked up its ears and galloped down toward them, shadowed by a young colt loping along beside her on his gangly legs.

Seth pulled a couple of sugar cubes from his pocket and held them out to the horse.

"This mare's True Faith," he told Faye as his fingers lightly brushed down the horse's velvety forehead. "Her daddy was Faith in Miracles."

"You're putting me on."

"No, it's the truth."

Faye was smiling now. "And the baby?"

"Well, if I decide to keep him I guess he'll be Blind Faith." He cocked his head at Faye and laughed. "That's how it seems I get by sometimes."

She reached out a tentative hand to touch the sweet-faced little colt. "You mean you might not keep him?"

"I usually sell my stock as yearlings at the July sales. That's how I get my operating capital for the next year. But this little guy, I don't know..." Seth reached out to stroke the baby, too. "I just feel it in my bones that he's something kinda special."

Faye cocked her head and studied the animal more judiciously, wondering what indefinable quality Seth sensed in him. But she shook her head in defeat. To her the colt was adorable, period. She saw nothing else.

"How can you tell he's special?"

"I guess it's instinct."

Faye turned to took at Seth, but he almost seemed to have forgotten she was there. His eyes roamed over the fields, but Faye had the impression he was really looking inward. So she said nothing, and gradually the peacefulness of their surroundings enfolded her. The horses whinnied softly and a robin sang a twittery practice note in a nearby tree. Even the sawing and hammering noises coming from the barn seemed pleasant this afternoon.

"You know," Seth said after a while, "I can remember as clear as if it was yesterday the first time I ever climbed up on a real horse's back—I mean prime-grade Thoroughbred. I was just a skinny fifteen-year-old and the horse's raw power scared me half to death. Then, bit by bit I realized that power and speed could be mine, too, if I could just learn to handle the animal, to control it."

"Interesting," Faye said, her eyes sparking in the late afternoon sunlight. "And you learned how to handle women the same way?"

Seth grinned back at her. "Haven't you found that out yet, Hundred Pounds?"

Faye gave an indifferent toss of her head, and Seth was reminded of one of his more unmanageable mares. "I met a friend of yours today," she said casually, not looking at him. "Said her name was Parris Harper."

"Yeah?"

"Yeah." Faye shot him a quick look from under her lashes. "She doesn't seem your type."

"No?" he said interestedly. "What is my type?"

"I don't know... some hard little mama who'd give whatever you dished out to her right back to you."

He smiled. "Sounds like you're describin' yourself, Hundred Pounds."

"I am not," she retorted in irritation. "So what is your type? You tell me."

"I like 'em beautiful, spoiled and just a tad bored."

Her eyes widened with surprise. "Why?"

"Because they're usually so self-centered they don't pay me much mind. I don't have to worry that they'll want to change me," he said with a quiet laugh. "Because I know we'll get bored with each other eventually and I can shoo 'em on their way, and go on just being myself."

"Boy, Carradine! You had a nerve calling me a weasel." She shook her head. "It sounds to me like you're pretty darn expert at oiling out of situations you don't like."

"No need to 'oil out' if I can arrange a satisfactory situation from the start."

She turned to face him, her eyes narrowing. "Don't you think it's pretty dumb to reveal your tactics to the opposition here?"

His only reply to that was a sly grin.

"I gotta run, Faye," he said suddenly, swinging his legs around toward the yard and jumping down off the fence.

"I've got an appointment with some buyers. How about dinner Saturday night?"

"Sorry. I've already made plans."

The corners of his mouth dropped a little. "Markham?"

"What's it to you?"

"Nothin' at all." The way he said it made Faye smile from ear to ear, which irritated him all the more. "And I'm not jealous."

"Oh, sure."

"But I'll pretend to be as long as you keep smilin' like that. For that smile I would do anything, Fayette Lee Hunt." He reached up to touch her mouth lightly with his fingers, and the light caressing stroke sent a quiver through her. Then, somehow, his hands found their way to her waist and he was lifting her down from the fence. Her breasts and hips brushed against him as he set her down, but she made no move to back away.

"Aren't you going to be late for your appointment?" she whispered huskily.

"It can wait. I want to tell you something first," he said, his thumbs lightly teasing her ribs. "I want to tell you the difference between Markham and me, Faye."

"You mean in case I haven't noticed?"

But Seth ignored her gibe. "As far as I can tell, Markham's always had things handed to him on a silver platter. He was the youngest; he got coddled. The guy never had to fight for what he wanted, so I don't believe he appreciates what he's got. Now me," Seth said, his hands tightening on Faye's waist, "I'm the opposite. Once something nice comes my way, I gotta stop and savor it. You understand me, Faye?" he murmured, his eyes as much a caress as his words. "I make the moment count, especially when I got a woman like you in my arms. I want to make her feel as good as she makes me feel.''

"Go on," she commanded softly, feeling excitement spark in her like a seed bursting with life.

"For example, I wouldn't say to you, 'Fayette Lee, I been staring at your mouth for ten minutes and I'm hungry for it. I remember how it tastes and I want more.'''

She licked her lips. "You wouldn't?"

"No. I'd say, 'Hundred Pounds, you look like you had a rough day, but you can put all that behind you. Because I'm goin' to love you back to life.''' Seth leaned closer, his mouth hovering over hers. "I'm goin' to make you feel good to be alive, same as you do to me."

Their lips met and as he kissed her Faye was enveloped by a melting sweetness. "Oh, dear God," she murmured, giving in to the pleasure that spurted through her as the kiss deepened. Faye wrapped her arms around his neck, aching for his hands to brush across her breasts and to feel them cup the slender curve of her behind.

Instead he pushed her gently, reluctantly, from him. "Can't tarnish your reputation in front of the Dalby boys," he teased her huskily, as he nuzzled her throat one last time before releasing her.

"You're a real gentleman," she teased him back, her voice unsteady and her face all flushed.

His low laughter washed over her. "That's the difference between Markham and me."

His eyes said he wanted to stay, but Seth turned and strode away. Faye stared after him in confusion. She knew what he was, and yet she knew, too, that he made her feel more deliciously alive than she had ever felt before. She suspected sweet-talking was his chief stock-in-trade and that he was just softening her up to get what he wanted. *So what,* she told herself. *I'll just enjoy the ride as long as it lasts. I can walk away, too. I'm not falling for him.*

If she were going to allow herself to fall in love, she told herself further, it would be with someone like Barry. Someone dependable and caring. She felt guilty now about not defending her old friend against Seth's scathing criticism. No one but Faye had an inkling of the torment and frustration beneath Barry's smooth, handsome exterior. Yet she couldn't defend him without giving away his secret, something she had no right to do.

Seth Carradine was as opposite from Barry as anyone could be. He was hard and scrappy with a huge chip on his shoulder. Faye would never have imagined falling for his type. He was as much of an outsider as she was. They were no good for each other. No, she would never succumb to her seductive neighbor, even if he did have the power to ignite her with just a look.

CHAPTER TWELVE

THE CHEVIOT COUNTRY CLUB looked as snobbishly elegant as Faye had remembered it. A long row of Cadillacs and Mercedes Benzes discharged their passengers beneath the white-pillared portico. Faye shifted impatiently in the passenger seat of the BMW and shot her companion a quick wink.

"You know, Barry, I think minidresses were in the last time I came here with you."

"Barely."

She smiled at his pun. "I hope you're not having second thoughts about showing up here on my arm."

"No, I'm not." He laughed resignedly as they inched forward to the valet parking zone. "I like fireworks."

A teenage car attendant opened Faye's door. With an appreciative glance at the shapely legs beneath her short dress, he gave her a hand out onto the brick driveway. Barry came around to join her. Together they walked up to the private club's beautifully carved double doors, which were opened by a pair of liveried footmen.

As the doors swung open, heads turned automatically to scan the latest arrivals. The low, steady stream of conversation was suspended for one long heartbeat while dozens of eyes took in Faye's trendy attire. Then, as if on cue, the club members withdrew their narrow-eyed appraisal and turned back into their small exclusive circles. White-jacketed waiters carrying sterling-silver drink trays circulated unobtrusively through the high-ceilinged foyer, taking orders for pre-dinner cocktails.

"This is what Californians call 'styling,'" Faye murmured to Barry as her low-heeled gray pumps sank into luxuriantly thick carpet.

Barry took a deep breath and guided Faye toward the fireplace where his mother stood conversing with another woman. Siperia Markham looked up and smiled coolly at the newcomers.

"So we meet again, Fayette. I should have known you'd be the one to introduce a Forty-second Street atmosphere to Lexington."

"I hope you're not disappointed, Mrs. Markham," Faye replied spunkily. "To tell the truth, though, I was hoping for a Fifth Avenue rating. It's more tony than honky-tonk, don't you think?" she added, turning slowly to reveal the sweater dress's startling V plunge. Faye was rewarded by a collective gasp.

Barry cleared his throat as Faye turned back around with a mock innocent smile. "Fayette, I don't think you've met Mrs. Tom Stone—she and her husband own Stoneleigh stables over Harrodsburg way," he said, adding correctly, "Mrs. Fairley, may I present Fayette Lee Hunt? She's a descendant of old Colonel Catesby Hunt. You probably remember he was a well-respected Standardbred breeder in his day."

"Fayette and I already met at the Summerton Club luncheon," Mrs. Stone replied neutrally, her eyes fixed on the younger woman. "Do you think you'll join our club?"

"You do a lot of great charitable work, but I've got a mammoth project of my own," Faye said at once. "For me, charity has to begin at home right now. Indian Creek's been run-down and neglected for too long."

"You plan to raise horses or tobacco?"

"Both . . . eventually."

"You farmed in California?" Mrs. Stone asked.

"No. I worked for a stockbroker."

The other woman shook her head. "It's hard to believe you'll find farming to be up your alley."

Faye smiled. "I've always been a great believer in midlife career changes. Keeps a person from getting stale." She wondered if she'd gone too far when, out of the corner of her eye, she glimpsed Barry's discomfort.

Mrs. Markham intervened. "Running a farm can be a hard, lonely life, Fayette. In fact, without the support of family I would judge it to be close to impossible."

"Mother, now why go discouraging her like that?" Barry spoke up. "Just because farming's always been a family venture doesn't mean it has to be that way forever. You know as well as anyone it's big business today. A person can hire professionals to help run it. Fayette could do it out at Indian Creek. But..." He hesitated for a moment before adding, "I think it makes a lot more sense at a bigger place like Oak Hill."

The words had been spoken, and Faye could have cheered at Barry's calm courage in saying them. Siperia's eyes glittered angrily, first at her son and then at Fayette.

Not wishing to get involved in the Markham family's power struggles, Faye glanced away, only to have her eyes connect with those of a petite, elderly woman who had been staring at her, obviously eavesdropping. Faye recognized her at once.

"Excuse me," she said to her companions and walked over toward the elderly woman.

"Mrs. Wainbridge, I'm Faye Hunt," she introduced herself with a forthright air, extending her hand. "I spoke to your secretary on the phone last week."

The woman's arthritis-gnarled fingers barely connected with Faye's warm vigorous grasp before withdrawing again. "Miss Hunt," she said imperiously, her sharp black eyes boring straight into Faye's, "you're not at all like Courtney. She was quite a beauty in her day."

The insult only amused Faye. "We Hunt women are more alike than you think."

"Indeed?"

"I've made Indian Creek Farm a going concern again."

"I've heard exaggerated rumors to that effect," Laura Bell Wainbridge said dryly.

The faint hostility beneath her imperious manner was unmistakable—and rather perplexing. Faye chose to ignore it. "Maybe you'd like to pay me a visit," Faye invited, "and judge for yourself."

"It seems like such a lot of effort to waste on such a small, insignificant piece of property."

"We can't all have the luxury of owning thirteen hundred acres and a racing stable of two hundred Thoroughbreds," Faye replied, bristling, unconsciously mimicking the woman's imperious manner.

"You know so much about Boar's Head?"

"My gran's life was a long and interesting one, Mrs. Wainbridge," Faye replied obliquely, wondering if she had detected wariness in the other woman's tone or if she'd just imagined it. "Naturally I couldn't help but be interested in the lives of her oldest and very dearest friends, too."

The irony wasn't lost on the elderly woman. Restlessly she moved her cane over the carpet, making deep tracks in the plush pile. Then she lifted it and poked Barry lightly in the back. He turned at once from his conversation with his mother and Mrs. Stone.

"Young Markham," Mrs. Wainbridge barked at him. "These damned impertinent waiters have been ignoring me. Will you bring me a whiskey and soda from the bar?"

"Delighted to, Mrs. Wainbridge," he said with his usual charming manner. "How about you, Fayette?"

"I'll have the same."

As soon as he had gone, Mrs. Wainbridge returned to the subject of Indian Creek. "I've heard you've been having some troubles, young lady."

Faye's answering smile was pure mischief. "Exaggerated rumors."

Before Mrs. Wainbridge could reply, the carved entry doors swung open again and another couple made their grand entrance. Faye's head turned with everybody else's, and this time it was her turn to be surprised.

Seth Carradine stood nonchalantly in the doorway, his deeply tanned face an attractive contrast to his surprisingly well-cut gray suit. The elegant look was diminished a little by the boots he had on, even if they were highly polished. But no one was paying attention to Seth. All eyes were riveted on his lovely companion. Parris Harper wore a turquoise print ruffled concoction and a faintly bored come-hither look in her eyes.

Seth had spotted Faye at once and strode through the milling crowd in her direction, unceremoniously pulling his companion after him. The sight of the beautiful Parris on his arm put Faye in a snit.

"Hello, Seth," she greeted him with an I-couldn't-careless smile. "Since when are you a member of the country-club set?"

"He's not," Parris interposed, her sultry eyes briefly twinkling. "I am."

"How lucky for you both."

Seth's green eyes moved with lazy contentment between the women as if he'd been judging the qualities of two very different mares. Faye glared at him before turning back to her elderly companion. "Mrs. Wainbridge, do you know Seth Carradine and Parris Harper?"

The elderly matriarch gave Seth a wintry smile. "I never thought I'd see the day you'd be working for a woman, Carradine."

"I'm not," he shot back amicably, managing a sly wink at Faye. "We have one of those mutually beneficial arrangements."

"Don't be too certain of that," Mrs. Wainbridge warned him. "Not where Hunt women are concerned."

Faye was about to demand what she had meant by that remark when the lovely Parris interposed again. "You should drop by my shop in the Hyatt Center, Mrs. Wainbridge, I've got a few Evan Picone suits in petite that would look superb on you."

"I'm afraid I do all my shopping in New York, Miss Harper."

Parris smiled. "You'd be surprised how much of New York can fit inside Panache." Her bit of self-promotion done, she turned back to Faye. "But I interrupted you. I'm sorry."

"I was only going to say to Mrs. Wainbridge that I can't stand cheap-shot innuendos," Faye said stiffly.

The elderly woman waved her hand as if the subject was not worth pursuing, which annoyed Faye all the more. She wanted to argue, but was aware of Siperia

Markham standing close enough to eavesdrop on every word.

At that moment a bespectacled young woman bustled through the crowd, balancing an old-fashioned glass on a cocktail napkin. "Here's your whiskey and soda, Mrs. Wainbridge."

"Oh. I forgot I'd sent you for that, Mary," the woman said sharply, not bothering to thank her.

By this time Faye had had more than enough of the elderly woman's high-handedness. "If you'll all excuse me," she said tartly, "I think my nose needs powdering."

To Faye's surprise, Parris offered to show her the way. "That tough old Laura Bell is something else, isn't she?" Parris said with a soft laugh. "She'd do wonders for my business, though I don't know if I could stand kowtowing to her like everyone else in this town does."

"Including Seth?" Faye asked, feeling a bit friendlier toward the elegant boutique owner after her wry remark about Laura Bell.

"Honey, he's just like you," Parris replied, rolling her beautiful eyes.

"Like me?"

"Yes. I didn't see you kowtowing just now, did I?"

Faye chuckled. "No, I guess you didn't."

"If I'd known what you were really like when you dropped in last week, I'd never have shown you that dress," Parris teased her. "It looks divine, by the way. You really stand out in this conservative little town."

"As if you don't," Faye retorted.

Parris shook her head deprecatingly. "Now don't you dare tell anyone where that dress came from if they ask. If it got around, I'd probably be blackballed out of the Chamber of Commerce."

Faye had expected Parris to be the archetypal "other woman"—bitchy, self-centered and manipulative. She had been prepared to despise her thoroughly. What she hadn't expected was Parris's infectious warmth of manner, her sense of humor and droll attitude toward the town. And she suddenly became very depressed; no wonder Seth hadn't given Parris Harper his famous bachelor's shove.

By the time they made it through the steadily growing crowd to the powder room, Faye and Parris were almost friends. The spaciously elegant sitting room with its flocked wallpaper and chintz-covered chairs, was empty.

After a desultory check of her lipstick and an automatic fluff of her bangs, Faye turned away from the mirror and leaned back against the marble vanity. Parris, on the other hand, took her beauty seriously. Faye watched her brush away a tiny fleck from her perfectly mascaraed lashes.

Aware of Faye's scrutiny, Parris grinned. "Let me guess if I can tell what you're thinking, Fayette Hunt."

"Go ahead."

"You're going through that little blue-blood registry in your head, aren't you? Wondering, 'How did *she* ever get a membership in the Cheviot Country Club?'"

"My turn to guess how you did it," Faye said, getting into the game. "Old family?"

"No."

"Old money?"

"Wrong again."

"No old anything?" Faye exclaimed, feigning a dismay that made Parris laugh again.

"Give up?"

"One last guess—you married into it."

"Smart girl," Parris said. "It was my husband's family, the Munroes, who had the membership."

"That name vaguely rings a bell. They had a son, Theodore, right?"

Parris nodded. "When Teddy and I split up, this was part of the divorce settlement. I got the club membership and little else. I guess the Munroes thought if I didn't have money I wouldn't dare show my face here."

"And obviously your in-laws were wrong."

"After the divorce I took stock of my life. And I thought—what do I really know?" She paused, carefully outlining her mouth with a lip pencil. "Clothes was the answer. Expensive clothes and how to buy them. The only difference is that before I used to shop in exclusive boutiques. Now I own one. And the Cheviot is the ideal place to drum up business."

Faye had to ask it. "Have you known Seth long?"

"Mmm. Better *after* my divorce. Then our affair cooled when he thought things might be getting serious—on my part, that is." Parris snapped her purse shut, as if she were closing a book on a dull subject. "Tell me about you now."

Faye shrugged. "Not much to tell. I'm a stock-market analyst. I advise people where to put their money."

"You mean as in hog bellies and soybean futures?"

"I mean as in blue-chip stocks and conservative mutual funds. Commodities are often too risky."

"Sounds like you know your stuff. You like that kind of work?"

Faye shrugged again. "I guess the challenge wears off anything after a while."

"I see," Parris said, giving her a long shrewd look. "So that's why you're here now."

"I don't exactly know how I got myself dug in here," Faye said with a sigh. "But it looks like I'll be sticking around for a while, at least."

"So Seth tells me." For no reason Faye flushed to the roots of her hair making Parris exclaim, "Aha! So just mentioning his name has that effect on you. Honey, take a warning—"

"The turf's already spoken for?" Faye finished for her tartly, making Parris laugh.

"That's not what I meant. May I tell you something about Seth?"

"Go ahead. Doesn't mean I'll listen."

"For all his playboy ways, he genuinely likes women. You can have fun with him. Seth's a great companion. But he's allergic to anything serious; if you show any sort of vulnerability he runs."

"And you're not vulnerable, obviously," Faye couldn't help observing.

"Neither are you!" Parris winked. "That's why I do believe that man is taken by you."

"What!" Faye was nonplussed.

"I asked him about you the other day after you came into my shop. I think Seth sees you as a real gutsy, shoot-from-the-hip type. A woman who can take care of herself. No complications." She sighed. "Believe me, even hint at anything else and Seth is out the door."

"Is this the voice of experience I'm listening to?"

"Listen," Parris said wryly, one hand on her hip, "there isn't much this lady hasn't experienced. Now come on, we'd better get back out there before they think we've been kidnapped."

As they made their way back through the crowd, Parris said offhandedly, "I hear they've hired a new chef here. He's supposed to be French, but I have a feeling the

Cheviot's idea of haute cuisine is French-fried chicken and black-eyed peas—*au beurre*. I'm tempted to take over the damned kitchen myself and give this place some—"

"Panache?" Faye finished for her, making Parris laugh again.

"You're quick, Faye. I like that."

"Seriously, you cook?" Faye asked, thinking of her own miserable attempts.

"Cordon Bleu. I studied in Paris once. That was one of my jaunts with Teddy in our happy days when Jessica was a baby and life was still a long picnic." They finally reached Barry and Seth.

Barry, gracious as always, invited Seth and Parris to join them for dinner. Before Seth even had a chance to decline, Parris replied in her best flirtatious manner, "Why, how sweet of you to invite us, Barry. We'd love it."

To everyone's surprise, dinner proved to be quite enjoyable.

Later in the evening, after the coffee and mints had been served, the couples danced. At some point Seth claimed Faye for a slow dance.

"Did I tell you I think you look beautiful tonight?" he murmured against her ear.

"Not in front of Parris you didn't."

"Well, I'm tellin' you now in private."

"Thanks," she said grudgingly.

"You glad you came tonight?"

She shot him a look from beneath her lashes. "I wouldn't have missed it for anything."

"Me neither," he agreed, his expression teasing. "It's nice to be fought over."

"What an ego you've got, Carradine!" she exclaimed. "What on earth makes you think we're fighting over you? If we were to fight over anyone, it would be Barry, not you!"

"What!" His contented look vanished. "Who'd want to fight over Markham?"

"Are you blind, Carradine? He's got everything any woman in her right mind would ever want."

"He ain't your type, Faye."

"Oh, yeah? Why isn't he?"

"Hell, I don't know." He sighed in frustration. "He just isn't. I figured you'd go more for some wild-ass guy who'd keep you guessin', someone who wouldn't be fallin' all over himself to make sure your every little wish was met. I figure you'd want somebody you could roll up your sleeves with and go thirteen rounds."

"Someone like you?" she asked innocently, and he grinned.

"Now why do I feel like I got myself backed into a corner?"

"That's what you get for messing with a smart woman."

"You want to know something, Faye?" he complained. "The more I know you the harder you are to take."

"Tough. Because you're stuck with me and my barn, neighbor."

"Lord help me, then," he retorted with that low laugh that drove her pulse up, and swung her around to the slow beat of the music.

Faye's eyes smiled up into his. How much she was enjoying their teasing banter, enjoying the way his arms felt around her and the earthy sexiness that flowed from him like rough wine. Each moment with him was like a scene from a movie. There was no past and certainly no future—just wonderful fleeting delight that made her senses leap with sheer pleasure.

Still, she was glad when the dance ended and Barry reclaimed her. She felt safe with Barry, protected. Not as if she were tiptoeing gingerly on the edge of a cliff, which was the way Seth made her feel. That dizzying blend of exhilaration and danger she experienced around him always left her breathless and slightly out of control. She tried to tell herself she didn't like that feeling, but she knew she was lying to herself. The truth of it was, that feeling excited her to the core.

At the evening's end, Faye stood in the foyer waiting for Barry in the rapidly thinning crowd.

"Miss Hunt?"

Faye turned to face the efficient-looking young woman Mrs. Wainbridge had treated so cavalierly earlier on. "Yes?" Faye said, waiting.

"I'm Mary Clark. Mrs. Wainbridge's secretary," she explained briskly. "We spoke on the phone once."

"Of course. I remember."

"The reason I came over is to invite you to visit Boar's Head Farm. Mrs. Wainbridge asked me to extend the invitation."

"Oh, really? I had the feeling she'd rather not have seen me again."

"You have to understand that Mrs. Wainbridge is elderly and at times a little eccentric." The secretary smiled apologetically. "We make allowances."

Well, I don't, Faye felt like saying. But for a change, she kept her mouth shut. She was very curious to see the testy old woman again and find out precisely what she had against the Hunt women.

CHAPTER THIRTEEN

SETH PAUSED in the narrow doorway of the kitchen, balancing two steaming plates of ham and eggs. Faye was stretched out on his lumpy old sofa as if she'd been born there. Briskly she leafed through one of his issues of *Spur*.

The sight of her there made him want to laugh. Hell, he couldn't remember the last time he'd entertained a woman at his place. He didn't like the idea of bringing them into his space. It was safer and cleaner to deal with women on their own turf.

But Faye was different, he told himself. He didn't feel threatened by her; she was as jealous of her independence as he was of his. And besides, she was a business partner. They were both adult enough to realize this crazy attraction between them wouldn't get in the way of their business dealings. He'd only invited her over to show her his barn setup, to mollify her in case she was still upset about the extra money they were pouring into the remodeling job.

He watched her drop the magazine on her chest and stare up at the ceiling, frowning. Seth's grin faded as he followed her gaze, wondering what the hell she was staring at. The bulges where the fake paneling had warped?

He felt tense, finally acknowledging the real reason he'd never invited a woman out to his place. He was ashamed of it. The ramshackle little mobile home had become a painful reminder of his Gypsylike childhood.

He guessed that was why he hungered so much to own the Hunt place. That farmhouse with its beautiful weathered stone had come down intact through two centuries. The warmth and mellowness inside those walls made him ache to own the place. He would have a real home for the first time in his life. Seth knew that his wanting the farm so badly angered Faye. Sometimes she reminded him of a spoiled little kid—not wanting her toy but unwilling to let anyone else have it, either.

He shook his head in frustration, and Faye caught the movement out of the corner of her eye.

She sat up and hurriedly cleared the pile of magazines from the battered maple coffee table. "That smells delicious, Seth. Maybe I can con you into making me breakfast every morning."

His grin returned. "Ain't it time you learned to cook for yourself?"

"Not as long as there's Chinese take-out," she joked. "I've got too much else to do. I was just glancing through some of your horse magazines. There sure aren't many solo women in the business."

"It can be a grueling life. I guess not too many of them could take it."

"And then there's Laura Bell Wainbridge. She's eighty-five and still going strong." Faye shook her head. "You know, she intrigues me. Barry says she really came into her own after her husband died."

"That's the story people around here like to tell," Seth said, joining Faye on the sofa. "The truth is, she ran Boar's Head from the start. She was stronger than her husband and smarter. That old gal had the courage to take risks."

"Laura Bell sounds like my kind of lady." Faye chewed thoughtfully on a bite of ham. "I wish she had't taken such an immediate dislike to me."

"Don't feel bad. Laura Wainbridge doesn't like any-body—except her horses."

"Maybe so, but you didn't see the look on her face when I mentioned Courtney's name to her." Faye picked up her mug and blew softly over it to cool the hot cof-fee. "And Gran's old friend Minah did say I bear a striking resemblance to Courtney."

"You think your grandma and old Laura Bell were ri-vals?"

"That could be," Faye agreed, letting her imagina-tion run wild. "Maybe Laura Bell was as much in love with my grandfather Catesby as Courtney was. What a romantic idea! Do you think I could get her to admit it?"

Seth looked amused. "What are you gonna do—ask her the next time you're shootin' the breeze over cock-tails at the club?"

"Maybe I can work the conversation around to it when I go visit her out at Boar's Head."

"What makes you think she'll see you?"

"I was invited," Faye announced with a regal air that made Seth whistle sardonically.

"My, oh my," he drawled. "Looks like you broke the big social barrier, honey. Laura Wainbridge is a real heavyweight in this county."

"And I need all the weight behind me I can get," Faye said, giving Seth a cool sideways look, "what with Pet-tigrew on my back...and now you. I can't stand the idea of owing you nine thousand bucks."

"No kidding. I'm not crazy about the idea myself."

"What would you say if I told you I'm thinking of putting my San Francisco property on the market?"

Seth's fork paused in midair, and he felt a little twinge of uneasiness. "That'd be awfully like pullin' up stakes, wouldn't it? Be kind of a rash move."

Faye's nose wrinkled suspiciously. "I thought you were worried about my out-of-state collateral."

"Your money's safe where it is," Seth hedged. Hell, she was so perverse. He knew if he encouraged her not to sell, she'd soon be a permanent neighbor. Which was the last thing he wanted. "Besides," he added with the caution born of years of wily bachelorhood, "wouldn't you be afraid of losin' everything?"

"Now you sound like my ex-boss, Harve," she retorted in disgust. "You know, I'm tired of listening to conservative men trying to tell me what to do. I should be following Courtney's and Laura Bell's example. I should be buying a Thoroughbred instead of offering to take care of yours."

"This ain't no glamour business, Faye," he warned her softly. "You can read all you want to about rich sheikhs flying into Lexington in their private jets to buy stock and about the Whitneys throwing their fabulous presale parties. But the reality is this." His eyes swept the cramped little mobile home. "The reality is having to live like a no-account Gypsy 'cause you've laid every cent on the line for your bloodstock."

"I know it takes guts."

"It's not just guts," he said angrily. "It's havin' to deal with people putting you down for the way you live. Having to deal with people who think you're a clone of your old man—a hick with no brains and less taste."

Faye listened to his outburst in fascination. "You intrigue me, Seth," she said quietly, her arms hugging her upraised knee. "You really do. I don't know what to make of you, and probably no one else does, either, so they write you off as a hick. Here you live in this run-down little place with this Salvation Army reject of a couch. And yet you cover it with an absolutely exquisite plaid blanket." Faye stroked the soft Scottish wool.

"And those curtains over there look like something left over from a lousy garage sale. But underneath them you have this incredibly beautiful collection of antique duck decoys." She laughed softly. "You may be a redneck, Seth, but you definitely do know something about taste!"

"Damned right, I do," he growled, embarrassed by her praise. "That farmhouse of yours has a fine walnut built-in bookcase I've had my eye on for a long time. I know my ducks'll look just great on 'em."

"Oh, damn you!" she swore. "Why is it every time we start to really talk about what we're feeling you have to put up a barrier. You have to remind me we're competitors. What are you so afraid of?"

He stood up angrily, knowing deep down inside she was right. Damn it, he was scared. Scared of being touched by her praise, of the effect she had on him. He was afraid that before he knew it he'd be wanting her to stay instead of wanting her to leave. Seth was afraid of the possibility of his own vulnerability.

And so he attacked.

"You're the barrier, Fayette Hunt," he muttered with eyes blazing. "It still bugs the hell out of me the way you moved into Indian Creek like it was a lark. You know who you remind me of? Your friend Markham—you've both had it all handed to you on a silver platter and then you bellyache when things don't go your way."

"I could have a worse role model," Faye replied, her look making it clear who she would consider a hell of a lot worse.

Seth swore under his breath. He knew he was being a boor, but he couldn't stop himself. Some little demon inside drove him on.

"Yeah, well, I'm not surprised you're defending him," he said, moving restlessly around the room. He picked up one of the decoys and then slammed it down so hard that

Faye jumped. "I can already pick the scenario. Markham's goin' to ask you to marry him and you'll accept. All your talk about taking risks and gambles'll be just that—talk. You'll take the easy way out, Faye."

She blanched, shocked at how close he had come to the truth. "You'd call living under the same roof with Siperia Markham taking the easy way out?" she retorted dryly.

"The lady's no fool. Pretty soon she'll figure out that you'd be nothin' but an asset to the Markham team. That steel-belted magnolia blossom is gonna realize you're exactly the kind who'd be strong enough to take over that matriarchal clan once she's ready to step down."

"How flattering," Faye said acerbically. "Especially when just a second ago you were calling me a gutless wonder."

Seth came over to the coffee table, shoved their empty plates aside and sat down in front of her, his legs spread and his elbows resting on his knees. "I didn't say that," he denied, his clenched jaw relaxing just a little. "Or if I did, I didn't mean it."

Faye drew up her other leg and hugged them tightly, resting her chin on her knee, so that their eyes were only inches apart. "You are the most aggravating man I have ever met."

"But basically lovable, right?" The dimple in his cheek barely revealed itself.

"About as lovable as a cornered weasel."

"I'm gonna have to watch what lines I use on you. You're stealing them right away from me."

"Guess we're two of a kind, then," she teased him.

"What else do you steal?" He teased her back, his eyes holding hers.

"I don't know." She put her knees down and leaned toward him. "What do you have worth taking?"

Seth didn't want to kiss her. He didn't want to feel her soft lips moving against his, to feel the heat rising in him like a gushing spring. But her hand had already slipped around to caress his neck, and she pulled him closer until their mouths touched. He had to fight himself not to give in to the light foray of her tongue.

Sensing his resistance, Faye let her eyes flutter open. "What's the matter, Hardboots?" She laughed softly. "Scared?"

He caught her hand and slowly drew it away from his neck, aware of the lingering tendrils of warmth left by her fingertips. "I just don't want to overindulge," he countered. "Your blue blood's a little too rich for my constitution."

The little dig struck home as he had intended it to.

"Damn you," she swore in exasperation, sitting back against the sofa. "You make it sound like I'm a disease!"

Seth's grin was ornery. "I'll get me a T-shirt that says Danger—Blue Blood Causes Cholesterol."

"If I hear you mention blue blood one more time," she threatened, "I'll scream. You're obsessed!"

"Hell yes, I'm obsessed."

"I don't understand you."

"I don't expect you to," he growled, his jaw muscles tensing again. "How could you possibly understand the obsession of a man who doesn't know who his grandparents were? Grandparents, hell, I don't even remember who my mother was." The words tore out of his throat before he could stop them.

"Seth, I'm sorry."

But he wasn't interested in her sympathy. "I'm just trying to make a point, Faye," he went on, his controlled expression not quite masking the fire underneath. "I'm a man without a history living in a place where a predigree is everything. And it galls me."

Faye bit her lip, remembering that Barry had warned her against talking to Seth and implied that the trainer's murky past somehow made him an unsavory character.

"You're the type of man whose past means zero," she heard herself saying. The shame and anger Seth felt acted like a forge, she realized suddenly, making him stronger instead of weaker. Out of it had come his fiery sense of pride at what he'd accomplished on his own. "Everything that matters is inside," Faye went on. "You know it, and you get angry as hell that other people haven't figured it out yet."

Seth lifted his eyes from his clenched fists and gave her a wary look. "I don't need you to believe in me."

"Believe in you!" she exclaimed wryly. "How could I believe in a man who's trying to steal my house and barn out from under me?"

"Yeah, and you'd be bored silly if I weren't trying to," he retorted. "You've already figured out that Pettigrew is a marshmallow man. That leaves you against me."

"Like you said, Seth, I guess I need a man I can go thirteen rounds with." Despite her cocky grin, inwardly Faye was a little dismayed. Even jokingly she had never before admitted needing a man for anything.

Abruptly she got up and went over to the shelf of decoys on the pretext of examining them. Seth came up behind her.

"You ever been duck hunting?"

"No. The only thing I've ever shot are those little clay plates they have in skeet shooting."

"Well, I'll take you sometime." He was teasing her again. "See what kind of a hotshot you are."

"No way! I'd never take aim at those pretty feathered creatures." She gave him a funny little look out of the corner of her eyes. "You're heartless."

"And you're no vegetarian, you little hypocrite. I bet you like to eat it." He grinned. "In fact, I happen to make a lip-smackin' Peking Duck. Got the recipe from a little China doll..."

"I'm really not interested in hearing any more about your culinary exploits, Carradine," she said dryly.

His eyes crinkled mischievously, but before he could reply they were both distracted by the sound of an approaching truck outside.

Seth glanced out the window. "It's Tommy. Want to say hi to him? He'll probably try to talk your ear off about horses."

"Good," she said as they headed for the door. "If you're not willing to give me advice, maybe he will."

"That's just what I'm afraid of."

Tommy climbed out of the truck cab, his shoulders drooping.

"Hey, Seth...Miz Hunt," he greeted them disconsolately.

Faye shot Seth a quizzical look. This Tommy seemed a far cry from the expansive, amiable man she'd met at Leroy's Café, but Seth apparently knew his friend's moods.

"You been gambling again, Tommy?"

The old trainer scratched his head sheepishly. "Hell, Seth, I thought it was a sure thing this time."

Faye thought she understood. "A horse race?" she asked, curious. "Did you bet on one of your own horses?"

Seth shot her a sardonic grin. "If Tommy only did that he'd probably make out pretty well. The problem is he'll bet on anything."

"Now that ain't exactly true," Tommy denied, indignant.

"So what *did* you bet on?"

"Who woulda ever figured an all-women climbin' team from Japan'd make it to the top of Mount Everest? It just beats all."

Seth shook his head. "How much, Tommy?"

"You really want to know?" The trainer rubbed his jaw nervously. "Two thousand."

"How the hell you gonna pay that off?"

Tommy looked miserable now. "Guess I'll just have to sell Sinbad."

"But he's the best two-year-old you ever owned," Seth said in disgust. "And you won't make a penny on him either if you sell before he's had a chance to prove himself on the track."

"I know, I know. Guess I'd better get back to those Gamblers Anonymous meetings afore I try to stake my own damned head." He heaved a huge sigh and then looked at Faye apologetically. "Didn't mean to talk about my little weaknesses in front of you, ma'am."

"I don't mind. I'm fascinated."

"Yeah?" He perked up. "Wish my ex-wife'd had that attitude, but she always seemed to be worryin' about things like groceries and payin' the rent."

Faye bit her lip to keep from smiling. "Women tend to do that."

Seth interrupted. "Tommy, I'm gonna show Faye my barn layout. Want to come along?"

"Hell, why not? I gotta kiss Sinbad goodbye sooner or later." He fell into step with them and then let out a low admiring whistle a moment later when he saw the shiny red Alfa convertible parked beside the barn. "That your snazzy car, Miz Hunt?"

"Guilty." Faye laughed. "Women have their little weaknesses, too."

Tommy grinned back. "I know what you mean. That fine machine'd pay for a nice colt easily."

Faye gave him a surprised look but said nothing. Her mind was whirling with new possibilities as the three of them stepped inside the cool spacious barn.

"Well, what do you think, Faye?" Seth asked, his voice full of pride.

Her eyes slowly moved around the interior. Morning light poured in through the high Palladian window set above the barn doors, an architectural detail at once beautiful and practical. More than ever she began to understand the driving forces inside Seth. That he would be willing to live in a cramped old trailer so he could afford a barn like this spoke volumes about his dreams.

"It's beautiful," she said finally. "Any chance my place will look this good when the remodeling is done?"

"Dream on, Hundred Pounds," he said good-naturedly, obviously pleased by her praise. "Nine thousand bucks doesn't go too far these days."

They made their way leisurely along the occupied stalls. For the first time Faye had the chance to see Seth's interaction with animals. She read the affection in his eyes as he patted noses and slipped each horse a treat. She sensed the knowledge and care flowing from his hands as he bent down to check a swollen knee or bruised hoof.

How could such a hard-eyed, cynical realist be capable of such tenderness, she wondered to herself. And then she remembered those same hands touching her skin, enveloping her until she'd wanted to cry out with the intense pleasure of his discovery of her. He'd made her feel more beautiful and alive than she'd known she was capable of feeling. And she found herself envying the mares and little colts who experienced his special touch every day.

Every night in bed she fantasized about Seth touching her. How could she want him and distrust him at the same time? How could she have grown to so deeply respect a man whose ambitions threatened everything she wanted to protect? Faye shook her head, dismayed by her conflicting emotions.

Tommy had drifted on ahead and was murmuring endearments to a wild-eyed horse who snorted and tossed his head. The trainer's blandishments obviously weren't enough to appease him.

Faye eyed the animal warily. "Is this your Sinbad?"

"None other." Tommy held out a sugar cube in the palm of his hand and Sinbad's mean-looking teeth crunched it with ferocious pleasure. "This colt's fast but temperamental. With the right kind of trainin' I swear he'd be dynamite." A downcast "if only" tone had crept into his voice again.

"Damn it, it's your own fault, Tommy," Seth broke in impatiently.

"I know it." He rubbed the white streak that ran down Sinbad's nose. "Guess I'll take him out to Keeneland, see if I can find a taker. Want to come along?" His woebegone gaze took in Seth and Faye.

"I'd like to," she said at once. "I haven't seen the track in years."

"Seth?"

"Yeah, why not. I got some paperwork to take care of out there, anyway."

FAYE LEANED FORWARD IN ANTICIPATION as they drove onto the grounds of Keeneland Track. The English parklike setting was a far cry from the seedy concrete-and-asphalt jungles that housed racetracks in most cities. Hundreds of elms and oaks shaded the grass and gravel lanes that led up to Keeneland's elegant gray stone buildings. The ambience reminded Faye of that in a rich man's mansion or a private club.

A day at the races in Lexington had always been a real social event, as if the Bluegrass crowd wanted to show they could compete any day with the Queen of England's Royal Ascot.

Faye smiled to herself, remembering the time Gran had brought her out to the track one fine day in late spring, the last Sunday of Faye's Easter vacation from junior high. A staunch traditionalist where fashion was concerned, Gran had insisted on white gloves for her granddaughter. And she had even prevailed so far as to curl Faye's hair in tight little sausage ringlets, which had embarrassed the tomboy no end. Mercifully, because of the fineness of her hair, the Shirley Temple curls hadn't lasted more than an hour.

"This place bring back memories?" Seth asked.

"Funny memories." She looked over at him, her private smile deepening. "Things I'd forgotten all about."

He gave her a quizzical look, and Faye wondered what he was thinking.

"Well, folks, here we are," Tommy announced briskly, drawing the old truck to a halt back in the stable area.

While Tommy and Seth went back around to the trailer, Faye wandered around on her own. The place was nearly deserted except for a few stable hands busy mucking out stalls. The utilitarian concrete buildings seemed to stretch indefinitely in every direction.

Usually a childhood landmark loomed larger in memory than it did in reality. But not Keeneland. The track and its support facilities had expanded tremendously since Faye had last been there. More proof of the town's wealth and another reminder that the Farmers and

Breeders Bank was riding the crest of that affluence. A reminder, too, that there was no logical reason to explain why Pettigrew and the bank board should have taken such a risk in trying to defraud Courtney's estate.

The question of the bank's unethical tactics inevitably brought to mind the uglier implications beneath: that someone wanted Faye off the property badly enough to make threats. She still woke up anxiously in the middle of the night, imagining noises, frightening voices. But she deliberately contained her fears there in the world of nightmare. She managed to convince herself the threats weren't serious, that they'd only been meant to frighten her. She had to do this if she was going to get on with the business of her new life. Faye pushed aside her fears and uncertainties determinedly and went around to watch the men back Sinbad out of the trailer.

He was skittish, kicking viciously with his iron-plated hooves. Faye couldn't understand what the men saw in the ornery horse. In her eyes he was a lot more trouble than he was worth.

"You gonna come watch us work him out?" Tommy called down to Faye.

"As long as you promise you won't put me up on his back. That horse looks crazy."

"Crazy like a fox," Tommy countered, grunting from the exertion of trying to get Sinbad down the ramp. "That's why I bought him in the first place."

"Oh." There was obviously a lot Faye still had to learn about this absurd, breakneck business. She watched them saddle him up, and then to her surprise Seth himself swung up onto Sinbad's back.

Tommy and Faye followed the horse and rider out to the track. "Shouldn't an exercise boy be running him?" she asked, eyeing the pair nervously.

"You see any around?" the trainer replied. "The last string rides out by eight-thirty. Come out any later and you ride 'em yourself."

"Isn't that dangerous?"

Tommy gave her a disbelieving look. "You know, a trainer can watch a horse run from now till doomsday. But it ain't gonna compare with feeling that horse move underneath you, understand? Of course I can't do that anymore." He patted his ample girth ruefully. "So Seth has to be my eyes and ears out there now."

He led her to a place alongside the rail, his eyes fixed on the horse. "Now watch this fella move."

"Sinbad or Seth?" she teased him, but Tommy was no longer paying any attention to her.

She followed his gaze, drawing in her breath as Seth leaned low over the saddle, urging his mount on with sharp whip taps on a flank. Even Faye's inexperienced eyes registered the animal's remarkable grace and speed, his low, plunging stride that exuded power.

Exhilarated by Sinbad's performance, Faye exclaimed to Tommy, "I can't believe someone let him go in a cheap claiming race! He runs like the wind."

"He runs like 'at now because there ain't no other horses out there, no noise and crowds and cameras flashin'." Tommy winked sagely. "But, you see, I figured out the trick to calmin' him down."

"What is it?"

Although the grandstands behind them were empty and there wasn't another soul nearby, Tommy leaned over to whisper conspiratorially in her ear.

Her eyes widened in surprise. "Something as simple as that?"

"Yup. You can see now why I figured I had a real goldmine on my hands." He sighed hugely. "Now I guess I won't have the chance to ever find out for sure."

"Um, Tommy..." Faye began tentatively, feeling her way. "You remember you said my Alfa could buy a nice colt. Would...would it be enough to pay for a horse like Sinbad?"

The trainer's eyes narrowed to a speculative squint, as if he were looking at the woman beside him in a totally new light. "I think it might," he said carefully.

"Are you looking for a partner, Tommy?"

After a long meditative pause, he smiled and held out his hand. "Miz Fayette, those are the prettiest words anybody ever spoke to me."

They turned to watch Seth ride over to them. A fine sheen of sweat glistened on his face, and he was breathing hard from the exertion of the gallop. He swung down out of the saddle and leaned on the rail, the reins still twined in his gloved right hand.

"You gambled away a winner, Tommy," he said, his green eyes hard and flat.

"That's what you think," the trainer replied gleefully. "I just been bailed out."

"What're you talking about?"

"Miz Fayette and me—we're gonna race Sinbad together."

Faye shrank a little when Seth's hard flat stare turned on her. The amusement usually lurking in the depths of his eyes was absent. He looked angry, wary.

"Just where the hell do you think you're going to get the money for that?"

Her nose lifted in the air. "My Alfa."

"Yeah, well, what gives you the right to plunk down money on a rogue horse when you're already up to your ears in debt to me?"

"Rogue horse! Just seconds ago you said he was a winner."

"Nobody wins every time." His jaw tensed. "You're playing way out of your league, lady."

"I'll take my chances."

"That cheap bravado of yours is going to get you in trouble, Fayette. And when it happens, don't expect anyone around here to bail you out. Understand?" Without waiting for her reply, Seth spun on his heel and stalked off, pulling Sinbad with him.

"Oh, I understand, all right," Faye shouted, running along beside the rail. "You're afraid I might win. You're afraid of losing your chance on the one thing that can give your life validity. If I win," she hurried on, trying to catch her breath, "you lose. And believe me, I intend to win."

She stopped running, aware of Tommy moving uncertainly between them. "I'll talk to him, Fayette," he promised, his look at once worried and optimistic. "I'll talk him round."

She leaned against the rail, staring past the empty track to the rolling hills beyond with their neat fields and sturdy barns.

What had happened to her? Seth was right, in a way. She was staking everything on a gamble. Yet she felt she had no choice. The land, her roots had somehow caught and entwined her when she wasn't looking.

They were all risk takers—Gran, Seth, Tommy, now Faye, too. She'd been infected by their madness. She would do anything to save what was left of Indian Creek Farm. It had become that essential to her.

CHAPTER FOURTEEN

THE TWO WOMEN faced each other across a low expanse of highly polished mahogany. The tea table was set with a silver pot and gilt-edged porcelain cups and saucers, the whole setting at once severely correct and cold. In the room were matching sofas of pale gray velvet. Laura Wainbridge sat on one. Faye sat opposite her on the other, quelling the urge to squirm beneath her hostess's sharp birdlike stare.

"Mrs. Wainbridge," she began, when she realized the woman wasn't going to ease this cool and somewhat awkward tête-à-tête with the usual small talk. "Do you mind if I ask what made you change your mind about seeing me? When I wanted to visit a few weeks ago your secretary fended me off, saying you were too busy."

"Mary is very jealous of my time, and she had no idea what you might want," the woman replied, leaning forward to pour from the silver pot. "Why *did* you want to see me, Miss Hunt?"

Faye took the cup that was offered from a rock-steady hand, aware that her own question had been turned back on her.

"Your friendship with my grandmother went back sixty-five years," Faye said carefully. "I had thought you might be able to help me."

"Help you?" the woman echoed, her expression at once wary and slightly incredulous. "In what way?"

"To find out who my enemies are."

Mrs. Wainbridge smiled thinly. "Do you realize how melodramatic you sound, Miss Hunt?"

"My life was threatened," Faye responded with a flash of annoyance. "I'm sorry if the melodrama of it offends you."

"You have proof of these so-called threats?"

"I—" Faye stared down into her teacup, remembering the soft male voice unraveling its ugly web of insinuation along the phone line. She thought also of the black rose petals and the smudged, perverted rhyme that she had swept into the dustbin. She wished she could sweep them out of her mind that easily and completely. She looked up again. "No, I have no proof."

Faye sensed that her companion had relaxed infinitesimally. "Well, then," Mrs. Wainbridge said, impatient, "I can't think what you expect me to do."

"You can tell me who Courtney's enemies were."

"Enemies?" The woman smiled that curious thin smile again. "Courtney was beloved by all."

"That's not hard to believe," Faye said with spirit, ignoring the faintly ironic tone imbuing her companion's words.

"Perhaps you're the one with a dangerous enemy or two, Miss Hunt."

"One or two? Try a cast of thousands," Faye quipped.

"And the arch villain?" Mrs. Wainbridge inquired. "Hollister Pettigrew, Siperia Markham, Seth Carradine?"

Faye gave her a long look. "Exactly how much do you know about my personal affairs, Mrs. Wainbridge?"

"Don't be naive, Miss Hunt," she replied urbanely, lifting a plate of paper-thin lace wafers to offer her guest.

"For all its cosmopolitan airs, Lexington is still a small town."

"Don't you mean small-minded?" Faye snapped, ignoring the proffered cookies.

The woman's lips tightened, and Faye sensed that for some reason the silly little dig had found its mark.

"Really, Miss Hunt," Mrs. Wainbridge said condescendingly, as if she were humoring a child, "it seems to me that all your little complaints might be the product of an overactive imagination. It's easier to blame your problems on a faceless bogeyman than to confront the fact that the farm you inherited is a dying enterprise."

"Indian Creek isn't dying," Faye pronounced levelly. "I think someone has deliberately tried to kill it."

"Aren't you just trying to make excuses? Courtney grew old and feeble, then senile. You can't blame malice for that."

"I can blame the bank for violating a trust, for taking advantage of an old confused woman to steal the only thing she had left." Faye leaned forward, her eyes full of anger as she confronted Mrs. Wainbridge's sharp stare. "Didn't you ever drive past Courtney's farm? Didn't you ever notice what was happening to the place she'd lavished so much work and love on?"

"I own three thousand acres, Miss Hunt," she replied with cold hauteur. "Do you really believe I would have had the time or the inclination to concern myself about Courtney's ramshackle little operation?"

Faye boiled, but she did her best to contain herself. "A few hundred acres might not mean much on your scale of operations, but they mean everything to me," she said angrily. "I'm not going to lose that farm."

"Really?" Mrs. Wainbridge replied with an air of bland humor that annoyed Faye all the more. "Forgive an old woman's curiosity, but how do you intend to save your precious heritage, Miss Hunt?''

''The same way you built up Boar's Head, Mrs. Wainbridge—Thoroughbreds.''

''I've heard talk about your lease agreement with Carradine. You'll be fortunate if you make your taxes.''

''What I meant is that I've gone into partnership on a horse. And I intend to race him,'' she said rashly, unable to resist that bravado announcement, even though her agreement with Tommy was far from settled.

''Big winners require big investments,'' Mrs. Wainbridge said with a shrewd air. ''I had no idea you were a wealthy woman, Miss Hunt.''

''I'm not rich. Just resourceful.''

''And so modest, too,'' the woman added dryly.

Faye flushed. ''For the first time in my life I've found something I really want. Nothing's going to keep me from it.''

''This business takes courage.'' The woman's gnarled fingers tightened on the delicate porcelain cup in her hands. ''Hasn't it occurred to you that you could lose everything?''

''I may, anyway, so why not go for it? Besides,'' Faye added with a faint smile, ''I was something of a gambler by profession. I put my reputation on the line every day as part of my job.''

''And what job was that?''

''Investments. Stocks, commodities, bonds.''

''How impressive. But then, Courtney always had that same calculating bent of mind, too.'' Mrs. Wainbridge paused. ''Calculating and rather heartless, I might add.''

''My grandmother was the warmest, kindest woman I knew,'' Faye retorted hotly. ''How could you say something like that?''

"Human beings are like prisms, Miss Hunt. If you look at them from different perspectives you see entirely different things."

"But you had to have loved her," Faye insisted. "Minah told me that you and Courtney and Quentin were the best of friends."

"Why bring Quentin into this?" Mrs. Wainbridge answered sharply, a faint quaver of pain in her voice.

Startled by the woman's reaction, Faye asked, "Whatever happened to your brother?"

"He was killed when he was twenty. An automobile accident."

"How tragic."

"You can spare me your sympathy, Miss Hunt," she said austerely. "Now if you will excuse me, this conversation has worn me out." She picked up the small, etched silver bell from the table and rang twice. Its high-pitched peal rang out in the elegant room that had become charged with tension.

Instantly the efficient-looking secretary appeared in the doorway. "Mary, please show our guest out."

Faye drove away from the imposing stone residence, not knowing what to think about the visit. She had come to Boar's Head hoping to find some illumination about the past, to forge at least some tenuous bond with the woman she had hoped might eventually be an ally. But Laura Bell Wainbridge's coldness had deepened with each minute Faye had spent with her. Faye had found her to be a woman every bit as calculating and heartless as she had accused Courtney of being.

And yet Faye couldn't help admiring her, too. It amazed her that the tough, mettlesome woman who must have weathered all sorts of crises through the years could still nurture such an ache of tenderness for a long-dead brother. Fascinating.

Faye decided that Laura Bell Wainbridge would be an interesting psychological puzzle to solve. On impulse she decided to drop by Minah Willis's cottage again and get her to talk some more about the past.

NO ONE WAS HOME at the little yellow cottage on Limestone Street. Faye turned away from the door in disappointment. After her visit to Laura Wainbridge, she had been looking forward to an infusion of Minah's warmth and her home-baked molasses cookies.

Still not up to facing her own empty house, Faye drove over to the three-level Hyatt complex and pulled into the busy parking lot across the street. She squeezed into a narrow space between two big clunkers, careful not to ding the shiny red lacquer finish on her door as she swung it open. She climbed out and gave the hood a friendly pat.

She hated the thought of selling the Alfa. Once the car was gone, another little piece of her old life would go with it. Faye felt as though she were peeling away layers of herself, not sure at all what the end result would be. The only thing she knew for certain was that she was changing, and that the transformation had begun the moment she had decided to fight the bank, to protect what was hers.

Once inside the mall, Faye made a beeline for Parris Harper's elegant storefront. She smiled, remembering how wry and funny Parris had been at the Cheviot. It had been a long time since Faye had had a close female friend, and suddenly she found herself missing that special woman-to-woman bond. She couldn't help liking the disgustingly beautiful redhead, even if she was her arch rival for Seth's attention.

"Faye!" Parris exclaimed with pleasure as soon as she saw her. "Out shopping again? I've had a marvelous new shipment in from New York. A designer named Evienne Marat. Real slithery feminine way-out stuff. They cost the earth and the moon, but who cares. Y'all only live once, right?"

Faye laughed at her enthusiasm. "Does it cost anything to try them on?"

"Enter my private boudoir," Parris responded with a flourish of her arm, smiling back. "It's almost quittin' time for me, anyway. I think I'll join you. I've been dyin' to slip into this lavender silk charmeuse ever since it got here."

An hour later Parris's small, mirrored office looked like the dressing room of a busy couturier show. Drifts of silk and satin floated down from the padded hangers hooked over lampshades and from the walls and closet doors, as if the gossamer outfits were extravagant artworks meant for permanent display.

Faye twisted and turned in front of the narrow oblong of mirror, and with each turn hundreds of bugle beads winked from her sweater. Hugging her slim hips and calves were a pair of the slinkiest satin pants she'd ever seen.

She bent over and shook her head until her hair pouffed out wildly around her head and then she studied her reflection again.

"Now all I need is some ice-pink lipstick and a sexy pout, and I could fit right into the pages of *Vogue*," she said, laughing. "What do you think?"

"Mm," Parris agreed, her face getting a faint shade of purple as she held her breath and struggled to get the zipper past her sucked-in stomach.

"Ohmigod," Faye breathed in admiration as Parris finished zipping up the curve-hugging sheath with its shimmery expanse of sequins. "You look like every sailor's vision of a mermaid."

Parris took short mincing steps toward the mirror to examine the effect. "Don't say that," she said, not daring to laugh. "I have a feeling I'd be in big trouble if this gown got wet. Oh, quick, unzip me before I faint from lack of oxygen."

Faye did as she was bade, and they both broke up in laughter.

"This has sure been fun," Parris said as soon as she got her breath back. "My heavens, I can't believe it's already seven! Good thing I'm on my own tonight. Jessica'd be wondering where I am."

"We should do this more often," Faye agreed, slipping back into her own blouse and skirt. "It's great for the ego!"

"Faye," Parris suggested suddenly while they worked to replace the garments back on the racks, "would you like to join me for dinner? Jessica's off to a slumber party and all I had to look forward to was a lonely evening by myself. It'd be fun if you came over."

"I'd love to," Faye said at once, secretly wondering how many evenings a woman like Parris would have to spend alone. Not very many, she judged.

FAYE PULLED INTO THE DRIVEWAY of the pretty two-story brick house on Fincannon Street, drawing to a halt behind Parris's compact station wagon. She followed Parris to the back door, glimpsing outlines in the darkness of a backyard swing set and a bicycle propped up against the garage wall.

"How old is Jessica?" she asked.

"Twelve and growing fast. She's goin' to be tall like her daddy."

The kitchen was bright and homey, potted plants in the window and beaten-copper utensils hanging from a rack above the telephone. A message had been scrawled there in a quick childish hand: "See you tomorrow, Mommy. Love ya." A pair of satin-ribboned pink ballet slippers were slung whimsically over the blackboard edges.

"Faye, there's a bottle of white wine in the fridge," Parris called to her as she wrapped an apron efficiently over her ultrasuede skirt. "Why don't you open that and we can be sippin' it while I cook? There's a corkscrew in that drawer near the phone."

Faye poured two glasses and joined Parris at the counter, amusing her with light banter while all the time watching in undisguised fascination as the woman deftly separated egg yolks from whites and then beat the yolks with a little wire whisk until they frothed like a milkshake.

"What are you making?" Faye asked when small packages of Parmesan, Gruyère and aged Swiss cheese appeared as if by magic on the butcher block.

"Just a simple soufflé *au fromage*," Parris said, cutting the paper-thin Swiss cheese into fancy shapes for garnish.

"How elegant," Faye replied faintly, wondering if this particular recipe had made it into Seth's culinary repertoire.

She tried to memorize the steps, but for a "simple" soufflé, the steps quickly grew more complicated. Soon Parris seemed to be doing a half dozen things at once, stirring the white sauce, shredding cheese, beating egg whites—until Faye thought she'd get dizzy just watching her.

"So I take it work's progressing well on your barn remodeling," Parris said, apparently able to carry on a conversation, too, while she went through the complicated series of steps. Faye was becoming more envious by the second.

"It'll be done soon. If everything goes the way I'm hoping, along with Seth's horses I'll be boarding one of my own, too."

"What! Seth didn't mention that when I talked to him yesterday."

"Didn't he?" Faye answered casually. "Tommy Thomas and I are thinking about going into partnership on a horse."

"You know anything about them?"

"Tommy's promised to teach me the ropes."

"Do you have twenty years?" Parris teased her.

"Oh, come on. The way I see it is Thoroughbreds can't be an any more complicated or risky business than the stock market." Faye smiled. "I remember I had a client once who lost a bundle in pork-belly futures because he didn't anticipate the hog slaughter in the fall would be as big as it was. Naturally, he came to me for advice *after* he bought the futures."

"Sounds to me like you might be missing that life a little."

Faye took a long thoughtful sip of her wine. "Sometimes I do, though mainly I guess what I miss is the people I worked with. Living out there on the farm by myself is so . . . isolating."

"Mm, I can imagine." Parris opened the oven door and slid her fancily garnished soufflé onto the bottom rack. "But at least you've got Seth as a neighbor."

"That has its advantages and disadvantages."

Parris straightened up, smiling. "Want to tell ole Parris about it?"

Faye shrugged. "What's there to tell? He's a very attractive, elusive, puzzling, frustrating man."

"And you wouldn't be attracted to him if he weren't all those other things," Parris said sagely. "No smart woman's gonna be interested in a one-dimensional man for long."

"Yeah, well, I think I'm going to continue to steer clear of this particular multidimensional male."

"Famous last words?"

"Parris, I'm serious."

"So what other momentous decisions have you made?" Parris went on, her eyes still teasing.

Faye looked away, her gaze taking in the homey kitchen with Jessica's drawings clamped to the refrigerator. She breathed in the sharp scent of chives in their windowsill box, their odor mingling with the delicious scent of the cheese soufflé in the oven.

"Well, you're not going to believe this," she said to Parris at last, biting her lip. "But to tell you the truth, I'm thinking of getting married and having babies."

"My stars," Parris shot back with a grin. "Who's the lucky man?"

"I haven't quite decided."

Parris's laughter bubbled over warmly. "Honey, you're more entertaining than a Saturday matinee. Anyway, I thought that out in California women think nothing of having babies with no hubby in the picture."

"I may be liberated, but I'm not that liberated." Faye paused, groping for the words to express the new feelings that had begun to steal over her the past few weeks. "Here I am almost twenty-nine years old, and all of a sudden I feel that old biological clock ticking. All of a sudden I feel like I've been rushing around all my life and never getting anywhere in particular."

"And Kentucky is somewhere in particular?"

"Kentucky's where my roots are," Faye replied slowly. "At first I thought it was going to be a pain in the neck putting in all that work getting the old house and garden shipshape after it had been abandoned for so long. And then I told myself the profit I made would make it all worthwhile. I was kidding myself there. Pretty soon it dawned on me that I didn't give a damn about the money. I found myself wanting to stay."

"I know what you mean." Parris nodded. "It's nice, feeling you belong to a place."

"Right. Then I started to think it would be nice to feel I belong to someone and that someone belongs to me." Faye paused. "Like what you must have with Jessica. I envy that sense of...centeredness."

"That's a touching way to put it, Faye. I sure hope it can work out for you. But first things first," she went on briskly. "We gotta find you a husband."

The kitchen timer dinged and they both started laughing.

Over the delicious dinner, Parris and Faye half playfully began to draw up a list of potential husbands for Faye.

"Okay," Parris said, refilling their wineglasses, "who should we start the list with?"

"How about Barry Markham?"

"Excellent choice if you can put up with his mother. Barry's always been considerate and thoughtful, and besides, we already know he's a terrific father."

"I'm glad you're so enthusiastic. Seth thinks he's an idiot."

"Oh, Seth's just prejudiced. He thinks the youngest son in every wealthy family is a catered-to, spoiled brat. Like my ex." Faye grinned crookedly. "Everything just fell into Teddy's lap. He was used to being taken care of and expected me to do the same. I kept waitin' for him to grow up but he never did. I wanted a man who'd hold me, and I wound up doin' the holding. I finally decided I couldn't be a mother to Jessica and to him, too."

Parris stopped and bit her lip. "Sorry, Faye. I didn't mean to go on about me that way."

"Please don't apologize," Faye said at once, her eyes full of sympathy. "I appreciate your insights."

"Anyway," Parris went on with a brisk, practical air, "what other men have you met since you've been here?"

"Hollister Pettigrew."

"Oh, my land!" Parris broke up laughing. "You can't be that desperate yet. Now be serious."

Faye shrugged nonchalantly. "Well, then, maybe I *should* give Seth a run for it, just to get his adrenaline flowing. I bet no one's seen him running scared in a while."

"You are joking, aren't you?"

"I suppose so." Faye twirled her glass on the table-top, not looking at Parris. "Besides everything else, we're too different. He's addicted to country music and Countrytime Lemonade. That just doesn't go with white wine and Frank Sinatra," she said ruefully. "I like antiques, he's into early Salvation Army."

"Seth had his antique phase, too," Parris replied with a worldly twinkle. "I recall there was this older woman he was dating for a while..."

Faye raised her hand to stop her from going on. "Who I'm sure was a gourmet cook. Enough, please!"

The two women regarded each other solemnly for a moment and then burst into laughter.

"Men are all bastards, aren't they?" Faye said with a frustrated sigh.

"The ones we love seem to be."

The evening ended on a more optimistic note, with Parris writing out her soufflé recipe for Faye.

"Thanks, Parris, but I think I'm going to need more than a recipe. Step-by-step on video would be more like it."

"Your fear's all in your head. Cooking's just a matter of following the steps. There's no magic involved."

Hah, Faye thought to herself as she drove away. *You could say the same thing about life, and look at how often people mess that up.* She laughed to herself. *Who knows? Maybe I will get the steps right eventually.*

CHAPTER FIFTEEN

JENNY GREETED FAYE with a happy yelp and pranced around the kitchen excitedly.

"Sorry I abandoned you all day, girl," Faye apologized, scratching behind the dog's ears and stroking her thick coat. "Come on, let's go up to bed."

Faye switched on the television while she brushed her teeth. After hurriedly splashing her face with warm water, she climbed into the old mahogany four-poster and snuggled beneath the quilt. Plumping the pillows behind her, she settled in as the fat sergeant on the screen began his weekly briefing of the cops in his precinct.

"Just in time," she murmured to herself in satisfaction, closing her eyes to enjoy the jazzy *Hill Street Blues* theme while the credits rolled by. The program was her favorite, and the main reason was Captain Frank Furillo. Over the years she'd developed a serious crush on the character. She allowed nothing and no one to interfere with her Thursday-night ritual.

Barely fifteen minutes into the show, however, the telephone on her bedside table jangled. She jumped and then stared at it balefully through four rings. Knowing she had no choice, she finally picked up the receiver.

"Hello," she snapped.

"Faye, it's me," Seth began. "I been trying to reach you all day. I want to talk to you about this partnership deal you and Tommy have cooked up."

"I'm in bed, Seth, and I don't talk business at ten o'clock at night," she said icily. "Besides, I'm busy."

There was a perplexed pause. "How can you be busy if you're in bed?"

"I've got company," she said and couldn't resist adding, "a very handsome, sexy Italian."

"Who!"

Faye held the phone out from her ear until the echo of his surprised bellow died away. "You heard me," she said, enjoying herself now. "He's the only man I've ever been in love with. Sensitive, strong, caring. One in a million."

"And he's lying there listening to all this?" Seth sounded disgusted and annoyed though not particularly jealous.

Faye sighed. "Actually, he's on TV."

"Shoulda guessed." Did he sound relieved? "Who is it, anyway?"

"The captain on *Hill Street Blues.*"

"You mean you put that mealymouthed dude up on a pedestal? I don't believe it, Faye. Somehow I never figured you for the type to go looking for fantasy heroes."

"As if you don't have your fantasies," she shot back, his criticism rankling. "I saw that poster of Dolly Parton in your bathroom. You've obviously got a thing for big breasts."

"I just like the way she sings," Seth defended himself. "I don't give a damn about big boobs."

"Oh, sure. I noticed that dress Parris Harper wore to the Cheviot. And knowing you," Faye sniffed, "I've got no doubts you've sampled her soufflé *au fromage*, too."

"Faye, what in hell are you talking about?"

"Good night, Seth. Don't you know it's rude to call people so late?"

She hung up on him and settled back down into the covers, trying to concentrate on the show. But Seth's call had shattered the mood. Finally she touched the remote-control button and turned over on her side, willing herself to sleep. She thought she might dream of the handsome police captain. Instead, visions of Seth haunted her thoughts. It was easy to love a two-dimensional figure on a television screen; in Faye's mind Frank Furillo was exactly what she wanted him to be. But real life was different. Faye wasn't used to falling in love with her next-door neighbor, and she wasn't quite sure how to proceed.

FAYE WAS WAKENED in the middle of the night from an uneasy sleep by Jenny's whining. She lifted her head groggily off the pillow and switched on the lamp. The distinct odor of smoke drifted in through the open bedroom window.

Immediately she jumped up and ran to look outside. Through the darkness she glimpsed a faint red light shimmering in the unfinished barn and she imagined the ominous crackle of fire as it licked up the new stalls.

In a panic she raced downstairs, not bothering to throw a robe over her white cotton nightshirt. She stumbled out the back door and raced barefoot down the uneven path, barely feeling the sharp little stones that dug into her heels as she ran. Jenny rushed ahead of her, barking madly.

"Dear God, please don't let it burn," she prayed, her palms scraped raw from struggling with the rusted faucet at the corner of the building. She was almost sobbing by the time she managed to crank it on full blast. Gripping the rusty nozzle in both hands she ran awkwardly into the barn as the leaky hose unwound itself behind her.

A pile of wood shavings and hay in the corner of the barn was already consumed by flames. Streams of sparks shot out from the highly combustible mass, hissing as they landed in a neighboring woodpile. Blinking against the brightness of the hot yellow flames, Faye directed her pitiful stream of water with shaking hands. Again and again she tried to put out the fire as it encroached upon the woodpile, but another licking tendril would find passage along the old dry floor.

Her stomach churned. Should she run back to the house to phone for help or stay where she was, holding back the growing fire as best she could?

She was so frantic that she hardly noticed Seth had joined her until she saw the welcome stream of white foam rushing out from the portable extinguisher in his hands.

"How'd it start?" he shouted over the hiss of foam. He was barefoot, too, and shirtless above his low-slung unbelted jeans. "I heard Jenny barking and came running."

Faye shook her head, too numb to talk. She couldn't yet face the possibility that it might have been the work of an arsonist, that he might not stop at the barn next time.

They worked grimly side by side, until Faye's arms began to ache from holding the heavy hose. She steeled herself to hang on. After what seemed like an eternity the last flame was beaten down and nothing remained but a few smoldering patches and a sharp acrid smell in the air.

Despite the tears burning her eyes and a rasping cough from the smoke, Faye grabbed a rake and went over to spread out the smoldering heap.

"Here," Seth said, "let me do that."

"No." She held tight to the rake. "I'll do it."

Mechanically she went through the motions until one of the rake tines caught in something. Curious, she dragged a tangled black ball toward her. Seth bent down to examine the charred heap of rag, and then looked up at Faye.

"Smells like gasoline."

She bit her lip. "Arson?"

"Sure looks that way." He stood up and gently pried her fingers from the rake. "Come on, Faye, we've done all we can for now. Let's go outside and get some fresh air."

She was surprised how soft and peaceful the night was, how pleasantly the cool wind rustled the grass and how innocent and clean the air smelled. Somehow she had expected the whole world to be engulfed in an inferno.

Seth put his arm around her shoulders and wordlessly she turned to him, slipping her arms around his waist. They stood together like that for a long time, just comforting each other.

At last she drew back a little to look up at him. "Thanks for coming, Seth. It started to get hairy in there. I was getting...worried." Now that the immediate horror had passed, she was reluctant to admit how frightened she had been. But Seth saw straight through her.

"Worried?" he teased her. "Is that all?"

"Okay, okay," she said, her eyes sparkling a little. "I admit it. I was scared to death."

"Did you see anyone—your friendly flower delivery-man?"

"Not a soul," she confessed, leaning her head back against his bare chest. "Jenny woke me up with her whining. She's been a godsend. I...I don't think I ever really thanked you for lending her to me."

Seth didn't reply. All he did was gently stroke her hair. After a while he asked, "You ready to go back up to the house?"

"No," she murmured wearily, her voice muffled because she had turned her face into his chest to breathe in the comforting scent of his skin, like horses and English leather. "Not yet." She felt protected there in his arms, safe.

It was a long while before she drew back again. "Guess I'm okay now." She looked up at him, trying out a smile. But it was pretty shaky.

Seth slipped his hands beneath her hair and with his thumb brushed away a smudge of soot from her cheek. "You don't look okay."

"Who would do this to me?" Telltale wetness gleamed in her eyes. "Hollister Pettigrew is a venal little marshmallow but not a villain."

Seth nodded his agreement. "He's got as sharp an eye for a buck as any guy out to feather his own nest. But you're right. I don't see him doing something like this."

"Then who?"

"I just don't know," he said slowly. "Guess it's time you called the sheriff."

"Guess so." Gently she disengaged herself from his hands and went to lean on the fence, trying to push away the fears tugging at her. Seth came up behind her and began to massage her shoulders and the back of her neck. His touch felt delightful.

"You're all tensed up," he murmured against the back of her head. "If you want to talk, I'm here, Faye. I'll listen. Maybe I can't match that TV cop. But I can try."

She reached up to put her hand over his where it lay on her shoulder, and she turned her head. "Seth, I'm sorry

I snapped at you on the phone tonight. That was pretty childish of me.''

"Maybe I deserved it.'' He chuckled. "I got this bad habit of wanting to do things when *I* want to do them. It isn't real polite.''

She smiled. "Well, you made up for it just now. I'm...I'm grateful.''

"Still want to stay out here a little longer?''

She nodded and he lifted her up on the rail fence. They sat there side by side, allowing the tension and the aftermath of fright to ebb away completely. Bit by bit Faye gave herself over to the quiet beauty of the night. The fragrance of summer was in the air and the paddocks shone like silver in the moonlight.

"Seth, look!'' she said suddenly, stiffening at the sight of something ghostly white moving in the distance. "What is it?''

"That's just Jezebel,'' he said in a relaxed voice. "One of my mares.''

The horse moved out of the shadows, and Faye sucked in her breath. "A white Thoroughbred! They're rare, aren't they?''

"Technically she's a gray because she's got a few black hairs in her muzzle and mane. But, yeah, I'd call her white, too. She's real susceptible to sunburn, so I've been letting her out at night instead of the day, now that the sun's getting hotter. Besides, she gets restless in her stall after dark. I think she's just an ole night owl.''

The familiar, lazy amusement in his voice warmed Faye to the core. "On a beautiful night like this, I don't blame her,'' she whispered.

They were both quiet for a while, just content to watch Jezebel graze. After a while Faye said, "You know, I don't remember seeing her in your barn last week.''

"She was out being bred. To a stallion called Polar Star. They should produce one hell of a get, if the mating took."

Faye shook her head. "It all sounds so mechanical. I guess there's no room for romance in this business."

"If you're curious, I'll take you out to see a breeding session. But you're right, there's no romance. Just a padded shed with the vet looking on as witness and a groom holding the mare," he explained. "They put a rope twitch in her nose."

"Why?"

"Well, it hurts her a little, so she concentrates on that instead of trying to kick the stallion," he said, and added wryly, "Can't risk damaging that valuable property."

"Sounds like the mare gets the lousy end of the deal."

"Like you said, no room for romance. Although..." Seth paused and gave Faye an amused sidelong look. "There was this crazy Italian breeder once..."

"Go on." Faye smiled over at him, grateful for the pleasant diversion of his conversation. "I'm all ears."

"His name was Teseo. Now this Italian had his own unique ideas about horse breeding. Claimed the offspring'd be stronger if there was genuine passion between the stallion and mare."

Faye cocked her head interestedly. "Was this Teseo right, or was he just crazy?"

"Well, there's a story that one time he was leading his mare to a stallion to be bred when they passed by another stallion in the field. The horses got wind of each other, and they both went wild. They were that hungry to get to each other. Well, old Teseo thought, 'Hell, why not?' So he bred the two."

"And?" Faye prompted, her lips curving in anticipation.

"And they produced a champ." Faye laughed softly and Seth went on. "There's more. Teseo bred the mare the next year to the original stallion. And..."

"The offspring was a dud?"

Seth grinned. "You got it."

"The power of passion." Faye laughed in delight. "I like that."

The wind shifted slightly and Jezebel lifted her head, catching the human scent. She sauntered down easily to them, a big sturdy mare with a placid air about her. She stood calmly before the two people perched on the rail fence.

"I thought Thoroughbreds were born nervous. You told me they've got that edginess in their blood. But Jezebel looks so...maternal." Faye leaned forward a little. "Even her eyes seem kind. Or am I just imagining things?"

"No, you pegged her right. I guess that's why she was just a good racehorse instead of a great one. Somehow the mean feisty ones got more oomph to them." He grinned. "Sorta like you, Faye."

"Hmm," she murmured tartly. "I can't decide if I've just been complimented or insulted."

"What do you say we go for a ride on Jezebel?"

"You mean now?"

Seth laughed at her disbelief. "Why not? She won't mind."

He called Jezebel over to the rail and lifted Faye onto her back. He climbed on behind her, lightly twisting a hank of white mane in his hand, and gently nudged his bare heels into her flanks. Jezebel obligingly leaped into a cantering gait that was as gentle and easy as a rocking-horse motion.

Faye laughed in sheer delight. She had never ridden bareback before and their impromptu ride was a wonderful lark. The wind streamed through her mussed hair, carrying away the lingering stench of the fire. She felt wild and free, as if the mare's powerful flanks were an extension of her bare thighs propelling her forward into an exciting unknown. And yet there were Seth's arms, gentle around her waist, a protective caress that spoke of shared adventure, of an experience belonging to both of them.

"There's a pond down at the far edge of the pasture," he murmured against her hair. "Should be pretty in this moonlight."

The pond filled a tiny hollow, its surface black and mysteriously luminescent. Seth took Faye's hand and pulled her companionably along the fields he'd walked every day since he'd bought the property.

He pointed to a low gnarled tree, its truncated limbs like broken teeth bared to the sky. "Lightning struck it summer before last during a storm," Seth said in a subdued voice. "Lost a prized mare that was shelterin' under it."

They walked on and his somber mood gave way to a deep chuckle. "See this hollow here?" he asked, lifting their joined hands to point to a steep dip in the pasture. "I had a colt that just loved this hollow. Once he'd lain down there you couldn't see him. I remember the first time he did it. I thought he'd got stolen."

"How'd you find him?"

"I crisscrossed every field. And there he was, lying on his side, snoring away." Seth chuckled again. "Damnedest thing I ever saw."

Faye turned and laughed up into his eyes. "I can't blame the little guy. I used to do the same when I was a kid. I'd lie in a hammock and dream the summer away."

Seth stared down at her, and Faye sensed that some undefinable emotion buried deep inside him had been awakened.

Indeed, something about the reflection of the moonlight in her eyes had touched him deeply. He'd never felt this way with a woman before—as if he was new and the world was new, and it was all stretched out ahead of him.

Faye read something of this in his eyes and suddenly her heart beat faster. Seth lifted his hands to trace her cheekbones and her jawline with fingertips at once sensitive and inquisitive. "Kentucky woman," he breathed, his voice as low and gentle as the spring wind. "Guess that song didn't lie. Guess you do shine with your own kind of light. Beautiful."

Her heart opened up to him then, and all the feelings she'd held in for so long gushed out. She rose on her tiptoes and he took her in his arms, his lips finding hers unerringly in the darkness. There was no hesitation, no preliminary brushing of tentative mouths. They kissed deeply, feverishly, as if afraid the night would consume them before the kiss was complete.

Her fingers dug into his bare shoulders, clinging to the solid strength she found there, and she imagined his powerful arms bearing her away to a secret place meant for the two of them alone. To an enchanted hideaway that had existed since the beginning of time.

In a twinkling the magic of the night had enveloped them. The ripe warm earth, the ghostly mare whickering softly in the distance, and the soft night air heavy with promise conspired to envelop them in a heady magic.

A low growl erupted from Seth's throat as if to acknowledge he was lost to the moment, and he pulled her down beside him into the deep fragrant grass. His hands were everywhere at once on her body, fingertips stroking her closed eyelids, palms cupping her breasts and her behind, his thumb grazing the soft mound of her womanhood like a musician caressing the strings of a harp until the whole instrument resonated with the wild soaring music begun by a single plucked note.

Passion seared between them, an unleashed sexuality that rocked them both. Faye cried out as she felt his hands climb up beneath the hem of her nightshirt, felt them impatiently tear her panties away so that she lay naked and vulnerable. Wholly open to him. He bent down and brushed his mouth against the soft warmth of her inner thigh, his tongue sending rivulets of fire along her quivering muscles.

"Oh, yes," she moaned. "Oh, you make me feel so wonderful, Seth. Please don't ever stop."

Impelled by their own hidden rhythm, her hips began a wild erotic gyration that excited Seth to the marrow. He breathed in her femininity and felt himself growing harder. He groaned with pleasure as Faye's exploring hands moved down across his chest and belly to stroke his compelling hardness where it strained for release against his jeans. She fumbled with the zipper and then unhesitatingly reached in to caress him, excited by that hot tumescent maleness.

"Please, Seth," she begged. "Make love to me. Now."

He rolled on top of her, and for all the fierce sexual urge to completion driving him on, he entered her slowly, like an armored knight chary of breaching an enchanted moat, afraid of destroying the tenuous magic of her ecstasy.

Then she lifted her hips to him, drawing him ever deeper. With a groan he thrust into her, over and over again. His climax came in a thundering explosion.

Faye strove to match his fury, reaching for the spiraling web of pleasure just beyond her reach. Then his thrusts ebbed ever slower, moving closer toward the cool dark rhythm of her rotating hips. She felt his hands beneath her bare buttocks, lifting her toward him, helping her find the elusive rhythm she sought. Tension gathered deep in her belly, a gathering crescendo of kaleidoscopic pleasure that burst through her like fireworks to shower her with warmth and light and almost unbearable pleasure.

They lay spent in each other's arms, limbs sticky with salt sweat and the animal musk of their bodies darkly sweet against the innocent freshness of the night.

Little more than an hour before they had been friends, battling together side by side to protect something vital to them both. Now they had become lovers. Could they be both?

Gently Faye combed her fingers through his hair, her lips pressed to his throat. "Seth," she murmured, half to herself, "I guess what happened just now was inevitable. It had to be."

He stirred beside her. "Don't know about inevitable," he said slowly, as if reluctant to break the mood their lovemaking had created. "I know it's something we've both been wanting—and fighting—for quite a while."

She drew back a little to look up at him. "But isn't that the same thing?"

He shrugged, not looking at her. His gaze was fixed on the lace ribbons of her shirt. "I wanted a lot of things in my life, Faye, and it seemed like every time I said I had to have something, then I was sure to lose it." He fingered one of the slender ribbons. "Nowadays I don't expect anything to be inevitable. It's like a superstition with me, almost. If I don't want something, I don't have to worry about not getting it."

"Maybe the boy inside you thought that way. But does the man?"

"The boy makes the man. The boy *is* the man." He lifted brooding eyes to hers. "When you've been abandoned, you expect to be abandoned. Once you're ridiculed, you expect to be ridiculed. You may grow a tough hide, but inside you're still afraid of being hurt. You learn it's safer to want only concrete things—a barn, a house, a horse. Pretty soon nothing else matters."

Faye stroked his shoulder and chest, as if the loving gesture could ease the long-buried pains. "How old were you when your mother left?"

"Four. Took my sister too when she went. Sally was three years older'n me. I can still see her," he said, and Faye felt his gaze turning inward again. "Had soft brown hair, a funny smile and sad eyes. Remember how the inside of a lunchbox smelled when you were a kid? Well, Sally smelled like that. I missed her."

Faye bit her lip. "And you never heard from them again?"

"Nope," he said matter-of-factly. "Once my dad quit drinkin' we went on up to Canada to work some tracks there. The kids laughed at my accent, at my patched clothes. They laughed at the hard lumpy biscuits I brought for lunch. Made 'em myself." He smiled a little. "I couldn't believe their neat little sandwiches, some of them with the crust trimmed off, the oranges their mamas had peeled for them. Guess that's when I got used to bein' an outsider. Now I guess I don't want to be any other way."

Listening to him, Faye felt her heart constrict. But when she tried to slip her hand back around his waist, Seth gently pushed it away, the same as he had done the time she'd tried to kiss him in his trailer.

"Come on, Faye," he said briskly. "We gotta get you out of this damp grass afore you catch cold."

Jezebel had gone and so they had to tramp through the pasture, swiftly crossing the dark empty fields. They climbed the last low rise and Faye saw the light from her bedroom window, shining in the distance like a beacon. She longed to take Seth home to bed with her, but she knew better now than to even suggest it.

They reached the fence and she'd already slid under it before she realized he wasn't going to follow. He stood there on the far side, looking at her. She leaned on the rail toward him. Briefly he reached down to touch her hair, and then he turned and strode away into the darkness.

CHAPTER SIXTEEN

FAYE'S MEETING with the county sheriff had not been satisfactory, so she was not in a good mood when Seth called later in the morning.

"You talked to the law yet?" he asked straight off, making no reference to their midnight interlude in the field. It might not have happened at all, as far as he was concerned.

"The sheriff just left," she said, her manner brittle. "He took the gas-soaked rag for analysis but he said even that wasn't ironclad proof of arson. He said Cal Darby or one of his men could have used it to clean their hands and left it out there accidentally. Or some kids could've sneaked onto the place. He said there's been a rash of vandalism reports."

"And you didn't listen to a word of it," Seth said, feeling her anger.

"If there hadn't been the phone call or the dead flowers, I might have gone along with his ideas. But I know better," she insisted, her hand tightening on the phone. "I've been threatened. And now that I see no one's going to help me, I've really got no choice but to handle this on my own."

"How—with a shotgun?"

His wry tone made her smile a little, but when she replied she was absolutely serious. "I think it's time I confronted Hollister Pettigrew head-on again, for one thing.

I have to find out exactly what he knows. I'll talk to you later, Seth."

"Wait a minute," he said before she could hang up. "There's this other matter we got to discuss."

Her pulse quickened. Maybe he *was* ready after all to confront the feelings they'd stirred up last night. "What is it you want to talk about?" she asked in a softer voice.

"We haven't had a chance to hash out what you're gettin' into with Tommy and Sinbad."

"Oh, that," she said stiffly. "Well, you can rest assured. You're not going to lose out. I've sold my car. The guy's giving me a good price, enough for me to go halves with Tommy on the horse and still give you five thousand. I think that's fair."

Her frigid manner annoyed him. "Dammit," he swore, "the money isn't the issue."

"Money's been the issue from the first and you know it, Seth. Why do you think we put everything down in writing?" she reminded him. "Neither one of us trusted the other. And with good reason."

"You still feel that way?"

"No!" She paused a fraction of a second. "Especially not after what happened between us last night."

She felt the silence, like a denial, on his end of the line. But she went on, anyway. "Seth, I've been doing a lot of thinking. I called my ex-boss and had his real-estate agent get in touch with me. I'm putting my condominium on the market. She says she can probably sell it in a month because the location's so great. Seth, are you listening to me?" she said almost angrily. "I'm pulling up my California stakes, shallow as they were. I'm committing myself to Indian Creek."

The deafening silence on the other end continued.

"Seth, don't you hear what I'm saying?" she said in irritation.

"It ain't too late to back out," he replied finally, his voice low and cautious.

"I don't want to back out!" she shouted. "You sound just like Harve. He said it still wouldn't be too late even after I signed escrow papers; he said he was sure another place on the planning board would open up soon. It's like nobody's listening to what I'm really saying!"

"I'm listening, Faye," Seth said heavily.

"Oh, never mind. Goodbye," she said in irritation and hung up on him.

He had acted as though she'd stuck a knife in him, for heaven's sake. She refused to accept he wasn't feeling the same way she was. She told herself it was just a matter of time until she won him over. Until she remembered Parris Harper's warning, remembered his own avowal that he was an outsider, a loner, and wanted to keep it that way.

HOLLISTER PETTIGREW seemed none too pleased to see Faye barging into his inner sanctum after she had sweet-talked her way around his inexperienced secretary.

"I'm a busy man," he complained peevishly, looking up from the pile of papers in front of him. "You could have made an appointment, Fayette Lee. Whatever happened to proper etiquette, I'd like to know."

"Oh, so you want to hear about etiquette, Mr. Pettigrew," she blazed, her face as red as the Windbreaker she wore over her jeans. "I'll tell you about the sort of etiquette I've gotten used to around here. I don't get phone calls from the neighborhood Welcome Wagon. No, I get a phone call from a bozo who threatens to shoot my head off. And I get a bouquet of dead flowers with a note saying they're for my coffin. And last night," she said between clenched teeth, "someone tried to set fire to my barn, and believe me, he didn't leave a calling card. I'm telling you, mister, I've had it."

Pettigrew blanched. "Why are you telling me all this? Have you called the sheriff?"

"I've already talked to him. Now I intend to talk to you."

"Just sit down, Fayette Lee." Despite the air-conditioned office, beads of perspiration had popped out on his forehead. "You're beginning to make me angry."

"Good," she retorted, throwing herself into the nearest chair. "Then maybe you'll understand a little better how I feel."

Pettigrew looked at her with tired, resigned eyes. "Now in the first place, I'm not any prankster. And I'm not any criminal, either. I'll admit this bank's got a vested interest in Indian Creek Farm," he said. "But I'm also tryin' to deal fair and square with you, Fayette. I'm givin' you the chance to make good with that place. Chances are you won't, but in the meantime I'm not interfering. When I get you off that land it's going to be legally. I got my trust department. I got my lawyers. I ain't got no taste for breakin' the law." His narrowed gaze met hers squarely. "You understand that?"

It was the first straight talk she'd heard out of his mouth since they had met. Faye stared at him for a long while, and he began to realize that she did believe him.

"Now I didn't set that fire," he said in a more relaxed voice. "There may be people with grudges that strong, but I'm not one of them."

"Grudges! Who?" she demanded. "I think you know more than you're saying."

"All I can say is the grudge may not be so much against you as against what you're tryin' to save."

"What do you mean? The farm? I don't understand."

"I'm sorry, Fayette Lee. There isn't anything more to say."

"But you know, don't you?" She jumped up and leaned her fists on his desk. "You know who's responsible."

His features took on a closed, obstinate look. "I can't help you, little lady."

Faye sensed he was as guilty of protecting someone as he was innocent of involvement with the fire. But she wasn't able to pry anything more out of him.

She left his office as abruptly as she had barged in, her mind churning. She had no idea where to turn next, what avenue to pursue. The whole situation was just too crazy. So far, all her brave talk about playing detective had come to nothing. With every passing day she was feeling more vulnerable. Another attack could happen at any time, and she was virtually powerless to prevent it.

Outside, she climbed into the eight-year-old station wagon she'd bought for herself with the little money she'd had left over from selling the Alfa. She had to pump the accelerator and crank the key several times, but finally the old clunker started up. Faye still couldn't quite believe she was driving such a monstrosity.

Out near Red Mile Track she saw Tommy Thomas crossing the street absentmindedly, his attention fixed on the wad of bills in his hand. His expression was gleeful. Faye pulled over and honked.

He ambled over toward her with a grin. "Hey, Faye, what's goin' on?"

"That's a nice pile of cash, Tommy. Did you win big?"

"Actually I..." He stopped dead and gave her a guilty look, stuffing the half-counted wad into his jeans pocket.

"Tommy, if I find out you've been gambling I'm going to pull out my share from Sinbad so fast your head'll be spinning," she warned him. "I'm not driving this wreck so you can support your bad habits."

"Aw, hell," he groused. "I thought I was gettin' me a business partner. Not a wife."

She ignored that dig. "Promise me?"

"But this was trotters. Horses," he defended himself. "The thing I know best."

"Tommy..."

"Okay," he promised, breathing a deep sigh of defeat.

"Where are you off to now?"

"Keeneland," he said promptly, the light rekindling in his eyes. "Gonna check our little goldmine out, make sure he's ready for the race on Sunday."

Faye's hands grew moist on the wheel. Tommy sounded so casual and yet to her so much rested on the outcome of that race. "You think he's ready?"

"Sinbad looks real sharp," the trainer said at once. "He should do just fine."

She relaxed. "I trust your judgment on that, Tommy."

He smiled. "We ain't got nothin' to worry about."

KEENELAND TRACK overflowed with people on race day. The elegant airs of the rich man's exclusive retreat had given way to the ambience of a festive country fair. Tiny jockeys in bright racing silks of orange and royal blue and vermilion hurried from the changing room to make the first race. In contrast to the tropical plumage of the jockeys, the racehorse owners and their wives lounged elegantly in subdued tone-on-tone outfits of nubby linen and raw silk.

Faye threaded her way through the milling throngs, nervously pushing up the sleeves of the white unconstructed blazer she wore over a sleeveless yellow sweater and straight khaki skirt. She looked like a racehorse owner, too—a working owner.

She found Tommy and Seth together in the saddling-up area.

"This is gonna be a historic day, Miz Faye," Tommy greeted her ebulliently. "I can feel it in my bones. Sinbad's operatin' on the cutting edge. Look at him."

Faye eyed the brown Thoroughbred critically. He looked as mean and cantankerous as ever. With hesitant fingers she reached out to touch his glistening flanks. They were damp. "Tommy, he's sweating, he's nervous. Did you . . . ?" she asked.

The trainer smiled and pulled Sinbad's head down so she could see inside his ears. They were stuffed with cotton wads. "He's goin' to be oblivious to the noise of the crowds. You'll see."

"If you say so," she said, rubbing her arms.

"Now you calm down yourself, Faye," Tommy ordered. "You're bein' nervous won't help him a bit."

"Me?" She stiffened. "I'm fine, Tommy."

Listening to her denial, Seth briefly glanced up from the girth he was tightening. But he didn't say a word.

His withdrawal angered Faye. More than anything she needed a quick hug at least, warm assurance from his lips that everything would be fine. He had been standoffish ever since the night in the field. Faye tried to tell herself it was simply because he was busy with the farm, but deeper down she feared a more damning reason. The moment their lighthearted friendship had shown proof of deepening into something else he had begun to shy away. He had made it plain from the first he didn't want her to stay in Lexington. She knew now that his whole life had conditioned him to shy away from emotional entanglements. Yet she had been so sure of being able to change him.

She swallowed her private pain as Tommy took her arm excitedly to introduce her to their jockey, Fred Kern, a shifty-eyed kid with bad teeth and a sullen expression. Faye tried to smile at him, all the while feeling her anxiety grow. So much rested on the outcome of a race she had no control of. She imagined the vultures circling: Pettigrew with his vow to be rid of her through legal means, and whoever was at the source of that other shadowy and far more menacing threat, which was no closer to diffusing after weeks of wrestling with it and worrying.

"Come on, Faye," Tommy said, pulling her along with childlike excitement toward the rail. "Let's go grab a place along the finish line so we can cheer our fella home."

"Where'd you find that jockey?" Faye asked, resisting the urge to add, *Under a rock?*

"He may not look like much," Tommy said, as if reading her mind. "But he's got good steady hands."

Despite her misgivings, Faye's heart leaped with excitement as the starting pistol fired and the horses charged out of the gate.

"Man, he broke good!" Tommy whooped, pounding Faye on the back. "Come on, Sinbad!"

Her hands clutched the rail, eyes fixed on the brilliant blur of colors on the far side of the infield. She picked out the orange-and-purple silks of her team, her gaze zeroing in on the raiment as if by sheer force of will she could urge horse and rider on.

Miraculously, Sinbad, who had broken eighth, started to pass the horses ahead of him one by one. Faye heard herself cheering, screaming his name. When Sinbad edged into fourth at the third furlong she turned and hugged Tommy, dizzy with excitement. They clung to each other, beating the rail and shouting until they were hoarse. The strung-out pack reached the final turn, the low pounding drum of their hooves a driving counterpoint to the raucous screams from the grandstand.

In the final stretch Sinbad started to edge into third when he seemed to take a bad step and then falter. Valiantly he tried to recover his momentum but the critical edge was lost. As the frontrunners thundered past the wire, Sinbad was half a nose behind the third-place finisher, heartbreakingly close to finishing "in the money." But close wasn't good enough.

Anguish and disbelief in his eyes, Tommy turned away from the rail to hurry to the unsaddling area.

"What happened to him?" Faye cried, running to keep up with the trainer.

"I don't know," he muttered between clenched teeth. "But I'm sure as hell goin' to find out."

They caught up with Kern outside the changing room. He turned sullenly when Tommy called his name.

"What happened out there, Fred?"

"Whip broke," he said laconically.

"What the hell do you mean, the whip broke?" Tommy repeated in disbelief. "Them things are unbreakable plastic."

The boy reached into the back waistband of his breeches and drew out the whip, or what remained of it. It had been sheared cleanly in two.

"Get outta here, you little two-bit skunk," Tommy snarled.

Faye stared at the trainer in disbelief. "Tommy, it wasn't his fault."

"Like hell it wasn't. Faye, you got a lot to learn about this business, about the ugliness that can go on. We were sabotaged, plain and simple. I'll bet you a hundred to one that little weasel was paid off."

"Sabotage," Faye repeated numbly. Her world had been tainted by the ugly word for weeks. Why should she have been naive enough to expect today would be any different? "I'm sorry, Tommy," she said, touching his arm. "I shouldn't have dragged you into my problems."

"Never mind," he said, pulling himself out of his gloom. "It ain't the end of the world, Faye. Not by a long shot. Next time we just gotta outsmart 'em."

Faye nodded, refusing to give in to the depression that she knew would sneak up on her later. She imagined herself sitting bolt upright in the middle of the night, wide-eyed, wondering if she had invested several thousand dollars in chasing rainbows.

Leaving Tommy to take care of his other business, Faye wandered off on her own. She spotted Parris Harper across the grounds, looking cool and elegant in a white muslin dress, a wide-brimmed straw hat shading her beautifully made-up features. She was walking side by side with a tall gangly man. Faye started to turn away, but Parris had already seen her and waved gaily, motioning for her friend to join them.

"Fayette Lee Hunt, I'd like you to meet Dr. John Turlock," Parris introduced them, her green eyes teasing Faye. "He's our local veterinarian. So busy taking care of everyone's stock he hasn't bothered to find himself a wife yet."

The vet smiled, his brown eyes twinkling but shy behind his wire-rimmed glasses. "I've been hearing a lot about you, Faye. Welcome to the Bluegrass."

"Thanks," Faye answered, trying hard to be friendly. "Who's been talking about me?" She shot the elegant redhead a mildly rebuking look but Parris returned the look serenely, the picture of innocence.

"Oh, word gets around," the vet said. "A newcomer, especially when she's pretty, is bound to attract attention."

Someone came up to John Turlock with a question, and he excused himself. Chuckling to herself, Parris watched him saunter away. "He's cute, isn't he?"

"Yes," Faye conceded, giving her friend a wry look. "But I'd prefer to do my own man hunting, if you don't mind."

"Look, as long as Seth and Hollister Pettigrew are the only two names on your 'male' list, I figure you need all the help you can get, honey."

"Speak for yourself, honey," Faye shot back, her tense features relaxing in a smile. "Besides, you forgot Barry. He's still in the running."

"That's better." Parris nodded approvingly at her friend's animation. "You looked like a sad sack when you walked up. I'm sorry Sinbad lost."

Faye nodded. "Me too."

"How about a lemonade? Would that cheer you up?"

"Only if it comes with a shot of Bourbon."

"Spoken like a true Kentuckian." Parris laughed softly. "Now I think that can be arranged."

Faye laughed, too, intent on enjoying the rest of the afternoon. But seconds later, the lighthearted mood was shattered when Faye spotted what she thought was a silhouette of the deliveryman whom she had seen skulking away after leaving the dead roses on the farmhouse porch. She clutched Parris's arm.

"It's him," she whispered, dry mouthed. "I think it's him."

Parris looked at her curiously. "Who?"

"The guy who left the dead flowers."

Parris's eyes followed hers, narrowing like a cat's. "You sure?"

"Positive. Let's go."

"Now wait a minute, Faye," Parris said reasonably as she tried to keep up with Faye's quick stride. "He's gonna run all the faster if he sees you."

Faye's step faltered. "You're right. We need a plan." She thought a minute. "I know. You pretend you're lost and ask him for directions. Strike up a conversation. I'll stay behind his back so he doesn't see me."

Parris's eyes sparkled. "Let's go."

Despite her high-heeled red pumps, Parris did a fair imitation of a run and managed to catch up with him. "Excuse me, sir," she called out to him in her best feminine drawl. "But I seem to have gotten all turned around. Can you tell me where the Carriage Farm Stables are?"

Faye, who had circled past to stand behind him, stiffened when she heard his flat, youngish voice. She had no doubts it was the same voice she'd heard on the telephone.

Faye could have kissed Parris when she saw her put a hand on his arm and say, "Honey, I still don't understand. Would you just mind showin' me?"

But he shook her hand off with a brusque, "Don't got no time, lady."

As he turned to hurry away, Faye ran after him. But the crowds were so thick and she was so short that she had a difficult time keeping him in sight. Seeing an empty bench, she ran to jump up on it. Her vantage point gave her a clean view of her quarry jumping into a muddy old pickup truck and disappearing down the road to the track exit.

"Dammit!" she swore in irritation. Bad luck seemed to be hounding her now.

Disconsolate, Faye turned back to find Parris but she'd gotten swallowed up in the crowd, too. Not knowing what else to do, Faye went back to the stabling area where she'd left Tommy with Sinbad.

Instead of the trainer she found Seth, deep in conversation with the vet. She ran over toward them. "Seth!" she called. "I just—" Faye stopped in midphrase. His tanned face above the crisp white polo shirt was drawn and a little downcast. "What happened?" she asked, guessing at once. "Cantilever didn't make it into the money?"

Seth ran agitated fingers through his curly hair. "Finished dead last. John here just took a look at him. He found a big abscess in his mouth I didn't even know about," he said tersely. "Damn bit must have been cuttin' into him something bad."

The vet shook his head sympathetically. "These things happen, Seth. I'll write you out a prescription that should clear it up quick."

After the vet left, Seth went back inside the stall to take another look in the young stallion's mouth. Faye watched him from the doorway, her arms folded across her chest.

"My grandmama told me there'd be days like this," she said, a wry smile playing around her lips. "But I didn't believe her."

Despite his gloom, Seth had to smile back a little at that. "You said it, Hundred Pounds," he said with a sigh, coming back out to join her. "It's just been one of those days all around."

"Whose idea was it for me to get into this crazy business, anyway?" she demanded, her eyes sparkling up at him.

"Hey, now didn't I warn you?"

"Go ahead," she teased him. "Rub it in."

"What were you rushing over here to tell me?"

"I saw my flower deliveryman."

"Out here?" His head jerked up. "Did you follow him?"

"Yeah, and I lost him. Some great detective, huh?"

Her woebegone look touched him. "Forget it for now," he said gently. "There's nothing else you can do."

"You're telling me."

"Listen, you want to stop by Leroy's for a bite?" he suggested. "His grits and biscuits'd cheer anybody up."

"No, I've got a better idea," she replied, her eyes sparkling again. "Why don't you let me come over and cook dinner for you?"

"You kiddin' me, blue blood?"

"No, I'm not kidding," she retorted, miffed by his tone.

"Oh, I get it now," he teased her. "You're figuring if my stomach's all cramped up, I won't have time to worry about a little thing like my horse losing."

"What an insult," she said airily. "Besides, I've learned a thing or two since you gagged on my pork chops à la mode."

"Yeah. Like what?"

"You'll see."

CHAPTER SEVENTEEN

"DAMN," FAYE SWORE for the umpteenth time. Parris had made it look so easy!

The foil collar she'd put around the soufflé dish was slipping again. Through the gap the egg-cheese mixture poured out onto the countertop leaving a gooey, slimy trail. It dammed up against the side of the preheating oven and started to harden like dried-out glue.

Not that it mattered at this point since the entire kitchen was an absolute, unholy mess. Where the deft and highly efficent Parris had sponged, rinsed and put things away as she went along, Faye rushed headlong from step to step, too preoccupied to even think of such minor concerns.

In her hands the homey *Joy of Cooking* had been translated into a Genghis Khan rampage of epic proportions, involving every innocent utensil, wall and countertop in her path.

Egg whites, shiny as white patent leather after being brutally whipped into stiff peaks, had congealed on the mixer blades and on the wooden spoon she'd used to fold them into the beaten yolks. Beaten? Pulverized was more like it. Exploded. Faye felt the panic rising in her throat when she glanced up at the ceiling. Even those far reaches hadn't been spared her remorseless attack.

To make matters infinitely worse, Seth chose that moment to saunter in, hungry and curious as to what was holding up dinner. He stopped dead in the doorway, his eyes bugging out.

"Holy hell," he whispered, awestruck.

"Everything's under control!" she lied wildly. "Believe me." Egg yolks dripping down from the ceiling like stalactites on a cave roof belied her feverish assurances.

"Sure, sure," he replied, gingerly taking a step into the room, only to feel his boot squelch into something on the floor. It made a sucking noise as he pulled it back up.

"Why don't you just go—watch the six o'clock news or something?"

"And miss this show? When are the chimps coming back—they're part of the act, right?" he deadpanned. "This pack of 'em comes through and overruns you while you're trying to cook a simple little meal. Knocks the audience dead every time."

"Very funny." Faye ran a hand through her hair, streaking it with flour. "I don't know what went wrong. Parris made it look so easy."

"What the hell's Parris got to do with this mess?" He leaned back against the doorjamb with a grin. "Don't tell me you're still trying to compete with her."

"All I can say is Cordon Bleu just blew it," she replied, half to herself, surveying the wreckage of his once-tidy kitchen. "The question is—now what?"

Seth sighed, feeling a strong sense of déjà vu. "Any eggs left?"

"Four."

"Good enough." Rolling up his sleeves, he plowed into the mess. "How does ham 'n' eggs and toast sound?"

"Sounds heavenly," she said, picking up a pile of used bowls from the kitchen step stool before sinking down onto it gratefully. "Have you got grits, too?"

He laughed. "It would have been a whole lot cheaper if I'd just taken you to Leroy's in the first place."

While Seth whipped up dinner she scraped, scrubbed and poured the evidence of her latest culinary disaster down the disposal. Within minutes the place was filled with the warm sizzling aroma of well-cooked food. Expertly Seth flipped the lacy-edged fried eggs out of the cast-iron pan, and they carried their smoking plates out to the living room.

"How come everything tastes better when you cook it?" she asked between bites. "I guess I should take lessons."

"What's this domestic kick all about?"

Faye ignored the question, still off on her own train of thought.

"I can see now it was a mistake to try starting off with Cordon Bleu," she murmured. "Maybe I should just tackle some good old American standbys like hamburgers or roast turkey. I can varnish wood; the technique can't be all that different in basting a bird."

"If you're gonna practice, how about using your own kitchen the next time," Seth put in good-naturedly. "My insurance doesn't cover those kinds of disasters."

"Okay." She nodded, laughing a little now, too. "In fact, next time I'll experiment with something new. How does Torquemada's Favorite Pasta sound?"

"Whose favorite pasta?"

"Torquemada." She grinned. "The chief honcho during the Spanish Inquisition. He just loved torturing innocent people."

"I can't wait."

As soon as they finished eating Faye picked up the plates to carry them into the kitchen. "Would you like me to make coffee?"

"Can I trust you in there?"

"Well, you have instant—don't you?"

"Parris..." Seth cried out in a feigned tone of weak longing, like a drowning man reaching out for a life preserver. Faye kicked his leg with her bare foot and he sighed lustily. "The instant coffee is in the cupboard above the stove."

MUSIC WAFTED from the living room as Faye picked up the two steaming mugs from the countertop. She paused in the doorway, listening to the strains of Neil Diamond's "Kentucky Woman" filling the air.

Vividly the memory of their night out in the fields swept over her, calling up all the sweetness and the intensity of the feelings she had experienced lying in his arms. They had never talked about what they had shared that night; they hadn't really gone forward emotionally from that moment.

Now with the music and the mellow afternoon light pouring into the living room, she felt as if the magic was set to begin again.

Seth was lying on the sofa, feet up on the coffee table. His eyes were closed, his hands laced behind his head. Faye set the mugs on the table and slipped down on the couch beside him, leaning over him to whisper, "Hey, I like your taste in music, for a change."

Without opening his eyes, he put his arm around her and she snuggled against him, content just to feel the slow steady rise and fall of his chest as he breathed. Gently his hand stroked her back in an easy and relaxed movement.

When the song was over, Faye lifted her head to look at him. Her eyes traced the curve of his lips, teasing even in repose, and the boyishly rounded cheeks that offset the harsh grooves angling downward from his nose to his mouth. They touched the delicate web of crow's-feet around his own eyes, a history of feelings etched there for her to read: a story of strength and humor winning over sadness. Her gaze reveled in those features she had come to love so well.

"You're a special man, Seth Carradine," she whispered, reaching up to kiss him. He responded to the warm soft pressure of her lips and the kiss deepened.

"You're special, too, Hundred Pounds," he murmured lazily. "You've turned my life upside down ever since the day you showed up next door."

"Are you sorry?"

For answer he buried his face in her hair and his arms tightened around her. The sweet, spontaneous gesture caused all those feelings to well up inside her again, as they had that night they'd lain together. A light summer breeze drifted in through the open windows, bringing with it the distant neighing of horses, the rustle of elm leaves and the scent of newly turned soil.

Faye felt as though she could stay right where she was forever. She remembered how she'd smiled once at Seth's run-down bachelor's pad, at the lumpy sofa and ancient cretonne curtains. But she no longer saw the dinginess. It was as though her heart had taken wing and finally come to nest inside the little trailer. Compared to it, the sturdy gray farmhouse up on the hill with its well-used hearth and big country kitchen, its rows of empty upstairs bedrooms was just a shell. She wished she could find the words to express what she was feeling to Seth, to the man-boy who'd been beaten down so much he only wanted such concrete things as "a horse, a barn, a house." How could such things matter without the rest—without someone to share them?

"Seth." She whispered his name and then said more strongly, "I feel like I could lie here like this forever. All the hassles out there in the big bad world just don't matter." She sighed. "This is what's important."

"I have to admit it feels good bein' your port in a storm. If it takes you getting a few knocks from the big bad world to make you all cuddly, why then I guess I'm all for it." He laughed softly. "I love seein' your softer side, Faye. When you're like this, you're so beautiful it takes my breath away."

"I didn't know I had this side to me myself." Gently she stroked his neck above the V in his shirt. "Maybe it took someone like you to bring it out—to show me what I really am."

"What are you, Faye?"

"Just this." She reached up to kiss him again, her lips warmly playful against his throat. She unfastened the top two buttons of his shirt and nuzzled against his chest. "Mm, I love the way you smell, Seth—all you and nothing clouding it."

"Faye," he growled, "what are you doing to me?"

She drew away and stood up, pulling him with her. "Come with me, Seth," she urged softly. "I want you to make love to me again. I want us to make love in a real bed."

They stopped in the doorway to kiss, his arms holding her tight. "Didn't you like that nice cool grass and the wind in your hair?" he teased her, reaching up to brush the stray wisp from her cheek. "Didn't you like the moonlight?"

"I loved it!" she cried. "But it was like a dream, like quicksilver rushing through my fingertips. I want—I need—something more solid, more real this time, Seth. Don't you see?"

As she spoke she took a step back into the tiny bedroom. His old double bed with its faded chenille spread practically filled the whole space. With a secret smile she pulled her yellow sweater up over her head. She unbuttoned her skirt and slipped it down over her hips, feeling the warm sun on her bare legs as it poured through the open window.

Stunned, Seth watched her every motion. She hung her clothes over the hook on the wall as if she'd done it a thousand times before, as if they'd lived together in another lifetime and were simply picking up where they had left off.

The unaccustomed intimacy of the moment, the very familiarity of it, disconcerted him. He half expected her to mention some problem with the kids or the mortgage payment, as if countless invisible filaments of daily life already bound them. And yet the sight of her there near his bed, naked but for the little-nothing wisps of lace, excited him to the marrow. Never had he desired a woman so desperately, a woman who had come to be so many contradictory things to him—friend and lover, testy adversary and exciting stranger.

Her big hazel eyes, vital and full of life, lifted to his.

In two swift strides he was beside her, his arms around her. "God, but you're beautiful, Faye," he said huskily. "So tiny and fragile looking—like a doe in the woods."

She reveled in the worship in his eyes, her expression at once glowing and impish as she reached up to unbutton his shirt and unfasten his jeans with impatient fingers.

When she had finished undressing him, he pulled her down beside him onto the bed. How good her bare skin felt against his, he thought exultantly. It was so warm and silky. But when she reached up to caress his chest he felt the rough calluses on her hand. He lifted her fingertips to his lips and kissed them. Then he kissed the short unvarnished nails.

"What happened to those long fancy red nails of yours?"

She laughed softly, delighting in the pressure of his lips against her fingers. "They matched the Alfa. I guess once it went, they had to go too. Now it's just the natural me and nothing else." She hesitated. "Are you disappointed?"

"You kidding?" he breathed and bent his head, his warm breath tickling the gentle swell of her breasts above the wispy bra.

"Oh," she whispered, running her fingers through his hair and down over his cheeks to touch his lips.

He unclasped the bra and lazily his fingers circled her breasts, letting one thumb occasionally flicker across the tips until they grew erect and she moaned softly again.

Her nipples were the color of wine and, as he bent to taste them, a thrill of intoxication swept through him. He felt out of control. Instinct and emotion had taken over from practicality and reason, and he was powerless to right the balance. He was drunk on her sensual vitality.

He fingered the sleek golden down bisecting her belly, all the way to the wisp of cloth at her hips. He traced the outline of the lacy garment against her skin. His fingers slipped beneath the lace to tangle in the springy fluff of her maidenhair, and he felt the soft flesh beneath quivering in response to his touch.

She began to move against his hand, excited by his tentative touch, inviting his deeper exploration. Ever so gently he responded until she writhed with pleasure, and his skilled fingers touched off a shower of tiny explosions deep inside her. She moaned again, feeling as she had that night in the fields, wholly open and vulnerable to him.

Still hungry for the touch of her, Seth's hand moved down her bare legs, molding the subtle swell of hip and the strong curves of her calf muscle. He bent his head again to taste her skin; she smelled faintly of vanilla and cocoa. He imagined white chocolate in a pool of sunlight, slowly melting beneath the warmth of his caresses, and he felt himself melting into her until it was impossible to tell where his flesh ended and hers began.

Gently he pulled her on top of him until she sat astride his thighs, her breasts tilting high and proud, her belly smooth and slightly rounded the way a woman's belly should be. He wanted to hold her in his vision like that while she made love to him.

He groaned as she drew him into her. Faye loved the feel of him inside her, pulsating. And his strength imbued her, making them one. She moved slowly at first, savoring the warmth and power of their joined bodies and then began to move at a more fevered pace, drawing him ever deeper.

"Faye, Faye." Hoarsely he murmured the word over and over again. It was half praise, half curse, as if he knew he was lost to her enchantment, ensnared against his will by the sheer power and beauty of her womanliness.

Her eyes swept down over him, and she watched the flush of sexual excitement spread across his chest—a dark wave of fire. She touched his shoulders and his chest. They were hot. Perspiration covered them both, so that their bodies moved against each other like water-slicked soap. Now the sense of his excitement filled her, drove her on until the rhythmic slap of her hips against his matched the quick feverish breaths escaping her lips.

They peaked together, earth and sun colliding, annihilating their individual natures. Out of their union came something new and unified, stronger than its parts. And Faye knew she would not be easily torn apart from him again.

With a final shuddering gasp she arched back, her face turned up toward the sunlight. And when she looked down at him again, their eyes met and dissolved into each other's as their bodies had done.

Seth's fingers closed around her upper arms and he pulled her down to kiss her between her breasts. "Where'd you learn to love like that?"

"Just took the right man."

Smiling lazily, Seth pulled her down to cuddle against him. She nestled her head against his shoulder, exulting in the way their limbs twined together so naturally. She sensed him drifting off to sleep and began to run her hand across his belly and down his thighs, her fingers tracing curlicues in the light matting of body hair.

"Hey," she whispered, biting gently on his earlobe, "don't go to sleep on me. Men never do in books. Talk to me a bit, Seth."

Responding to her touch, Seth stirred and cupped his hand around her warm breast. "Talk about what?"

"About us." Her feathery touch was a coaxing bribe to keep him listening, her caresses as slow and gentle as her voice.

In answer, his thumb stroked enticingly over her nipple and she reveled in this quiet intimacy that was the aftermath of their lovemaking. She knew with a certainty beyond thought that she wanted it always to be that way.

"Seth . . ."

"What about us?" he asked drowsily.

"Seth, I said it before," she whispered. "You are an extraordinarily special person. I—I've never said this to a man before. I think I love you." He stirred lazily, and she bent to kiss his closed eyelids. "In fact, I couldn't imagine spending the rest of my life with anyone else. Seth, I've decided I want to marry you. There's nothing else in the world I want more. Seth, sweetheart," she said, her voice rising on a faint questioning note, "did you hear what I said? I'm asking you to marry me."

His eyes flickered wide open in astonishment, and for a timeless instant they stared at each other nose to nose. Her words finally sank in, and Seth moved as suddenly as if someone had stuck him with a cattle prod, giving him a wild and totally unexpected jolt. He pulled himself up with such abruptness that Faye was dumped accidentally onto the floor.

She got up to her knees and leaned her elbows on the edge of the bed. "You're dangerous," she fumed. "Now I know what a fighter pilot must feel like when he ejects."

Still reeling from shock, he asked shakily, "Faye, did you say what I thought you just said?"

"Stop being so dense," she replied, her annoyance a cover for the nervousness beginning to churn up her stomach. "You know I'm the type who believes in taking the bull by the horns. I don't care how darn different we are. These past weeks I've begun to realize I couldn't imagine spending my life with any other man but you."

"Holy hell!" His frustrated tone scared her a little bit. She had laid bare her most tender secret emotions. She had confessed something that under ordinary circumstances wild horses couldn't have dragged from her. And in return she had expected at least a modicum of tenderness, an acknowledgment of a special shared feeling between them. She hadn't expected this . . . this disgust.

Yet it was too late to retreat. What she had begun she had to finish. "Seth, you can't tell me you didn't feel it, too—the change that's been coming over us. You're special to me," she whispered, as if saying the words again could make them true and meaningful in his eyes. "What do you think I do—fall in bed with any man I happen to meet?"

"Hell, I don't know!"

"What do you mean you don't know! Seth, you made it all feel right. You made me feel good about myself, about you and me together. It's a terrific feeling. You can't deny you didn't feel it, too."

"I can't deny it; you're right," he said, not quite looking at her. "What you just said I agree with one hundred percent."

"Good," she said, relief flooding through her. "Then marry me. We're already business partners, after all. A wedding would be the natural next step."

"Faye, Faye, stop. Please." Though he spoke more gently now, his voice was still chiding, as if she'd done something wrong. "Faye, I thought this whole thing was a fun, exciting game for you. I thought for sure you'd be headin' back to California once you'd proved your point—that you couldn't be pushed around by Pettigrew and his bank. Dammit," he said more forcefully, "you told me yourself you were a loner who didn't need anybody—least of all a man."

"A woman's got a right to change her mind." The words choked in her throat, but she was damned if she would cry in front of him. She'd revealed enough of her soul to him. She wasn't about to let him stomp on the rest.

"Faye, I'm sorry," he said at last. But the apology had come far too late. She already knew what he really felt—

not regret or pain but only disgust and irritation that she should want to invade his life! "You know, I'm not interested in permanent ties. I don't want a wife. Never have, probably never will. My life's just fine the way it is."

"You're turning your back on a mighty good thing, Seth Carradine," she said proudly, though tears were stinging the back of her throat. "You're going to feel real sorry if I marry somebody else."

"No, I won't," he promised, trying to tease her into smiling. "In fact, I'll even give you away."

"Thanks," she snapped, her eyes flashing. "And I suppose a bouquet of bachelor's buttons is next on your agenda for the lady." She was almost grateful now that he'd said something to make her so damned angry. For a second it helped dim the overwhelming sense of humiliation and rejection, the sense of loss.

With an air of majesty she pulled the chenille coverlet from the bed and wrapped it around her body before standing up. She had stood before him once, naked and vulnerable, offering herself to him body and soul. She wouldn't make the same mistake again.

"Faye," he called to her as she grabbed her clothes from the hook. "You know we had a pretty good thing going between us. Now I don't want you to go."

Her head snapped around. "But you don't want me to stay, either."

Tension charged the moment. He sensed the question in her voice; he knew she was poised to run back into his arms if he would somehow make it right between them. But it was impossible.

"I'm sorry, Hundred Pounds," he said now with genuine regret. "You knew what I was like."

SETH WINCED when the front door slammed.

"Hell, what was I apologizing for?" he groused to himself. Angrily he got up and dragged on his jeans.

He felt as if he'd somehow been tricked by Faye. He had been so sure she was somebody just like him—a good-time Charlie who wasn't interested in commitments. Then all of a sudden in midstream she had turned the rules upside down.

Even when she was doing all the talking about staying on at the farm, he'd figured it was just talk, that she was the type who'd move on after a while. How could he have misread her so badly? And what the hell had happened to his infallible weasel instincts? Usually he managed to extricate himself from a sticky situation like this long before they had a chance to develop. For an instant he wondered if he hadn't let it happen because deep down he might have half wanted the same thing she did. Before the idea could even form itself clearly in his mind, he brushed it aside. That was crazy!

Still he realized he hadn't thought all that much about his life once Faye was no longer there. Sure, he enjoyed needling her about the day Indian Creek'd be his and he could move into that big beautiful farmhouse. That was just part of their dynamics together, the fun of keeping the other on edge. Hell, she was as much an irritant to him as he was to her. But she was a delight, too, he thought, idly rubbing his hands over his chest, remembering the way she'd caressed him. And a woman constantly full of surprises. With a will, he shook off the delightful haze her memory evoked.

And what if she did stay in Lexington—then what?

A thought struck him. What if she turned that cocky kitten charm on Barry Markham, just to get even? Markham'd fall like a ton of bricks. "As if I'd care," he grumbled aloud. "The damn fool'd be doing me a favor."

Then Seth realized he was lying to himself. He knew he'd rather see Faye move on than settle down with Barry. He might not want her, but he couldn't stand the thought of her in any other man's arms, either.

"Hell, now I'm jealous, to boot," he said in aggravation, feeling himself getting madder by the second, mad at Faye for putting him in this spot and mad at himself for being so riled by it.

For one insane second he was even tempted to sabotage Sinbad in the next race himself. A little tranquilizer in a sugar cube and it'd be all over for Faye here. She'd be forced to sell out and he'd get the farm. But his conscience quickly smote him. "Don't be such a dumb-ass skulking fool," he chided himself.

He decided he'd just have to be tough and face up to her. No woman was going to get the better of him!

FAYE STOMPED OFF across the fields, giving free rein at last to her tears. They erupted in great gulping sobs. Oh Lord, she'd never felt so hurt in her whole life. So bitter. What on earth had ever made her bare herself like that to him? Had everything she felt been a lie?

She wondered how she could possibly face him again. She had made such a colossal fool of herself. And yet she realized she couldn't have done it any differently. Dear God, how she'd felt in his arms. How deeply she'd wanted to give, to share everything she had with him—her life, her emotions, even the farm they'd been squabbling over like children with a new toy ever since they had met. Now it all tasted like ashes in her mouth. She wanted to run as far away as she could, to forget all the disappointment and hurt he'd caused her.

She would prove her point and then get out. If Seth Carradine wanted Indian Creek Farm she would make him pay through the nose for it, she vowed, her bitterness deepening with each step she took. She let it fester, using the bitter anger to mask the hurt, the awful aloneness buried deeper.

Should she call Harve, admit to him she had been living in a dreamworld, and beg for her old job back?

No! That life had palled. No matter what, she knew she couldn't go back to her old life-style, working long hours and rehashing the day's events over happy-hour hors d'oeuvres with her colleagues, going home night after night to an empty studio apartment. These past weeks in Lexington had changed Faye irreparably. She wanted something deeper, more lasting, even if Seth wasn't the man capable of sharing those hungers and satisfying them.

"To hell with him!" she swore, swallowing the last hiccuping sob and wiping her nose on the back of her hand. "No man's going to get the better of me."

She slid under the fence rail, and as she straightened, her eyes were drawn to the barn. Cal Darby and his men had nearly finished the remodeling job. The structure gleamed in its new coat of traditional red paint. Faye slid open the rear doors and stepped inside. It smelled of unfinished wood and varnish, crisp clean odors of newness and promise for the future. With a deep sigh she leaned back against one of the posts, wondering what to do.

Somehow the air of stability and permanence inside the remodeled barn reminded her of Barry. She pictured him that day after she'd visited him at Oak Hill, so dissatisfied with his life and yet so devoted to his son. He had grown into a disciplined, complex, sensitive man, a man she respected and cared for. She wasn't in love with him, but then maybe that didn't matter. He would never hurt her, never tear her apart emotionally.

She smiled a little, remembering his impetuous proposal. The three of them would fly off to another continent, living the life he'd always dreamed of.

The notion was tempting now to Faye, very tempting. Impatiently she brushed aside the memory of what Harve had said to her on the phone the day she had moved back into Courtney's home. *"You set yourself up for this kind of scenario so you have an excuse to run away."*

But I won't be running away, she insisted to herself. *I'd be able to have my cake and eat it, too—a footloose lifestyle and permanence, as well, and a ready-made family in Barry and Corky.*

So tempting.

Faye went outside again, firmly sliding the door shut behind her. Her gaze swept over the land that had been the Hunts' for countless generations. And she thought of Seth again—so hungry for what Indian Creek represented.

She realized that more than running away, she wanted to hurt him, to get back at him for his coldhearted rejection. And instinctively she knew what the best revenge was.

She would build up a farm that surpassed his piddly spread. She would show him what a woman scorned was capable of.

CHAPTER EIGHTEEN

FAYE FELT LIKE the cartoon character on the ice floe again, being pulled crazily in opposite directions. Tommy was badgering her to join him at the upcoming horse sale at Kennington. He was eager for them to invest more money in another promising colt. ''Who knows, maybe we'll find ourselves a Derby contender,'' he'd said, stars in his eyes, and Faye had been mightily tempted by his dreams. If she could build up Indian Creek into the best little horse farm in the Bluegrass, she would feel vindicated. She'd show Seth, show them all.

And then there was Barry, sensing something had happened to deeply upset her, and gently urging Faye to reconsider his proposal. But she needed time. Time to think, to deal with the loose ends of her life. Time to decide what she really wanted.

To escape them all, Faye climbed into her old clunker and drove over to the Kentucky Horse Farm. She'd lose herself for a while in the hundreds of tourists paying five dollars a head for the thrill of getting nose to nose with legendary Bluegrass horses. There were acres of fields and barns to explore, a museum and an art gallery, a walking tour.

As she strolled through the grounds, munching on popcorn, a fanfare of trumpets sounded. She looked around and saw a stream of people heading up toward the stable area. Having nothing better to do, she fell in with the crowd, letting them jostle her along.

People filed into the small grandstand, cameras bouncing against their chests as they settled down for the show.

"What's going on, anyway?" Faye asked the family beside her.

"Parade of Breeds Show. Starts in ten minutes. Folks say it's real colorful."

Instead of climbing up into the stands, Faye wandered down toward the corral, debating whether to stick around for the show. A young girl in jeans and plaid shirt worked busily inside the fenced area, raking the sawdust into a neat smooth surface.

The murmur of the crowd and bustle of activity, the aroma of popcorn and hot dogs reminded Faye of a country circus. She would have loved this if she'd been ten years old again. She could almost hear herself badgering her dad to buy her a pony, telling him in all sincerity that she would join the circus when she grew up. She remembered the feel of his warm hand on her head, ruffling her hair, and his nickname for her. *"My little vagabond,"* he used to call her. And Faye heard herself shrilly piping back, *"Just like you, Daddy,"* making his disciplined features relax in a slight smile. She had a thousand little memories like that of her father, and none really of her mother, a woman who had died when Faye was barely four years old. She found herself wondering what her mother had been like, how Faye herself might have been a different woman if she'd had that feminine influence in her life. Less cocky, less argumentative, less stubborn, maybe?

"Hey, Miz Hunt!" Faye was jostled out of her reveries by a shrill little voice at her side.

"Corky!" she exclaimed, laughing and automatically looking around to find Barry. "Where's your daddy?"

"At home." He made a face. "Workin'."

"Too bad. You're going to have to tell him he missed one exciting show."

"Yeah, but . . . but he's got work. He says the quicker he gets done the quicker we can leave on our trip."

"That's right," Faye agreed. "It's going to be so exciting crossing the ocean in the Concorde. I bet not too many of your friends have done that."

"No!" His little chest puffed out proudly. "We're gonna . . . we're gonna fly over the Atlantic . . . Atalanatic Ocean in the fastest jet there is, my daddy says."

"Corky!" a woman's voice called out, and they both turned. Faye eyed her curiously. Long shiny brown hair falling loosely to her waist made her look very young. But what Faye noticed most were her eyes, a brilliant blue full of restless life. "Corky, darn it, you're too quick for me. I'm goin' to be worn out before this day's half over." The petulant complaint was softened by the hand she placed on his head, at once protective and possessive.

Faye met the woman's questioning look with a friendly smile. "Hi, I'm Faye Hunt, an old friend of Barry's."

The woman nodded slightly. "I'm Belinda Nichols, Corky's mama. Now come on, Corky," she said, having nothing more to say to Faye, "let's go sit up in the stands. It's goin' to be too warm and smelly down here by the corral."

"Let me stay here with Miz Hunt, Mama, so I can . . . so I can see everything." His voice rose excitedly.

"No, Corky."

"Come on, Mama," he wheedled. "Daddy woulda let me, I jus' know it."

"I'm *not* your daddy."

Corky clung mutinously to the fence, an inch away from causing a scene. Faye sensed what was going on; without realizing it himself, Corky was punishing his mother. Impulsively Faye stooped down to talk to him. "You know, I think your mama's right. You'll get a great overview from the top. See all the horses and riders come in," she said with infectious enthusiasm.

"Yeah?" His interest was aroused.

"Yeah. You can pretend you're an old king reviewing his soldiers."

Convinced, he smiled broadly and let his mother take his hands from the fence. But when he realized Faye wasn't following he turned back to her. "Aren't you comin', too?"

"I don't think so."

"Aw, please, Miz Hunt!"

"You'd better, Miz Hunt," Belinda mimicked lightly. "I'm gettin' tired of fightin' him."

So Faye followed them up into the shaded grandstand, wondering what on earth she should say to Barry's ex-wife. But her concern was unfounded because a Sousa march blared over the loudspeakers just as they settled onto the crowded bench. The music was followed by a chirpy announcer's greeting to the waiting spectators.

The show was fast-paced and colorful. A veiled girl in silky harem pants galloped into the arena, her Arabian steed performing in time to the keening Middle Eastern music. She was followed smartly by another rider in gaucho pants and a flat, black-brimmed hat. Cameras clicked, and Corky squirmed with excitement in his seat, pointing every time another differently costumed horse and rider appeared.

As the music finally faded and the last mount paraded out of the arena, Corky turned to his mother with a happy sigh. "Am I . . am I gonna see them in England, Mama? Just like that?" he demanded, eyes sparkling.

"I don't know, Corky." Belinda's eyes met Faye's as the boy squeezed ahead of them to race down the grandstand stairs and get a last peek at the brightly decked-out horses being led back to their stables. "I think he's much too young for a trip like that," she said half to herself and half to Faye.

"It's hard to say," Faye replied. "I think kids remember more than we think. He's certainly having a good time anticipating his adventure."

"Adventure!" Her remarkable eyes flashed. "When I called to tell Barry I was picking up Corky for the day, he told me he was thinking of working overseas and taking *my* son with him."

When Faye didn't say anything, Belinda smiled sheepishly. "Real smart of me, isn't it, to go spoutin' off to a friend of Barry's." She eyed Faye with more interest now. "You datin' my ex?"

"We dated in high school," Faye parried. "I haven't been back to Kentucky in years. I'm just here to take care of some personal business, then I looked up Barry for old time's sake." She smiled. "I was surprised to find out he was a father."

"Guess bein' parents kind of snuck up on us both," Belinda said, more friendly now. "I was only twenty-one."

"I can imagine how you felt."

Belinda laughed, though her eyes had an angry look. "Maybe you could. If you dated Barry, you must've tangled with his mother a time or two."

"She didn't like me," Faye confessed, her answering smile rueful.

"You were problably better off," Belinda said feelingly. "She did like me—at first. Then it all went to hell."

"I'm sorry."

"Don't be," she said shortly. "I gave it my best shot. I tried to do things Siperia's way—joinin' committees and plannin' big dinners at the house with her. Tried to be the perfect little wife and daughter-in-law—" She broke off when they reached the bottom of the stairs, her eyes restlessly scanning the crowd until she located her son.

Sensing Belinda's pent-up bitterness, Faye groped for words to make her feel a little better. "At least you got Corky out of it. He's something special."

"Want to walk along with us?" Belinda invited, her manner softening in the glow of Faye's sympathy. "Corky seems to think you're pretty special, too."

"I like Corky. Barry's doing a terrific job raising him."

Belinda shot her a quick look from beneath thick lashes, as if trying to divine whether there was implied criticism in the remark. Apparently encouraged by what she read in Faye's open, honest features, Belinda confessed tightly, "To tell you the truth, I don't think I was ready to be a mother. My dream was to be a country music singer."

"Couldn't you do both?"

Belinda tossed her long beautiful hair. "I tried. I even got myself a job singin' in the lounge at Campbell House Inn. But Siperia put a stop to that," she said bitterly. "She knew the owner and put pressure on him until he fired me."

"How rotten."

"She must've thought my havin' the baby would settle me down. Maybe it would've if they'd've let me alone with my son. But no, she had to hire a nurse to make sure Corky was taken care of properly." The bitterness in her voice deepened. "It was like Barry was never really mine, and neither was my own son. They both belonged to Siperia. All I had of my own was my music."

"It must have hurt Barry terribly when you left."

"I don't know. Sometimes I used to think he only married me because his mother thought it would be a good match."

"You wouldn't say that if you'd heard his voice when he told me about the divorce," Faye told her quietly. "It's just too bad you couldn't have waited around for Barry to grow up, for him to realize he didn't have to stay tied to Siperia's apron strings out of some misguided sense of duty."

Belinda shot her an impatient look. "I'd had it with him and the whole Markham clan. I ran as hard and fast as I could."

"To Nashville?"

"He told you," she said flatly. "Yes, that's right. I found an agent. Wound up marrying him." She shot Faye another expressive look, at once wry and wise. "Life's ironic, isn't it? It's like gettin' to sing has somehow settled me down. I'm even thinkin' of goin' to court to ask for joint custody of Corky." She shook her head. "I just don't like Barry's ideas of livin' overseas, draggin' Corky from pillar to post."

Faye looked at her in surprise. Saying that, Belinda had sounded just like Siperia when she had criticized Faye's "army brat" life-style.

The intimate exchange between the two women broke off as Corky rushed back to them excitedly, bubbling with news of the horses and how they were being "undressed" in the stables.

"Come on, mama," he cried, tugging at Belinda's arm. "I want you to see."

"Okay, okay," she said, obviously trying hard to be patient with him. "You go on ahead. I'll be there in a second."

The two women looked at each other in silence. Finally it was Belinda who spoke. "Funny isn't it, how you can sometimes talk to a stranger more easily than to anyone else.''

Faye smiled. ''Do you want me to mention to Barry that I ran into you?''

''My talkative little son'll probably take care of that!''

''Mm, I forgot about him!'' Faye's amused laughter died away. ''Would you rather I not say anything about what we discussed?''

''I don't care. I'm probably goin' to talk to Barry tonight when I bring Corky back. I don't even like the idea of him taking Corky on a trip overseas, let alone livin' there.''

''It's difficult.''

''We'll work it out.'' Belinda half turned as Corky called her again. ''Well, goodbye. It was nice talkin' to you.''

''Bye.'' Faye watched her hurrying away to join her son and suddenly felt sorry for Barry. He had been so intent on making the break from Oak Hill for his son's sake, and now here came his ex-wife threatening to prevent his escape, to confine him to the life that had become so abhorrent to him. But maybe he could talk Belinda around; maybe he would be able to convince her it would be far better to raise their son outside the sphere of Siperia's influence.

As she made her way back to the parking lot, Faye remembered something Siperia had said to her. The woman had been afraid Faye would lure her son into managing Indian Creek Farm. Faye toyed with the idea for a minute. It would certainly have been a way for Barry to escape Oak Hill, to be his own man in charge of his own operation. But Faye shook her head; she simply couldn't picture Barry at Indian Creek. Far more easily could she picture him in elegant European drawing rooms. His easygoing charm and temperate nature would make him a diplomat. She imagined him rising quickly in the ranks, coming to terms with himself in that milieu.

How strange that Faye had come back into his life at the point when he was ready to make such dramatic changes—a man hankering for freedom just when such freedom had begun to pall for Faye. That was part of what had prompted her crazy impetuous marriage proposal to Seth. She had begun to hanker for roots, for permanence. A family of her own.

To hell with him, she cursed Seth for the millionth time. *If I want it, I can have it without him.* The anger felt good. It drowned out the dull ache of pain.

STILL, THE LAST THING she needed was to see Seth's truck parked in front of the barn when she drove up.

He climbed out of the cab and strode over, yanking open her door. "It's no use in our feuding," he began as if he'd been rehearsing the words a thousand times. "Emotions get in the way of practicality."

"What are you talking about?" she snapped.

"I'm talking about this here barn we put up together. You need the rent money, I need the space. I'm going to bring in eleven of my horses."

"No, you're not," she said, wishing she could just tell him to go to hell and be done with it. But he was right; it simply wouldn't be practical. "You can only have ten stalls. I'm keeping one for Sinbad and one for the new colt Tommy and I are going to buy out at Kennington."

"What colt?"

"You think I'd tell you?" she retorted. "Next thing I know you'd be outbidding us."

He let that one go. "All right, is it settled then about the barn? How do you want payment?"

"How about in blood?"

He let that one pass, too. "Come on, Fayette, just give me a straight answer so I can get out of here."

"I'll give you the spaces rent free," she said stiffly, not daring to let him see she'd been cut to the quick by his eagerness to be gone. "It'll be part of what I owe you."

"What about the rest of that loan?"

"You'll have it back within nine months. I'm going to use some of it to plant tobacco on a couple of acres."

"You're stayin', then," he said flatly. And when she didn't reply, he went on in the same dead tone, "I been hearing rumors about you and Markham."

"What of it?" she flung back, her jaw thrust out.

"Nothing. It just seems to me that one way or another you're goin' to lose this place," he said cruelly. "So why don't we just make a deal right now—fair and square? I'm damned tired of you keeping me on tenterhooks while you play games decidin' what to do with the rest of your life."

"Keep pressing me, Carradine," she said, her expression fierce. "Keep pressing and you'll be looking out at this farm for the rest of your life, not an inch closer to having it." She was just warming up now. "Maybe I'll even expand," she went on arrogantly. "Maybe I'll buy back that one hundred acres you got under the table. Maybe I'll go after the rest of your spread. Now wouldn't that be ironic—to see you pushed out on the road again, Carradine?"

Seth shrugged, determined not to show his dismay. He should have known she was mean and stubborn enough to dig in for the fight. He should have known.

Faye watched him stomp off to his truck and roar away, restraining the childish impulse to pick up some dirt and throw it after him. After he'd disappeared around the bend in the driveway, she picked some up and threw it, anyway.

CHAPTER NINETEEN

FAYE AND TOMMY sat together at the back of the auditorium, their heads bent over the sales catalog as they compared the trainer's scribbled notes with the prices the stock was selling for. He nudged her arm when the door opened and another young horse was led out into the sawdust-covered arena beneath the auctioneer's stand.

The auctioneer launched into his pitch, smoothly helping things along whenever the bidding started to falter. "Five, five. FivefivedoIhearsix?" A quick breath and then, "DoIhearsixthousand for this good-lookin' filly out of Denver Dust. Six, six . . . six, five . . ."

Faye's eyelids drooped, and immediately visions of horses' rumps and cannon bones, great liquid eyes and big horsey teeth danced in her brain. They'd been at the Kennington sales since early morning, tramping from stall to stall to view the merchandise up close before the bidding began that evening. Tommy was looking for possible bargains, and Faye had gotten her first in-depth lesson in Thoroughbred conformation, learning to recognize the signs of potential problems, as well as those of potential greatness in the horses.

They had asked to see at least two dozen horses, and dutifully she had mimicked Tommy's every move in examining the animals. She had felt their cannon bones and tried to look professional when she bent back the knees to check for flexibility, all the while praying she wouldn't get kicked for her pains. She had confronted two dozen gleaming rumps and had watched them move away from her as she observed the animals' walking gaits. Balance, Tommy had reiterated tirelessly, and straight legs. "You gotta feel the movement of 'em."

Now all she felt was tired, and the auctioneer's raspy drone was making her very thirsty.

"Tommy, I'm going up to the bar to get a Coke," she said, stretching and standing up. "Want me to bring you one?"

"Sure, but hurry back. Number 117 is comin' up quick. You wanted to try your hand at biddin', didn't you?"

She nodded with more enthusiasm. "I'll be right back."

She had just put her foot on the first step of the staircase when she heard a familiar voice floating down to her, low and lazily amused. Her first impulse was to turn and walk quickly away, but she steeled herself to keep climbing. She couldn't spend the rest of her life trying to avoid him.

By the time they met halfway, she had a bright smile stuck on her face. Seth, taken by surprise, looked shaken for an instant before he recovered.

"You go on ahead, Joe," he said distractedly to his companion. "I'll meet you down there."

"Hi, Seth," she greeted him coolly. "You here to sell or buy?"

"A little of both." The look he gave her was wary. "How about you?"

"Oh, Tommy and I are definitely buying," she said, cocky as hell. And then her smile became genuine when she realized the effect her next pronouncement would have on him. "I just got word that my condo back in San Francisco sold."

"Good," he said, his expression flat. "Now maybe you can pay off the rest of that personal loan right away, instead of making me wait."

"Don't worry, you'll get every cent back. With interest," she said, bristling. "I've got enough to build up a pretty nice stable now. I may have a lot to learn about this business, but I'm determined to make a go of it," she told him, giving him a long look, the meaning of which he couldn't mistake. *No one's going to chase Faye Hunt off.*

With a curt nod he stomped down the stairs and out the front door, not bothering to stay to see how much his horse would sell for at auction.

Faye half turned to watch him leave, feeling all the fight go out of her. She wondered if every time she bumped into him now she would feel this emotionally drained. Surely after a while she would be able to forget the effect he'd once had on her, forget the loving warmth that had blossomed so briefly between them. Wouldn't she?

She went into the lounge, a big, dim, smoky room, and nudged her way through the three-deep crowd to the counter. While she waited to order, Faye glanced idly down the length of the curving bar. Her eyes zeroed in on a face. She did a quick double take, feeling the hair rising on the back of her neck. It was him, all right. The voice on the phone, the skulking deliveryman, the elusive figure at the track. Shaking a little, she turned and fought her way back to the outer rim of the milling crowd.

She stood there, trying desperately to think. What should she do now—march over to confront him? Or just hang around, hoping to pick up a clue? Surely he hadn't been acting on his own—sending dead flowers, setting fires. He had to be somebody's henchman.

Faye started getting angry as she remembered all the threats against her, and anger gave her courage. Courage and cunning.

Using the crowd as a shield she moved down the length of the bar until she was only a few feet away from her quarry. A tall broad-shouldered man stood directly in front of her. She tapped him on the shoulder.

"Excuse me, mister, do you think you could fight your way up to the bar to get me an ashtray?" She smiled winningly up at him. "I'm afraid I'll get crushed in there."

"Sure thing, little lady."

The big man parted the crowd as if it were the Red Sea, and Faye was right behind him, peering under his arm. She glimpsed her quarry, not a foot away, deep in conversation with a couple of other guys at the bar. They were all dressed in the same gray shirts and slacks, some sort of uniform, with an insignia above the pockets.

As her friend leaned across the bar to get the ashtray, she leaned forward, too, keeping out of sight while she desperately tried to read the initials on their shirts. Finally she made out the highly stylized letters: BH.

Faye felt the color draining from her cheeks as the big man turned around to hand her the ashtray. "Say, little lady, you okay?" he asked.

"I'm...I'm fine. Just trying to quit smoking," she ad-libbed, backing away. "But you know how hard that can be."

She hurried outside, suddenly feeling choked by the atmosphere inside the bar. But it wasn't the jammed bodies and the smoke that had upset her so. The implications of what she had just discovered washed over her.

She had seen those stylized letters once before, when she'd gone calling. BH stood for Boar's Head Farm—and Laura Bell Wainbridge. Faye shivered as the image of an industrious black widow spider weaving busily away crept into her mind. She remembered the woman's ill-concealed hostility toward her, and over and over again asked herself, "Why?"

Faye went back down to join Tommy, but her interest in the sale had evaporated. She barely heard his teasing reprimand that she'd missed their horse, his glee at getting them the good-looking colt for far less than it was worth.

In a fog she dropped Tommy off at his place. Around the corner she pulled over to think. One thing she had to do was pay a long-overdue visit to Minah Willis. The psychological puzzle she had once thought interesting but unimportant had suddenly become vital for her to solve.

"MY LAND, CHILE. Come in, come in!" Minah opened the door to greet Faye warmly. "Can I fix you some tea?"

"No thanks, Minah. I . . . I just needed to talk to you for a bit."

The black woman's eyes narrowed. "Now, sit right down in the parlor. You look like you had a fright."

"I'm okay." Faye rubbed her arms, and then blurted out as she sat down, "Minah, does Laura Wainbridge have any reason to hate me, to hate Courtney? Hate us enough to want to destroy everything Courtney lived for?"

"Dear Lord in heaven, what's happened, Miz Fayette?" Minah demanded, her whole manner agitated as she sat down beside Faye and took her hand.

Taking a deep breath, Faye launched into a terse account of the escalating acts of sabotage against Indian Creek.

Minah listened intently, her expression getting grimmer by the minute. "And you think Miz Laura Bell's responsible?"

"Minah, I know the features of the guy who delivered the ugly threats. I saw him. He had on a Boar's Head stable uniform. He works for Laura Bell Wainbridge. I mean, do you thinks it's coincidence?"

Minah rubbed a hand over her forehead, and Faye noticed it was shaking slightly. "I don't know what to think, chile. I can't believe..."

"Minah, what happened between Courtney and Laura Bell?"

The woman sighed. "Remember I tole you once that Miz Laura Bell's younger brother Mr. Quentin was in love with your gran?"

"Yes?"

"Well, Courtney hurt him. She hurt him real bad."

"But that was a lifetime ago," Faye protested. "What could that possibly have to do with me, with Indian Creek?"

"Miz Laura Bell was always a funny woman—a little twisted inside. Once she took a notion, why, I believe she wouldn't let go. Like an ornery dog worryin' a bone. She's not a one to let go easily."

"It still isn't making much sense to me. How did Courtney hurt Quentin? People survive emotional hurts. They..." Faye swallowed hard, wondering if it were true. "They get over them."

"Not in Mr. Quentin's case. Like I tole you, he was a reckless boy. But for all his wild ways, Miz Laura Bell adored him. She hoped Courtney'd marry him and bring him around. Make a man out of him."

"But it didn't happen."

Minah looked troubled. "No matter what she says, it wasn't Miz Courtney's fault. It wasn't her responsibility."

"What wasn't her fault?"

Minah shook her head. "The past is dead and long buried, Miz Fayette. Why she had to go stirrin' up trouble for you—I have half a mind to call up and lay into that woman!"

"No, Minah, please don't. I'd like to handle this my own way." Faye stood up.

"You be careful now."

Faye leaned down to kiss her cheek. "I can take care of myself."

"I believe you can. I believe you can, chile."

"Good night, Minah. I'm sorry to have upset you."

"Never you mind. I'm jus' glad you confided in me."

Faye drove away from the little shotgun cabin, her thoughts awhirl. What had Minah meant—that it hadn't been Courtney's fault? She didn't have the time to puzzle that out now. Faye felt the burning need to act. And the first thing she decided to do was enlist Parris Harper's help. Before she could formulate some plan of action she really needed independent confirmation of her suspicions about Laura Wainbridge.

THE LIGHTS inside the pretty brick house on Fincannon Street were still on when Faye pulled into the driveway. She climbed out of the station wagon and rang the bell on the side door impatiently.

Parris, her hands clutching the top of her soft wool bathrobe, peered cautiously out the window. As soon as she recognized who it was, the door flew open.

"What's going on, Faye? It's after ten o'clock."

"Oh, is it that late?" she said distractedly. "I'm sorry."

"Come in," Parris said at once, pulling her friend by the arm. "You look upset. How about some tea?"

"Thanks."

Five minutes later the two women faced each other across the small butcher-block table, a steaming pot of herb tea set cozily between them.

"Okay, Faye, give. What's up?"

Faye bit her lip. "You're my friend, aren't you?"

"Of course."

"I need your help."

"Anything."

"I'd like you to make a play for Hollister Pettigrew."

Parris fell back against her chair and stared thunderstruck at Faye. "Are you out of your mind?"

"You did say you'd do anything," Faye reminded her.

"Will you please tell me what this is all about?"

Parris's eyes widened as she listened to what Faye had stumbled onto. "So, don't you see, Parris? Right now it's just a hunch. I talked to Gran's housekeeper, Minah, and she pretty much confirmed my suspicions. She's known Mrs. Wainbridge as long as anyone, and she seems to think the woman is capable of anything. Still, it's just my word against hers. I've got to know for sure if Laura Wainbridge is the one. And I'm betting that Pettigrew knows a lot more than he's letting on."

"But asking me to make a play for that self-righteous little hedgehog! Faye, you *are* pushing the limits of this friendship."

"You did promise," Faye reminded her, trying not to smile.

Parris sighed. "I can see someone's gotta do it, and I guess it might as well be me."

"Bless you, Parris. You're a doll."

"Now don't you worry." The redhead gave her a sultry wink. "Darling Holli will be putty in my little ole hands."

Faye laughed wryly. "Just don't turn him into mush. I want him to talk."

"And I'm such a fine listener," Parris drawled, laughing now, too.

Faye left in much better spirits than when she had arrived. For the first time she felt as if she were close to getting to the bottom of the ugly threats that had been making her life so tension filled. She was grateful for the promise of action. It was just what she needed to get her thoughts off her neighbor. "He's out of my life now," she said fiercely, only wishing she could believe it.

CHAPTER TWENTY

FAYE HAD GRAVE MISGIVINGS about racing Sinbad again.
Yet she couldn't convey them to Tommy without giving
away her suspicions about Laura Bell Wainbridge. She
had expressed her fears to no one but Minah and Parris.
She didn't dare let it go further than that without proof.
So Faye had to bide her time, to cultivate patience when
what she sorely needed was action.

She stood at the rail with Tommy, her hands clenched
tightly, and tried to brush away the sinking sensation of
déjà vu. Last time their hopes had risen so high, only to
be dashed to smithereens in the final seconds of the race.
She couldn't bear to watch it happen again. Despite the
trainer's assurance that nothing would go wrong this
time, Faye didn't believe it.

"You put the cotton in his ears?" she asked, nervousness making her words clipped.

"Yep."

"But what about the jockey?" she blurted. "How can
we trust him any more than that last jerk you hired?"

"Never you mind." Tommy smiled. "There ain't
gonna be no sabotage this time. I guarantee it."

"But if she, er, they offer him enough?"

"He knows they can't beat my counteroffer," Tommy
said mysteriously.

"What do you mean?"

His grin widened, but before she could press him for an explanation, the starting pistol cracked and the horses broke out of the gates in a thundering whoosh.

Faye closed her eyes. She felt as if the downhill ride on a particularly wild roller coaster had just begun and she had left her stomach somewhere back at the top.

"Why didn't I keep the condo?" She mumbled her cowardly litany. "Why didn't I listen to Harve? I'm going to lose everything."

"Come on, Sinbad!" Tommy was screaming at her side, oblivious to her loss of faith. "Come on, Jock, bring that beautiful baby home!"

Faye's eyes sprang open. "Jock? The guy's name is Jock? That sounds like an alias if I ever heard one, for Pete's sake. Are you crazy, Tommy?"

"Not Jock," he said distractedly, his eyes glued to the binoculars. "Wow, Sinbad took 'at last turn like a champ! You know, it's like 'zhock.'"

"Jacques. You mean he's French?" she asked in disbelief.

"French Canadian. Dependable kid. No, no, no, Jock!" he thundered, belying his own testimonial. "Don't let that cussed little worm trap you against the rail, dammit!"

"I can't look." Faye closed her eyes again. "I can't stand this horrible suspense."

The crowd in the stands began to scream until Faye felt as though she were being bowled over by the rising crescendo of sound. Yet distinctly, as if in a dream, she heard Tommy muttering beside her, "Ohmigod, I can't believe it."

Her eyes still shut tight, Faye let her shoulder slump against the rail. "I knew it, Tommy," she said disconsolately, "I knew we never should..."

But she never got the rest of the sentence out. Her breath escaped in a whoosh as Tommy scooped her up in a bear hug and swung her around. "That little sweetheart done it, Faye! We won!"

"You mean he finished in the money?" she demanded, once she'd gotten her breath back.

"Faye, I'm tellin' you, he took first!" Tommy whooped. "Sinbad was king out there today."

"Damn. I had my eyes closed," she confessed. "I missed the whole thing."

"Never mind—we'll watch a replay later in the clubhouse. Now come on," he laughed, dragging her by the arm, "we gotta go get our pictures took in the winner's circle. And you can congratulate that little fella you were so prejudiced against."

As soon as he saw Tommy the attractive dark-eyed jockey jumped down out of the saddle, and the two men embraced warmly. A chubby little blond woman, her hair caught back in a bouncy ponytail, detached herself from the milling crowd and flung herself on the two men.

Faye stepped back, bemused, wondering what on earth was going on. Tommy turned around, his broad face creased with merriment. "Now, Faye," he chided, "why're you hangin' back for? I want you to meet my daughter, Candy, and her fiancé, Jacques LaBelle."

Laughing with relief, Faye didn't hesitate a second in flinging her arms around the three of them. "Tommy, you sneak! Why didn't you tell me he was family? I could've been spared a lot of worry, darn you."

"Daddy just wanted to surprise you, Faye," Candy said happily. "Soon as he heard we were comin' to Lexington to visit, he got Jacques to promise to race."

"Well, I'm glad he did. Your fiancé is a terrific rider. I can't believe his performance out there today," Faye said with such conviction that no one would've guessed she'd missed the whole thing. Except Tommy, who gave her a broad, teasing wink.

"What do you say we all go have a drink to celebrate?" the trainer suggested.

"Maybe I'll join you three later," Faye demurred, not wanting to interfere in the little family get-together.

Slowly she made her way through the dispersing crowd as it moved en masse down toward the parking field beneath the trees. Sinbad had run in the last race of the day, but with summer fast approaching, the sun still rode high above the rolling Bluegrass hills.

Faye shoved her hands in her blazer pockets as she strolled along, in no hurry to get anywhere. She should have been elated by their victory, but somehow the success rang hollow. She was glad at least that Tommy's family had been part of his triumph. Once in a while beneath that jovial bonhomie she sensed his new bachelorhood wasn't everything he had hoped it would be. And she could tell that winning meant so much more to him because his daughter and his future son-in-law were part of it, especially now that he and Seth were barely on speaking terms. The rift between Seth and Faye had inevitably spilled over to affect the amiable trainer, and she felt terrible about that.

Faye tried to shrug off the depression that was beginning to gnaw at her. Her life was on track again. She was going to beat them all—Pettigrew, Mrs. Wainbrige, Seth. So why did she feel curiously incomplete?

She was so sunk in thought that she barely heard the slow crunch of gravel as a long elegant car drew up and finally stopped beside her. Faye looked up in surprise when the rear window of the silver Rolls slid down and she found herself staring face-to-face at Laura Bell Wainbridge, as if her thoughts had somehow conjured up the woman's presence.

The wealthy horsewoman regarded her austerely for a long moment before speaking. "I suppose congratulations are in order."

"Yes." Faye gave her a level look. "The more the wolves try to close in, the more I fight back."

"You're clever, Miss Hunt. Still, there are a lot of surprises in this business."

"I hope you don't forget that, either, Mrs. Wainbridge."

The air between them was charged with veiled and subtle threats. They stared at each other, as if measuring strengths and weaknesses.

Finally Mrs. Wainbridge leaned forward to tap her driver on the shoulder, and the expensive car glided away.

Faye stared after it, chewing thoughtfully on her lip. She still hadn't quite decided how to deal with her nemesis. All Faye knew for certain was that she wanted her revenge to be stylish and clever and thus worthy of her adversary. Because despite all the strange animosity between them, Faye still felt a grudging respect for the woman. Laura Bell was Gran's contemporary and had once been her friend. She was a woman who had worked long and hard, just as Gran had, to build up something she believed in. Faye had to respect that.

CHAPTER TWENTY-ONE

THE AIRY HYATT RESTAURANT was practically empty when Faye and Parris sat down for a late lunch.

"Oh, 'a piece of quiet,' as my Jessica used to say. How heavenly," Parris sighed, leaned her elbows on the table. "I've had a rush of clients in this week. Everyone madly shopping for a gown to wear to the big to-do coming up. It's worse than the Christmas-New Year's rush, I swear."

"Mm," Faye replied, her head hidden behind the oversize menu. "What are you having?"

"Fresh fruit and cottage cheese. Calorie-wise, that's all I can afford." Parris laughed. "How else am I going to look scrumptious in that lavender gown I modeled for you a while back?"

"Oh, where are you going?"

"The big do I was just talkin' about," the redhead said patiently. "The big Horsemen's Ball that anybody who's somebody goes to every year. I just *love* the chance to snub my ex-in-laws."

Faye had lost interest again. "Guess I'll order a Kentucky hot brown. Minah used to make them the best," she said, licking her lips as she remembered the cream-sauce-slathered sandwiches layered with sliced chicken, ham, tomato and bacon.

"That has a zillion calories," Parris replied, giving her friend a narrow look. "But on second thought, you look like you've lost a little weight lately, so you better eat up."

Later, after the waiter had set their orders down, Faye offered her a bite, but Parris laughingly shook her head. "Don't tempt me. It looks delicious."

"Even though it's not Cordon Bleu?"

"Are you kidding? I'm not that much of a snob, Faye. If I'm feeling weak willed and ready to pig out you can bet it ain't gonna be haute cuisine. In fact it's usually fried oysters, hush puppies and mint julep pie."

"I never heard of mint julep pie."

"My creation, sugar." She grinned. "Eggs, whipping cream, Bourbon and a dash of crème de menthe in a chocolate crumb crust. Out of this world."

Faye shook her head. "You are too much, Parris Harper. Tell me, did you try your fancy cooking on my friend Pettigrew?"

"Honey, I pulled out all the stops. Darling Holli was in hog heaven."

"And?" Faye laughed.

"And it took three evenings of wining and dining the man to get information out of him. Candlelight dinners, soft music, good wine." She made a comical face. "Holli was a hard nut to crack, but in the end..."

"In the end?" Faye prompted again.

"Putty." Parris flashed a Cheshire cat grin before getting down to business. "Your hunch was absolutely right, Faye. Hollister Pettigrew is not so much a villain as a pawn."

Faye leaned back with a mingled feeling of triumph and relief. "How are you so sure?"

"Because he confided in me that Laura Bell Wainbridge is the chief stockholder in Farmers and Breeders Bank. She's the one who calls all the shots. Very few people know she's in that position. She likes to pull the strings without being seen." Parris paused to sip her iced tea. "Sounds like your hunch about ugly collusion was right all along. What do you think, Faye? Doesn't it look like the pieces of the puzzle are beginning to fit?''

"A little." Faye sighed. "But I'd still like to know more about what happened between Quentin and Courtney. It gives me the creeps to think of Laura Bell plotting away to erase Indian Creek Farm from the face of the earth as if it never existed, because of something that happened so long ago she's almost the only one alive to remember it.''

"Maybe she's just gotten eccentric in her old age.''

"No. I have a feeling she's a woman who doesn't know the meaning of the word 'whim.' She engineered the slow deliberate sabotage of Indian Creek over the past several years. She must have hated Gran, I mean really hated her. And then the whole business was stepped up as soon as I came back to town, ready to take up where Gran had left off. It was like Laura Bell couldn't bear to see another Hunt woman carrying on the tradition.''

"Very strange.''

"Yes, it is. And I've got to put an end to it. I've got to confront her some way." Faye toyed nervously with her iced-tea spoon. "How do I make this whole vicious vindictive game stop?''

"Maybe you can't, Faye," Parris said slowly. "You might be able to reason with Mrs. Wainbridge, the strong matriarch. But maybe deep down inside there's still that angry hurtin' girl, Laura Bell Swann. Maybe she's the one who's causin' you all the problems, Faye. She's the one who probably can't be touched by reason because the whole thing's too emotional and buried deep.''

Faye looked over at her friend thoughtfully. "Parris Harper," she said after a while, "you are a genius.''

"I am? What did I say?''

"You just gave me the key to what I have to do. My idea's a little wild and it's definitely got gothic overtones," she added, biting her lip, "but I think it could just work."

Parris laughed. "You mean gothic as in haunted mansions and mysterious ladies?"

"Exactly."

"Can I help?" Parris volunteered immediately, leaning forward in anticipation.

"Didn't you say something a while back about a fancy ball coming up for all the tony upper crust in this town?"

"I told you twice," Parris said reprovingly. "It's the big annual charity deal. The Horsemen's Ball is the poshest society event the Bluegrass ever invented."

"So you think our Laura Bell will be at this Horsemen's Ball?"

"Haven't you just been listenin' to what I've been saying?" Parris said in utter exasperation.

"How do I get a ticket?"

"You might as well forget it. The guest list was compiled last year—there's a waiting list a mile long," Parris explained. "The only way I wangled an invitation is because I got on the decorations committee last year."

"I could cry."

"Faye, listen," the generous-hearted Parris said on impulse, "I could give you my ticket."

"You'd do that for me?" Faye really did feel like crying now.

"There is one condition."

"What?"

"You'd have to take Seth along as your date."

"What!"

"Faye, I don't know what's goin' on between you and him or why you're feuding. But I promised Seth I'd take him to the Ball. It meant a lot to him and I'm not about to disappoint him just because the two of you aren't on speaking terms anymore." Parris spoke coolly. "Now if you'll agree to that, fine. You can have my ticket. Otherwise, forget it.''

Faye looked pained but finally nodded her agreement. "Okay," she said slowly, "it's a deal. But do me another favor, will you please, Parris? Please don't tell Seth about me going instead of you.''

"Why not?''

"Because he might change his mind.''

Parris looked exasperated. "I know it's none of my business, but what *is* goin' on between you two?''

"I'd rather not talk about it, if you don't mind," Faye said stiffly, the pain evident in her eyes.

"I'm sorry, Faye. I shouldn't have asked. Let's change the subject," she said. "How about you telling me how you plan to come to terms with our dragon Lady, Laura Bell?''

Faye perked up a little. "It's simple, really, if I can pull it off.''

Parris listened openmouthed. "You know," she said, when Faye had finished outlining her sketchy plan, "that sounds just crazy enough to work.''

Faye smiled bleakly. "It had better.''

She was tired of being a target, of wearing the epithet "outsider." She wanted to belong; she wanted the town's acceptance, to be looked up to by the likes of Laura B. Wainbridge and Siperia Markham. Faye had come full circle. Never had she understood Seth's hungers more clearly than she did now. She had mocked him once; now she shared those same needs. Had he been the one to make her change, to make her see the value and the beauty of her own roots? If he had it was too late to tell him. You couldn't say things like that to a stranger, which is what they had become.

Parris reached across to touch her arm. "What's wrong, Faye? Are you all right?''

Faye stood up abruptly. "I'm fine. Just too much to do, that's all."

"Where do we start?"

THE TEN DAYS leading up to the Horsemen's Ball went by in a blur. On the afternoon of the big day, Faye stood in the fitting room of Panache, studying herself carefully in the mirror.

Parris's own hairstylist, Wes, stood behind Faye, patting the cold waves he had arranged in her temporarily lightened hair.

"God, it feels like starched underwear," he said disapprovingly, his long hair falling over his shoulders as he leaned down to brush away a stray wisp. "If this ever gets out, my professional reputation in this town'll be ruined."

Faye shot him a nervous grin in the mirror. "There's always Hollywood."

"Yeah," he replied sardonically, "if the Harlow look ever comes back in, my fortune'll be made."

Parris poked her head around the door. "My land, how terrific! Too bad it isn't a costume ball," she said. "You'd win first prize, Faye. I mean, you reek of the Roaring Twenties."

Faye glanced down at the sleeveless white silk charmeuse dress sashed coquettishly at her hips. "You really think the dress is okay? I mean, there were several others up in the trunk in the attic. My gran was a real clotheshorse in her day. Guess I know where I inherited my expensive tastes from."

"The dress is perfect. I'm amazed at how close a fit it is." Parris laughed. "But the fun part is that it's so antique it's almost contemporary. You wouldn't look out of place at all if it weren't for that geeky hairstyle."

Faye reached up gingerly to pat the rows of symmetrical waves and winked at the hairstylist. "Don't rub it in. Wes is already having kittens."

"I'm leaving, you two," he said, washing his hands of the whole crazy affair. "Hair was never meant to be treated that way." He shivered. "We have one of those old 'cold wave' machines back in the shop basement. Looks like something Frankenstein would have invented."

After he left, the women buckled down to business.

"Okay now, what about shoes?" Parris asked, her brow dipping as if she were mentally ticking things off on a last-minute checklist.

"I can just squeeze in a pair of black pumps I found in the trunk. Gran's feet were a size smaller than mine. They're probably going to kill me, but I want to look authentic."

"Accessories?"

"I thought I'd wear Gran's choker of antique crystals."

"Perfect." Parris's brow cleared and she nodded approvingly. "Well...guess the moment of truth is approaching."

"I guess so."

Faye took one last practice twirl in the mirror, imagining Courtney dancing the night away sixty years earlier. Putting on her clothes and her jewelry made Faye feel close to her grandmother, as if she were really a part of her. Faye hugged herself, at once nervous and excited about the coming evening, and she met her own eyes in the mirror.

I'm doing this for you, Gran, as much as for me, she told the reflection.

CHAPTER TWENTY-TWO

FAYE FELT LOST in the spacious back seat of the limousine. The rented car had been Parris's idea. No way could she drive up to the Horsemen's Ball in that battered old secondhand station wagon, Parris had insisted. If Faye couldn't go in style, then she shouldn't go at all.

She bit her lip when the driver—or rather, chauffeur—pulled into the straight gravel road leading to Seth's place and drew to a stop out front. The sleek black car was almost as long as his little mobile home.

The man turned around and slid open the communicating window to the back seat. "Do you wish to call for the gentleman, or shall I?"

"You do it, please. I, um, want him to be surprised."

She craned forward, watching as the uniformed chauffeur walked up to the front door and knocked smartly. Seth came out at once and Faye ducked her head, suddenly intent on rechecking the contents of a small plastic carryall she had brought along in addition to her Gran's beaded evening purse.

Listening to their approaching footsteps over the gravel drive, she tensed. What on earth was she going to say to him?

The chauffeur opened the back door and Seth ducked to climb inside. He'd had an amused grin on his face until he looked up and saw Faye.

"What the..."

"Just get in, Seth," she ordered curtly.

He slid onto the seat, staying as far from her as he could. "Is this some kind of a trap?" he asked suspiciously.

"Don't look so damn scared. I'm not carrying you off to a preacher or anything," she said, irritated. "In fact, here—" She thrust a tiny bouquet of bachelor's buttons at him. "I wouldn't marry you if you were the last man on earth."

He relaxed a little as he pinned on the boutonniere. "Where *are* we going, then?"

"To the Horsemen's Ball, of course."

"Wait till I get my hands on Parris."

"Will you stop grousing and listen a minute?" she retorted, barely aware that the limousine had begun to move again. "I've finally figured out who's behind all the sabotage at the farm."

He leaned forward to peer at her, obviously not listening. "What the hell did you do to your hair, Faye? It looks weird."

"Will you please listen to me?"

With a sigh he leaned back against the door. "Shoot."

Swiftly she recapped for him her accidental run-in with the young guy she suspected, described the uniform he was wearing, her conversation with Minah, the plan she had concocted with Parris's help.

"I didn't even know you two gals were friends," he said, a hint of betrayal in his voice.

"Seth, please," she sighed. "I'm asking for your opinion. Do you think my approach'll work?"

He ran agitated fingers through his hair, his eyes gleaming at her in the darkness. "You want to know what I think? I think you're damned foolhardy. I think you're a magnet for trouble. Even since we met I feel like I've been caught in the middle of one of those disaster pictures—fire, sabotaged horses, booby-trapped meals." He sighed. "I don't know why this stunt should surprise me."

Her face reddened as he heaped his sarcastic abuse on her. "Nobody's perfect," she countered fiercely, wincing as he began to laugh rather wildly.

"Is that all you got to say for yourself?"

"I'm doing the best I can, dammit. I've uncovered what's been going on all on my own—without any help from you or Barry or the sheriff or anyone else," she said, her tone at once proud and scornful. "But I guess I shouldn't have expected a redneck macho man like you to recognize that fact, or to give me an ounce of cooperation."

Seth leaned his elbow on the doorframe and stared out glumly into the night, his chin resting in his cupped hand. "Ain't I *ever* gonna get you out of my hair?"

"I told you once a long time ago—you're stuck with me, Carradine, for better or worse."

It was his turn to wince. "Don't use those words."

She crossed her arms stiffly and turned toward the window on her side, her eyes drawn to the yellow squares of light shining cozily from the farmhouses along the way.

They sped through the dusk, following the dips and rises of the narrow country road. Finally the limo slowed, and they turned onto the grounds of Larnach Stud Farm. One of the last of the legendary Bluegrass farms to survive intact from the early nineteenth century, Larnach had been built by a tightfisted Scottish millionaire who had lavished thousands on horses and begrudged every cent due the government.

Lush pastures rolled away to either side of the well-kept lane, but Faye didn't see them. Her eyes rose to the brow of a nearby hill. A row of columns stood black against the early evening sky. They were all that remained of a mansion torn down by John Larnach in a fit of pique to protest a law taxing houses by the number of windows.

Faye felt a little shiver down her spine. Courtney must have picnicked on these hills dozens of times as a young girl. Faye recalled all the stories her grandmother had told her. She imagined Courtney—beautiful, carefree and full of mischief flitting among the columns after a late-night party in the neighborhood. Surely Laura Bell and Quentin had been along on many of those outings.

She tore her eyes away from the ghostly columns on the hill and looked ahead toward the tent pavilions that had sprung up like mushrooms in the Court of Lions, an elegant square formed by the intersection of four roads. As the limo inched forward, Faye glimpsed the other party-goers, the women resplendent in furs and diamonds, the men in white dinner jackets. The ball was a throwback to another era when elegance and manners reigned supreme, when gay opulent parties ran until dawn.

Faye took a deep breath to relax. She'd heard the stories so many times it was as if the year *was* 1921, as if she was not Faye but Courtney and that the man beside her was—who?

She sneaked a glance at Seth. He straightened his tie and shot her a rueful half smile. How she'd missed his smiles, his little teasing digs, the brooding anger that erupted from time to time—at once repelling and fascinating. Who was the man beside her? A dream character she'd built up in her mind like the TV cop he had once needled her about?

Seth's smile faltered beneath the intensity of her gaze. "You okay, Hundred Pounds?" he asked, slipping unthinkingly into his old teasing nickname for her.

"I'm fine," she lied, glancing away.

The limo drew to a stop. She leaned her forehead against the window, anxious for the chauffeur to open the door. Gracefully she climbed out, not bothering to see if Seth would follow. But as she started to walk away, his voice stopped her.

"Faye..." She half turned to look at him. "Good luck."

One corner of her mouth lifted in response to his words, and then she turned back toward the crowd.

Seth had tried to harden his heart to her, but the sight of that plucky crooked smile touched him way down deep. Dammit, he had thought he was over her. But now he realized the hunger still festered, still burned in his belly. The feeling wasn't anything like love, he tried to assure himself. Hell, he didn't even know what love was. All he knew was that Faye'd made him feel good and then she'd made him angrier than he had ever been, and for all that he still wanted her.

His feelings were all mixed up inside; the memory of her in his arms was a sweet ache. And yet he still felt betrayed by her: a woman who'd stolen from him—kept him from the farm he coveted, took away his best friend, Tommy, took away... herself.

He shook his head, his eyes still following the back of her head. What the hell *had* she done to her hair, anyway? It had been so shiny and soft...so kissable. He shook his head again, more fiercely this time. *Damn that Parris,* he fumed. *Who'd've thought she'd set me up this way?*

FAYE WALKED ALONG the row of columns, staring down from time to time at the party lights blazing in the circle of striped awnings far below. She'd created her own mysterious ambience there among the ruins, setting up the candles she had brought with her in the plastic car-ryall. Their flames flickered in the light breeze.

She glanced down the hill again, wondering if her message had been conveyed. Faye steeled herelf to be patient, though her thoughts were flying off in a hundred directions. Mainly she remembered Seth's sarcastic re-buke on the drive over. A lot of it was true, she had to admit, though most of it wasn't her fault—except the "booby-trapped meals."

Her life *had* been one crazy adventure after another since she'd come back to Lexington. Maybe this last little scenario wasn't strictly necessary. After all, she'd won, hadn't she? Laura Bell Wainbridge had done her darnedest to thwart Faye's plans, but all her shenani-gans had come to nothing. The new barn was up and ready to be occupied, she and Tommy had a promising champion in Sinbad, the fields were fertile...

No matter, she told herself. *This is something that has to be resolved once and for all.* The former Laura Bell Swann would get the comeuppance she so richly de-served.

Faye was getting more nervous by the minute. She wished she had a cigarette even though she didn't smoke. Anything to dispel the tension building up inside.

Music wafted up from the orchestra playing in one of the pavilions. Beyond the lilting strains of the waltz, she heard other, more familiar sounds—the rustle of the wind across the brow of a hill, the whickering of horses in a neighboring field—and they comforted her.

Faye had stood so deep in thought that when the voice called out from below, at once strident and querulous, she nearly jumped.

"Who wants me?" Mrs. Wainbridge demanded. "Who is it?"

Tensing up again in dread of the scene about to unfold, Faye reached up to touch the double-stranded necklace at her throat. The crystal necklace, mellowed over two centuries to a soft brown color, was her talisman. She found her courage and stepped out of the shadows into the candlelight to face the woman.

She heard the sharp intake of breath, then a quavering, "Courtney! My God, it can't be!"

Slowly Faye approached her between the row of flickering candles. Laura Bell stared in shock at the approaching wraith. Faye stepped a few feet in front of her. Their eyes met, questions and accusations blazing between them for a long tense moment. Then the elderly woman's shoulders slumped.

"That was a cheap, vile trick, Fayette Hunt," she accused. "And to what end? To what end?"

"I felt it was time to confront the past, Mrs. Wainbridge," she said softly. "To look back down that tunnel of years and forgive both Quentin and Courtney."

"Forgive Courtney?" came back the outraged response. "Don't you understand? Quen offered that woman his love and she spurned him callously. Your dear, wonderful Courtney killed my brother."

"He destroyed himself."

"No! He would never have crashed his car if he hadn't been distraught over her refusal to marry him. She killed him, I tell you . . ." The words trailed off brokenly.

"His death was an accident," Faye said, her voice more gentle. "A tragic accident no one could have prevented. I asked Minah Willis what Quentin was like. She said he was reckless, that he loved danger and excitement. He died because of the way he was, not because of anything Courtney did to him. Can't you see that now? Courtney was a strong woman. And Quentin was a boy to her, just a headstrong, lovable boy."

"He was my brother, my darling brother," Laura Bell moaned. "I should have taken care of him. Courtney should have taken care of Quentin. She betrayed him." Without warning, she began to weep, groping for support against one of the columns.

Feeling terribly guilty now, Faye reached out and put a gentle hand on her shoulder. "Mrs. Wainbridge, I'm sorry. I was just hoping we could confront the truth together," she pleaded. "Quentin's death was no one's fault. Not Courtney's, and certainly not mine. Courtney is dead and so is the past. Can't you let it go, too?"

The woman raised her ravaged face. Black mascara streamed down her cheeks like bars on a window. "You must think you've been very clever," she rasped, "the way you maneuvered me into this position of weakness. Believe me, no one *ever* sees Laura Wainbridge weep." As she spoke those words her haughty air returned in full force.

"You're a strong woman, Mrs. Wainbridge," Faye conceded softly. "I just wanted to show you I'm strong, too."

"But why go to all the trouble of creating this cheap scenario?" It was obvious she had to degrade the encounter to prove to Faye that she really wasn't affected by it. "That rogue horse of yours won stakes money last week. You've made Indian Creek pay off. There's no danger now of losing your farm."

"But don't you see? What really matters to me is seeing the hatred and malice end. I wanted to make you face the truth." Faye's eyes flashed. "I think deep down you're angry at Quentin and what he did to himself—his own irresponsibility—not at Courtney. You have to stop destroying her. You have to stop trying to destroy her legacy. It's over."

The woman withdrew a handkerchief from her bag and carefully blotted her face. "May I ask how you figured all this out?"

"Once I found out you were the chief shareholder in the bank, the rest fell into place."

"But how...that was a well-guarded secret."

"I'm sorry," Faye replied, biting back a smile, "but I can't tell you that."

Mrs. Wainbridge wrung the hanky, her gnarled fingers moving agitatedly. "Now I suppose you'll go to the newspaper with this, and then to your lawyer." She glanced down the hill as if to hide the dismay so clearly written on her face. "Create a scandal. Drag the Wainbridge and Hunt names through the mud."

Faye shook her head. "Unfortunately I have no proof of anything. That's why I simply wanted to confront you woman to woman. I'm not vindictive." Mrs. Wainbridge turned back sharply at that, her eyes watchful, waiting for Faye to go on. "I don't want revenge. I just want to be left alone. I've found something I love, something that matters to me, and I want to keep it. Can't you understand that?"

Mrs. Wainbridge didn't reply immediately. Her gaze was fixed now on Faye's shoes. "I should have realized at once this was just a masquerade," she said finally. "Those pumps are from the thirties, not the twenties."

Faye looked down at her feet in amused surprise. "Are they?"

"But those crystals," the woman went on, extending a veined hand to touch the jewels. "I remember how Courtney loved them. How they suited her." She lifted her eyes to Faye's face. "They suit you, too."

The last vestige of tension between them had ebbed. The two women faced each other as equals, survivors united by the common bond of a tragedy that had touched them both.

Faye held out her arm for the woman to lean on. "Shall we walk back down to the ball?"

"As you wish." After a while Mrs. Wainbridge spoke again, as if they were two old friends reminiscing. "These parties nowadays pale next to the ones we used to go to. Oh, they'd go on until sunup, and the servants would make us such marvelous country breakfasts. Hospitality was so lavish then." She sighed, remembering. "Courtney and I were like sisters. Her family was a lot poorer than mine, but in those days it didn't matter. What counted was who you were, not what you had. But I'm afraid those old values have fallen by the wayside."

A bittersweet nostalgia swept over Faye, and she found herself missing Gran terribly. She recalled some of the talks they'd had.

"You know, Mrs. Wainbridge, Gran used to say the opposite. She'd laugh and say her generation was a terrible bunch of snobs. They'd travel across the state just to party with the 'right' families." Faye shook her head. "The only thing Gran mourned was that people today seemed to have lost that nice sense of tradition and family. I think Gran always did have a knack for seeing things in a balanced way. I . . . I've always hoped I'd be like her someday."

The older woman gave Faye a sharp sidelong glance. "You already are, Fayette. And call me Laura," she added gruffly. "I think you've earned the right."

Arm in arm they walked down to the main pavilion. Hollister Pettigrew stood at the bar, his round cheeks ruddy. He nearly choked on the cherry in his cocktail when he saw the two women in intimate conversation.

"Fayette Lee, how did you get here?" he declared with false heartiness as they joined him. "I didn't know you were invited."

"I wasn't." She paused a half beat. "But my friend Parris Harper came through for me."

The man looked positively green around the gills, Faye thought to herself, struggling to stifle a giggle. He reached down to loosen his collar as if it were choking him and hailed the bartender. "A double!" he shouted. "And make it quick."

Faye excused herself with a smile and wandered off into the crowd, feeling drained after the emotional confrontation. She was tempted to slip away quietly, but she knew it wouldn't be fair to leave Seth stranded.

Lulled by the soft orchestra music, she walked in the direction of the dance pavilion. She stood in the shadows watching all the couples drift by.

A hand touched her shoulder lightly and she turned, startled. "Seth!"

"Would you like to dance?"

"I . . ."

"Just one."

Perhaps she owed him that much. Faye moved into the circle of his arms and they began to dance. She refused to meet his glance. Instead she stared at a point just beyond his left shoulder. All the same she was acutely aware of him—the way his big hand nearly engulfed her fingers, the gentleness with which he held her waist. As if she were a fragile doll that might break.

"All through chasin' ghosts?" he asked, his eyes playing over her bemused expression.

"They've all been laid to rest, where they should have been put a long time ago." She still refused to meet his look. Now her eyes scanned the crowd on the dance floor restlessly.

"Lookin' for something?"

"Don't worry about it," she said airily. "It's nothing you could supply."

"Hey," he said in a conciliatory voice, "I'm sorry I said what I did back in the car. I didn't mean to hurt your feelings."

She pretended not to hear him. At all costs she had to protect herself against this gentle, whimsical side of him, to steel herself against the cherished memory of how tender and loving a man he could be.

"Faye," he teased her, "you gotta admit you looked like a little old-time bride when I first saw you tonight." Now he chuckled. "Did you mean what you said in the car—that you wouldn't marry me if I was the last guy on earth?"

That got a rise out of her. "Of course I meant it," she snapped, marshaling her defenses. "I realize how I was blinded by a stupid animal attraction. Parris convinced me you're not husband material at all."

"Smart woman," he agreed. "I'm glad you listened to her."

"Yes." Faye's eyes glittered with mischief. "As soon as I looked at you with my eyes open I realized the defects at once."

He stiffened. "What defects?"

"Hah! I could go on all night. But to name a few— you're not rich enough or high class enough for me, your taste in sofas stinks and, besides, I'd never stoop to consider marrying a man who wears—" she leaned over to glance disapprovingly at his feet "—boots to a fancy-dress ball."

"You little snob," he accused her, outraged. "Your nose is so high up in the air that you don't even have a clue what's good for you."

"Don't I?" She smiled smugly. "I've made an appointment to see Barry Markham next week."

"About what?" Seth tried not to sound worried.

"About marriage. I intend to propose to him," she lied, observing with satisfaction how appalled he looked.

"You just can't do that, Hundred Pounds! You can't just go traipsin' all over the country asking men to marry you. It isn't ladylike."

"Who are you—Dear Abby or something? I'll do what I damn well please."

As the music ended she primly withdrew from his arms. "Excuse me," she said, turning to walk away.

"Where are you off to?"

"To set up an appointment with John Turlock."

"Is Jenny sick?"

"I'm not going to talk to him about Jenny," she said meaningly. "John's single, too. He's a veterinarian with a good future ahead of him. If Barry refuses my offer, John's next on my list."

"What!" Seth sputtered, aghast.

"If you don't believe me, just ask Parris. She helped me write up the shopping list." Faye threw out that final zinger with a sly grin.

Her bravado announcement was given further weight when Dr. Turlock wandered innocently into the pavilion, a drink in hand. Without a second's hesitation, Faye glided over toward her unsuspecting co-actor and invited him to dance. For Seth's benefit she would play out the charade she had begun. Maybe she would find some enjoyment in this evening, after all, even if the pleasure was only in seeing Seth squirm.

She could even pretend to herself for a little while that he cared enough about her to be jealous.

CHAPTER TWENTY-THREE

AT ODDS WITH HERSELF, Faye wandered from room to room in the old farmhouse. The drama was over. It had almost been worth the fears and hassles she had endured the past few months just to see the look on Hollister Pettigrew's face when she and Laura Bell Wainbridge had walked arm in arm into the ball.

Faye had won. She could quit fooling around and get on with her life now. Everything was falling into place as she had planned. She should have been gloating. So why did she feel so defeated?

The mellow old house had been part of the promise of fulfillment she had made to herself. Once these walls had resonated with life and promise. Now she sensed only the dimmest echoes of that vibrant warmth.

She walked over to the bedroom window and pushed aside the curtain. From her vantage point she could see the road in the distance. No sign yet of the trailers that would be delivering Seth's horses.

Dear Tommy had been jubilant the afternoon Cal Darby and his boys had driven the last nail into the spanking new interior of the barn. The trainer wanted to have a little party, but Faye hadn't been in the mood to celebrate. Ever since the Horsemen's Ball, she had felt a little down; the sparkle had gone out of her life somehow. She remembered reading that some women got postpartum depression after childbirth. Maybe she was just suffering the pangs of postvictory blues.

The phone rang on the bedside table. She let the curtain fall back into place and moved unhurriedly to answer it.

"Hello," she said tonelessly.

"Faye? It's Harve. Are you okay?"

"Yes."

"You don't sound okay," he commented. "What's wrong?"

"I guess it's over."

"What d'you mean 'it's over'? Last time we talked you said everything was working out."

She bit her lip. "Everything did work out, except for one minor detail. I'm not happy," she confessed. "Somehow it all went wrong, Harve. I thought I was entrenched here; I thought it was home. But I'm beginning to think what I felt was a lie. I feel like a piece of me is still . . . still missing."

"Well, maybe you should stay there and find it."

"I don't think so," she said at last in a quiet strained voice that was unlike her. "I'm thinking of getting out."

"Running away?"

The censure in his voice smote her. "Harve, I thought there'd be enough to hold me here. I honestly did!"

"What happened?"

"I guess I just lost my taste for the game."

"Game! Faye, this is your life we're talking about. Your whole damned future."

Tears smarted her eyes. "It just didn't work out, that's all," she said thickly.

"Hey now, don't cry," he murmured, contrite. "We'll . . . we'll work this out."

She sniffed hard. "Okay," she whispered, her voice sounding small and distant even to her own ears. "Look, I have to go. I hear some cars out in the driveway."

"Call me back."

"I will."

"And don't worry."

"I'm *not* worried," she retorted with a glimmer of her old feistiness. "I'm depressed as hell. Bye, Harve. And thanks."

She hung up and went back to the window to look outside. A short caravan of trucks and trailers, led by Seth's Blazer, trundled up the driveway. Faye went into the bathroom to splash some cold water on her face. Luckily she hadn't cried enough to make her eyes puffy.

BY THE TIME the vehicles drew to a halt in front of the barn, Faye had already pushed open the big wooden sliding door and stood waiting for them, her hands shoved into the back pockets of her jeans. A couple of high-school kids jumped out of the Blazer and went back to open the trailer gate.

Faye followed. "You guys need some help?"

The huskier boy, who looked like a linebacker, grinned and shook his head. "You new here?" he said flirtatiously. "I haven't seen you in school."

"I was in juvenile hall," she said with a deadpan expression. "They just let me out on good behavior."

He obviously didn't know whether to believe her or not. She winked and turned away, nearly colliding with Seth who had climbed out of the other pickup.

"You're attracting 'em all ages now, aren't ya?" he greeted her softly. "Not a male around that can resist."

"Except you."

He scratched his head. "How's everything look inside?" he asked hurriedly. "If you change your mind, I can start giving you that rent money."

"I don't need it."

He gave her a narrow look. "You sure about that?"

"When I say something, I mean it," she snapped. The words were underscored with deeper meaning, thrusting them back to that golden afternoon of lovemaking in his bedroom and the bitter aftermath.

They looked at each other as if they were standing on opposite sides of a wide canyon with no way to get across.

Finally Seth took refuge in the mundane. "Where's Tommy? I thought he was going to meet us."

"Don't worry. He'll be here," she defended the absent trainer. "He had to take Candy and Jacques to the airport."

Seth looked disgruntled. "Wish he wouldn't take care of his personal business on my time."

The words were barely out of his mouth when Tommy's mud-splashed white pickup came roaring up the rutted lane. He had an amiable grin on his face as he climbed out of the truck.

Seth put an end to that. "You picked a hell of a day to start playing chauffeur," he snapped at Tommy.

"There was a time when you'd been pleased to see me making it up with my family," Tommy replied, clearly hurt by the other man's coldness.

After a long tense moment of silence Seth asked gruffly, "Did they get off okay?"

Tommy sighed. "Yeah. Ole Candy's gettin' more like her mother every day, though. Made me promise not to gamble."

"Guess she just cares about you," Seth grumbled, "though only the Lord knows why."

Eyeing Seth keenly, Faye realized most of his anger and hostility had evaporated. The old telltale glints of humor were back in his eyes. Tommy must have realized it, too, because his face lit up with pleasure.

The trainer looked around the barn with an expansive, satisfied air. "Nice setup we got here," he observed at last, as if there had never been a rift between him and Seth. "It's a mighty big step on the road to what we used to dream of."

Before Seth could reply, one of the boys came over. "We need your help now, Mr. Carradine."

Faye stepped back into the shadows inside the barn. She listened to the rhythmic clip-clop of the horses' hooves as they were led across the well-worn floor. She watched the two men spread new straw inside the stalls, watched their dream take shape. It was a dream she had once shared passionately. Now it no longer seemed to matter to her.

Another car pulled up into the crowded driveway, and Faye glanced outside to see who it was. Recognizing Barry's BMW, she hurried out to greet him.

"Fayette, how are you?" he called, looking tanned and relaxed as he climbed out of the car.

She smiled up at him. "How was England? Did everything work out? When did you and Corky get back?"

"We got back yesterday." He grinned. "And I can answer your other questions with just one word: perfect."

"You got the position with Randall in London?"

He nodded proudly, and she flung her arms around his neck. "Oh, Barry, that's wonderful! I'm so happy it's all going to work out. Come on, let's go on up to the house. I want to hear everything."

SETH CAME OUT OF THE BARN in time to catch the tail end of the cozy little scenario. He didn't know what they were talking about, but he thought he had a damn good idea. His mouth tightened as he watched Faye and Barry walk up to the house, arm in arm.

He should have felt vindicated. He'd known all along she'd eventually succumb to Markham's "charms."

Hadn't she told him once the guy had everything goin' for him? How'd Faye put it? *"He's got everything any woman in her right mind could ever want."*

Seth supposed he should have felt relieved, too. The sooner she got hitched up to Little Lord Fauntleroy, the sooner she'd be out of his hair permanently. He wouldn't be tempted anymore.

Yeah, I'm damned lucky, he told himself, slamming a tight fist angrily into the palm of his other hand. *Then why am I so damned depressed?*

"Hey, Seth, you nappin' out there?" Tommy called out cheerfully. "Come on, boy, we got work to do."

FAYE POURED two glasses of iced tea and arranged some chocolate chip cookies on a plate.

"They're not homemade," she warned with a dire laugh as she sat down at the scrubbed kitchen table opposite Barry.

"I don't love you for your homemakin' abilities, Fayette."

Though he had said it teasingly, she glanced away in discomfort. She supposed they had to have this painful conversation sooner or later. Still, she wished it could be later.

Grabbing at the first topic that came to mind, she said, "I'm so thrilled you got the job. But what about Corky— how did you work things out with Belinda?"

He sighed, and Faye was relieved to see his "courtin' and sparkin'" look recede a bit. "It's going to be tough. She hates the idea of me takin' him so far away. But I think she'll come around. Now that her singin' career is on the upswing I suggested she could even get a little gig in England—they're big on American country music right now."

"Did she buy that?"

"I think she liked the sound of it. But—" he paused "—if I want to avoid her takin' me to court, I'm going to have to make some mighty big concessions—lettin' her have him over Christmas and half the summer vacations."

"Not an overwhelming price to pay."

He nodded. "I guess you're right."

"And Mother Superior?"

He laughed sharply. "See, Fayette? I'm not wincin' anymore when you call her that. I think I've given up carin' what she thinks."

"Barry..."

"She's threatenin' to write me out of the will. As if I give a lousy damn," he said angrily. "I know this is the best decision I've ever made—to get out of here." He stopped and reached across the table to touch her hand. "It'd be perfect if you'd come with me."

Unable to face the pleading in his eyes, she got up and went to stand in front of the sink. She stared out the window, idly watching the men finishing down at the barn. Dusk had crept up gradually, making them look like ghosts scurrying about in the gathering gloom. An engine turned over; one of the big trailers was being maneuvered out of the driveway. In five minutes they'd all be gone. She turned away from the scene abruptly.

"I can't marry you, Barry," she said, the bluntness of the words softened a little by her gentle tone.

"Why not? Is it that important for you to stay here in Lexington?"

"No. As a matter of fact, I may not stay."

Barry jumped up excitedly and strode over to her. "Then what's to prevent us—"

"Please, Barry, listen to me!" she interrupted him. "You're one of the dearest friends I could ever hope to have but I'm... I'm just not..."

"'You're not in love with me," he said, hurt welling up in his voice.

Her heart went out to him, and she reached up to cup his face gently between her hands. "I'll always love you. You're a special man. You deserve more than I could give you."

"Faye, I'd be satisfied..."

"No, you wouldn't be satisfied," she said forcefully. "After a while you'd come to resent me."

He took a long, shuddering breath, finally realizing he had to admit defeat. "So what are you goin' to do?" he asked flatly.

"I don't know." She forbade herself to cry.

"Well...I guess there isn't much more to say." He went toward the back door. "Except goodbye."

"Goodbye, Barry, and good luck." She felt the tears brimming in her eyes. "Give...give my love to Corky. He's a special little man, too."

Barry nodded, and then left as quietly as he had come.

She sank onto a chair and crossed her arms tightly, letting the night gather around her. Why did life have to be so messed up—why couldn't she at least have tried to make Barry happy? There was no reason he would ever have had to know her heart was spoken for elsewhere.

She roused herself after a short time, drawn by the unfamiliar sounds of life coming from the barn.

The evening air was warm and humid. Southern nights were magic, heavy with the perfume of magnolia blossoms and the changeless rhythm of old-fashioned country life. Crickets chirped in the old family cemetery plot up the hill, overgrown now with hollyhock and morning glory vines.

Faye wandered down into the yard, breathing in the night air as if that breath would have to last her a lifetime. She turned at the sound of a snapping twig and saw

Jenny loping toward her, tail wagging furiously and her tongue lolling.

Faye bit her lip. Jenny had been such a loyal and devoted friend. It would be so hard to give her up, too. She knelt and ruffled the dog's hair affectionately.

"I'm glad you didn't bring me any gophers, girl," she said, laughing a little now.

Jenny's ears pricked up and she started to whine a little, running down toward the far end of the barn and then rushing back toward Faye, insisting that she come.

Faye followed her, a little nervous. She'd lived on edge for so many weeks that it was hard to shrug off those ugly fears that had haunted her every minute.

Moonlight reflecting off a chrome bumper caught her eye, and she stopped short. A second later she recognized Seth's familiar blue Blazer, parked with its nose facing his farm. Curious now, rather than afraid, she strode around to the passenger side and pressed her nose to the glass.

She nearly jumped a foot when Seth turned to stare back at her from behind the wheel. He reached across to open the door, and wordlessly she slid onto the seat.

They sat like that for a long time without saying anything, both of them staring out across toward his property.

It was Faye who finally broke the silence. "I've decided to sell out, Seth," she said, not looking at him. All the same she felt his eyes on her. "So you can name your price."

"What're you gonna do?"

"What do you think?" Her eyes snapped over at him for an instant. "I'm getting out. The big adventure's over." When he didn't say anything, she pressed angrily, "Well, aren't you going to cheer, do a couple of cartwheels out across the yard? You won, Seth."

"What changed your mind?" he asked tonelessly, bracing himself for what he knew she was going to say. He tried to picture her bursting through the hallowed doors of Oak Hill, telling both Markham and his old lady in no uncertain terms what she thought was good for them. Despite his depression he smiled a little. He'd pay to see that.

Out of the corner of her eye, Faye saw the smile and her heart twisted with pain. "What changed my mind?" she said at last in a strained voice. "A lot of things, I guess. Nothing you'd be interested in."

He scrunched around the seat to face her. "So you're takin' the easy way out."

"If you say so," she said stonily.

For one last long second they stared at each other. Then she pushed the door open and jumped out.

She ran as hard and fast as she could up the hill, afraid the tears would burst from her before she could reach the dark sanctuary of the house. She heard his truck roar to life and tear off down the road, and it was like a knife twist inside. The bitter finality of their parting galled her. She knew she had to get away fast, before her heart broke completely.

CHAPTER TWENTY-FOUR

FAYE SAT ON THE FRONT PORCH, her suitcase beside her, waiting for the taxi. Tommy had wanted to drive her to the airport, but she wouldn't let him. She had to make a clean break. Goodbyes were too painful.

The old clunker sat in the driveway. She'd told Tommy he could have it. She would probably buy herself another Alfa with some of the money she got from the sale of the farm. The lawyers would work out a fair settlement. She wouldn't have to deal directly with Seth Carradine again.

Idly she glanced down at her fingertips, worn to nubs by all the farm work. She'd have to get herself another set of acrylic nails, too. For her country life was finished—kaput.

Belonging no longer mattered to her. She had learned the hard way that it was impossible to belong to something inanimate. The land meant nothing without the people who breathed life into it. She bit back a sigh, trying not to think about what she was giving up. She wondered if Gran would have understood. Courtney must have suffered terribly from loneliness.

A tear trickled down Faye's cheek, but she brushed it away impatiently. Where was that damned taxi, anyway? She didn't want to miss her plane.

Harve and Lynette would be meeting her in San Francisco. They had invited her to stay with them for a while, and she'd agreed at once. The last thing in the world she felt like doing was returning to her cold bachelor apartment. When Harve had called back she'd even managed to joke with him, offering to take a job in the mailroom if nothing else opened up. Life would go on somehow.

Faye heard a car turning off from the main road, and she jumped up. "Finally!" she said in relief. She was so eager to escape, to forget the beautiful, painful memories.

Her eagerness turned to dismay when she saw Tommy's familiar pickup round the last curve and bounce into view. She'd specifically told him not to come. How could he do this to her?

The truck bed seemed to be filled with something. She took a step forward, squinting into the morning sun. What on earth did the man think he was doing?

Faye descended the first step and, cupping her hands to shade her eyes, she could just make out his silhouette. He was standing in the truck bed now, and he was shoveling something out. Good Lord, they looked like flowers, white flowers raining down along the path and accumulating like drifts of snow. She stared in wonderment. Had Tommy gone nuts?

Slowly Faye went down the walkway, her nostrils flaring as she breathed in the mingled scents of orchids and stephanotis, baby's breath and roses. Still squinting against the sun, she ran toward the truck. He turned and shoveled another bouquet.

Petals drifted around her, floating in slow motion. She blinked in wonderment, feeling as if she'd been caught inside one of those miniature glass domes where it's a winter fairy tale all year round. She blinked again as he came into focus and she made out his features. It wasn't Tommy at all.

"Seth! Are you crazy?" she shouted up at him. "What are you doing?"

He stopped and leaned on his shovel. "You told me once I didn't know how to send flowers to a lady."

"Yes, but..." she sputtered. "These aren't bachelor's buttons. These are what you put in a wedding bou..." She stopped and stared up at him.

Grinning, he bent down to swing her up into the truck bed beside him. He lost his footing and they fell together laughing into the flowers that were as soft and yielding as a feather bed.

"Faye, honey," he whispered, hugging her to him as if he never wanted to let her go again, "I ain't ever done this before, so you've got to bear with me."

"Done what?" she teased him, her eyes laughing. "Seth, what are you trying to say?"

"I'm saying I want to marry you. I'm saying I want us to build the best damned little horse farm in Kentucky—together. I'm saying I want you to quit shopping around for a husband. Because I'm right here."

She reached up to brush a sprig of baby's breath out of his hair. "Seth Carradine, is this a proposal?"

"No, dammit, you beat me to it. This is an acceptance," he said slowly. "I couldn't imagine going through this with anyone else, and what's more I wouldn't want to."

"You mean you love me?"

"Now isn't that just what I've been saying?" he replied in aggravation.

"Not in so many words."

He took a deep breath. "Fayette Lee Hunt," he began, his voice only a little shaky. "I love you. Guess I never loved a woman before, and I know damn sure I'll never love another. It's too nerve-racking."

"Oh, Seth." She was laughing and crying at the same time. "Just hold me tight again. It feels wonderful."

After a while she drew back to look into his face, her eyes still sparkling with tears. "You know, you are crazy."

"That's too damn bad, 'cause I ain't gonna let you get away. You said it once yourself. We're stuck with each other, lady, for better or worse."

"I'm in a state of shock. Are you sure you want to marry me?"

"I've never been surer about anything in my life."

"But, Seth, you said . . ." She couldn't get the rest out because he was kissing her, his mouth warm and possessive on hers. She kissed him back, hungrily, reveling in the feel of his arms around her, in the pressure of his lips, in the taste and texture of his skin. It was sheer delight. She never dared dream she would be held like this again, loved like this.

"Seth, Seth," she said, drawing back at last, breathless and laughing. "Talk to me. Tell me why you changed your mind."

"I ran into Markham last night in Leroy's. He must've had a few beers and he didn't look none too happy."

"So?"

"So I bought him another and a couple for myself since I wasn't feeling so great, neither." Seth's smile was rueful. "I figured it was goin' to be a bachelor's party for one or the other of us. And I was only praying the best man would win."

Faye bit her lip. "He told you what happened?"

"Said you didn't love him," he said soberly. "Said he'd done his damnedest to convince you, but it was hopeless. By the time we had a few more beers I felt downright sorry for the guy. He ain't a bad sort."

"So you decided you wanted me just because Barry couldn't have me," she accused in a small voice.

"Hell, no! That ain't true, Hundred Pounds. I've been crazy in love for weeks but I was just too confused to realize it," he said, pulling her close again. "Then last night after you and I talked I understood what I'd be missing. I realized this damn farm wouldn't mean a thing to me if you weren't here to work it with me. You're what makes it worthwhile and important to me. And it hurt me to think you could just turn and walk away from it, from me. That's why I had to go drown my sorrow at Leroy's.''

Faye reached up to stroke his cheek. ''But don't you see, Seth?'' she murmured softly. ''That's exactly why *I* was leaving. None of it mattered to me if I couldn't have you with it. You were the missing piece that gave my life here any real meaning.''

He kissed her fingertips.

She nestled her head against his chest, feeling the sun warm them as it rose higher in the sky. ''Seth, I want us to be married down by the creek where the Indians had their sacred stone. I want to wear Courtney's white dress and have Minah and Parris as our witnesses. Then I want to throw my bouquet into the creek and watch it float away down toward the river—the way life flows, lots of ups and downs. Full of surprises.''

He bent his head again and kissed her tenderly, a lifetime of promise and sharing whispered in the soft mingling of their breaths.

Their sweet kiss was interrupted by the sound of another engine laboring up the driveway. They sat up hurriedly and brushed the flowers from them.

''Who is it?''

Faye craned her neck. ''Looks like the mailman. Awfully early in the morning for him, though.''

The post-office Jeep pulled alongside them and Mr. Clark leaned out. ''Mornin', Miz Hunt, Mr. Carradine,'' the gray-bearded mailman greeted them, his eyes widening as he took in the pile of flowers. ''Is it a funeral or a weddin'?''

Faye scooped up a big bouquet and held them to her waist. ''What's it look like?''

He laughed. ''Congratulations.''

''Thanks.'' Laughing, too, she handed him the impromptu bouquet. ''For Mrs. Clark.''

"Why, thank you. The missus is real partial to orchids." He smiled and laid the flowers on the seat beside him. "Oh, I almost forgot why I drove out here. I got a special delivery letter for you."

"Special delivery! From who?"

"Don't know. No return address."

He handed the letter over and after having Faye sign for it he drove off with a jaunty salute, screeching to a halt a hundred feet down the driveway to call out the window, "Let us know when the weddin' is."

"Will do!" Seth yelled back, grinning.

Meanwhile Faye had eagerly torn open the envelope. "Talk about surprises," she said, scanning the contents. "Seth, it's from Laura Wainbridge! She says she's giving me a breeding season to her stallion Softshoe Dancer—as restitution for all the trouble and grief she put me through."

He whistled in disbelief. "Do you know what his bloodlines are? He goes all the way back to Man O' War."

"Where's the stud book?" she said excitedly, poised to jump out of the truck. "Come on, we've got to figure out which of your mares to breed him to!"

"Now hold on right there. You're not going anyplace," he said, his eyes twinkling. "If there are any bloodlines to be established, I think we're going to start right here." He pulled her back into his arms and kissed her deeply.

"Mm," she murmured, melting against him. "Should be a high-voltage line, if your old Italian was right about his theory of passion."

Seth grinned. "What do you say we test it out?"

"Your place or mine?"

He got up and leaped over the tailgate onto the ground, then swung her down into his arms. "How about ours?"

Their laughter floated out over the sunlit yard as he carried her over the threshold.

Harlequin Superromance

COMING NEXT MONTH

Take 4 novels and a surprise gift FREE